I0775708

The Devil and the Dark:

Devil to Pay
Dead Reckoning
Enemy Colours
More to come …

ENEMY COLOURS

R.M. OLSON

1

Gracie hissed in a breath at the *crack* of a fist against her cheekbone. The bright burst of pain was enough to leave her seeing stars, and blood, warm and wet, trickled down the side of her face.

She breathed shallowly, trying to force back the pain.

"Captain Mad Dog." Commodore Matisse's voice was hard and cold. "Are you still certain you have nothing that will help me?"

She kept her eyes closed and ignored him.

It wouldn't matter. He'd do what he'd do regardless.

And besides … she'd done everything she could for her crew. She'd done everything in her power to keep them safe. She was Matisse's target, she knew that well enough, and she'd done what she could to keep them out of it.

Surely now, at the end, she deserved to be just a little selfish.

She could see Jenny, the day Gracie had first met her—standing on the captain's deck, brow furrowed, watching the organized chaos below. Her hair was pulled back into a utilitarian ponytail, her hands clasped behind her back, chin up as if she was the master of all she surveyed. Her officer's hat cast her face into shadow, but when she moved, the light caught her—pale skin cast a bluish tone by the harsh ship lights, blond hair glowing almost silver.

Gracie had stopped in her tracks, staring at the woman who was to be second mate on her ship. The ship she'd just been appointed to as first mate.

Judith had a self-possession about her, the quiet sense, in the lines of her mouth and eyes, that she knew more than she was prepared to let on, and a cool, casual self-assurance that sent a thrill of recognition through Gracie.

Gracie had heard of Judith Usher, of course—everyone had, the woman had risen through the ranks of petty officers quickly enough to become a legend. The fact she'd made second mate before ever having been recommended to the Academy, and as young as she was, was nothing short of astonishing.

Gracie's rise had been just as precipitous, but then, she'd never expected anything less. She knew damn well she was a better sailor and a better officer than half the commissioned captains in the navy. When she'd been appointed first mate, similarly young and similarly without Academy credentials, she'd known it was no more than her due.

And it seemed this Judith Usher, with whom she'd be serving, had a comparable lack of doubt in her abilities.

Gracie had been entirely prepared to hate her.

But this … this had the potential to be much more interesting.

She grinned, and swung herself into the ratlines, headed for the captain's deck. She swarmed up the riggings with the ease of someone who'd practically been born there, making sure she'd pass close to Judith. When the woman looked up at her, Gracie winked.

Judith's eyes went wide and startled, then she lowered her brows disapprovingly.

But Gracie caught the hint of a blush rising on her pale cheeks, and she grinned to herself.

She was going to have to get to know Judith Usher better.

***

Gracie smiled, a small, private smile.

She'd never forgive Judith. The knowledge was a fire that burned in her stomach, low and banked most of the time, but always ready to flare to life. She'd never forgive her for what she'd done—for the betrayal that had led Gracie to a life of piracy and exile, and Judith to the top position in the Admiralty—not in this life or the next.

But here, at the end—she figured after everything she'd done, she'd earned the selfishness of loving Jenny again, just for a few moments.

"Captain Mad Dog. If you insist on being stubborn, I shall instruct my people to continue until you have a change of heart."

She kept her eyes closed, and didn't answer.

"Carry on," the man snapped. "Inform me if she decides to cooperate."

The fact he'd spoken in her language rather than his own told Gracie the words had been meant for her.

She heard the scuff of his boots as he turned for the door, then the sharp click of it closing behind him.

She barely had time to brace as another fist hit her in the stomach, and she doubled over as much as she could, bound as she was, retching.

They hit her again.

The sharp, bright pain of a rib cracking jerked her consciousness back into her body, and she gasped despite herself, then gagged on the brittle, blinding pain of the movement.

Again, she forced her breathing shallow, tried to bring her mind back from the white roar of pain.

She knew pain. She knew it as intimately as a lover, the contours of it, how it settled into your very bones and pulsed through your veins like blood. How it drew the life-force from you, like the cold of deep space drew the warmth from you, lapping it up as it seeped from your body.

This Rosette System commodore wanted something from her. Everyone wanted something from her, and Matisse thought he'd win it by hurting her.

"Mate Madox! Modox, can you hear me?"

The effort to open her eyes was almost more than she could manage, but it was Jenny's voice. Somehow, she couldn't disobey when it was Jenny asking, and she fluttered her eyes open, wincing at the pain the movement brought.

Jenny was leaning over her, face paler than usual, expression grim. "Thank God! Come on, let's get you below decks to the med bay."

When Gracie listened, she could hear the sounds of the battle still raging around them, feel the way the ship shuddered at the release of broadsides.

"What happened?" she muttered, struggling to sit up. Her head spun, and there was blood dripping down her forehead and tracking down her cheek, warm and wet.

"You got the boarders off, if that's what you're asking, you goddamned fool." Jenny bit off the words, and Gracie grinned despite herself.

Jenny'd been worried about her.

"Why in God's name didn't you call for reinforcements, rather than charging in yourself?"

"Because," Gracie managed, finally getting herself upright, "I knew what I was doing, and the rest of the crew was needed at their posts."

Jenny shook her head, lips pinched together, and moved closer. "If I put my arm around you, do you think you could stand?"

Gracie gave the woman her most pathetic look. "Only if you call me Grace, instead of Mate Madox."

Jenny scowled. "You're hopeless."

Grace grinned. "I repelled a skiff they'd sent out to board us, and I did it singlehanded. That's not completely hopeless."

"And you almost got yourself killed!"

"You were worried." She grinned wider.

Jenny blew out a breath. "Of course I was worried. You're a fellow officer on my ship."

"That wasn't the only reason, was it, Jenny?"

A flush rose on Jenny's cheeks, and Gracie's chest warmed with the quick rush of triumph that came every time she made the woman blush.

"Mate Usher to you," Jenny snapped, threading her arm around Gracie's shoulders. "Come on, let's get you to the med bay. The battle's turned in our direction, so there are sailors to spare at the moment."

Gracie bit back a gasp of pain as Jenny lifted her to her feet, leaning against her hard to keep from staggering. The sharp pull of the movement against the cutlass-slash on her side was enough to bring tears of pain to her eyes, and the knot on her head, where she'd been struck by the closing airlock door, sent waves of nausea through her every time she moved, but she pushed it back.

With Jenny holding her, she took a step forward. Her vision went dark, and she swayed.

Jenny caught her. "Stay with me, dammit," she hissed. "How badly are you hurt?"

"'M fine," Gracie mumbled.

The world was spinning with pain, but she clung desperately to consciousness. She wasn't about to pass out, not here. Not in front of Jenny Usher.

"Stay with me, Grace, just until we can get you below." There was a frightened, pleading note in Jenny's voice.

She smiled, despite the waves of pain.

Grace.

Maybe the pain had been worth it.

"For you, Jenny, I'd do more'n that," she murmured.

***

Matisse had no idea what she'd lived through. He had no idea how long she'd survived people hurting her.

She shifted, just enough to brush the brand-scar on her forearm against her sleeve, and the familiar sharp, gut-deep tingle of pain from the injured nerves was enough to ground her.

Gracie knew exactly how far her body would be pushed. And she'd realized, quick enough, that these people in front of her didn't.

An experienced torturer would know, she assumed. Someone with experience keeping their victims alive would know the signs—the rapid breaths, the tight flutter of her pulse. They'd stop before they pushed too far. But these were just sailors—brutal, sadistic, but just sailors.

And she was Mad Dog. She'd gained that name when she first arrived in Blackrock, feral and vicious from pain, all bared teeth and rage and hate.

She'd not let them win.

She'd seen the look on Sil's face when he'd turned and caught her eye one last time before he was marched off. She'd seen the set of Ari's shoulders.

They'd escape, she'd no doubt of that. And once they were out, they'd need to get off the ship, but they wouldn't do it trying to carry her along with them, injured as she was. She'd known that from the moment Commodore Matisse had mentioned torture.

So she'd ensure that the torturers miscalculated. She'd use the skills she'd learned over the long, brutal years since she'd fled the Level, and she'd ensure that they didn't realize they were going too far until it was too late. She'd ensure that when Sil and Ari came— and they'd come, she had no doubt of it—they'd find nothing but her dead body.

She trusted Toothpick with her ship and her crew. He'd find a way to get them back to Blackrock, get Temple to a place he could be taken care of, repair the *Sweet Jenny*. He was perfectly competent to captain the ship, should she not make it.

Ari might not thank her for it, not at first. Ari was absurdly loyal. The rest of her crew were loyal too, not a one of them wouldn't die for her if she asked it, but she'd known Ari since she was a small, skinny, frightened thing, even then with that sharp edge to her, a stubborn determination that Gracie recognized. Ari'd all but grown up on the *Sweet Jenny*, and Gracie was the closest thing to family the lass had.

But this was the final thing she could do for Ari—for all of them —and she'd see it done.

2

Silas

The click of the lock, as the Rosette officer pulled the door closed behind them, was loud in the sudden silence.

For a long moment, Silas, Ari, and the two Level naval officers stood looking at each other.

They'd been held under guard, first in the crowded officers' mess, then on the captain's deck, for interminable hours as the Rosette commodore oversaw the surrender of the *Verity.*

This was the first time the four of them had been left alone.

Silas could feel the tension humming through Ari's body. Hell, he could feel it in himself.

Then Hollis swayed on her feet, and Price cursed. "We're locked up, and there's nothing we can do about it right now," they said, turning on her. "Lie down, for God's sake."

Hollis didn't protest, just let her first mate help her over to one of the hammocks. From the look of it, she was unconscious by the time her head hit the hammock ropes.

Price fussed over her for a few moments, then turned to glare at Silas and Ari. It wasn't until then that Silas noticed the exhaustion in

Price's face, the drawn lines of strain and weariness etched into their expression. "Captain Ives saved your damn lives," Price said, their tone flat. "It's more than I would have done, and I won't say I know why she did it. But you'll damn well not try anything while she's asleep, or by God I'll gut the both of you." They opened their hand to reveal a short, wicked-looking shiv.

Ari bared her teeth, but Silas sighed and stepped forward. "We have no intention of hurting you or Captain Ives," he said, raising his hands palm-first. "I swear it."

"Speak for yourself," Ari muttered, but he could tell by the tension in her voice that it was more worry for Gracie than anger at the naval officers in front of them that was driving her.

Price watched them for a few moments, then at last sank down against the wall beside the hammock, so that they were between Silas and Ari and the sleeping Hollis, and tipped their head back, letting their eyes fall closed. The weariness in their posture was so pronounced that Silas found himself grimacing in sympathy.

He waited until he guessed from the slackness of Price's posture that they, too, were asleep. Then he turned to Ari.

"They're going to kill her," he said in a low voice. "They're going to kill Gracie. I saw the way that Rosette commodore was watching her. He wants something from her, and you know Gracie as well as I do. She's not going to roll over and give him what he wants, and they're not going to be patient about it. They're going to kill her."

"They're damn well not." Ari's voice was hard and clipped. "Because I'll burn this damn ship and everyone on it before I let them kill Gracie." Her posture was one tight line, her hands trembling, just a little. She reached into the inner pocket of her shirt and drew out a long, slim knife. "Figure I can pick the lock with this easy enough." She grinned without humour. "Then I guess you'n me'll see how many we can kill before they manage to take us down."

Silas drew in a long breath, forcing his jaw to unclench. "I agree with you," he said, voice still low. "But I think we're better off waiting a bit. Between taking the *Verity* and taking the *Sweet Jenny*, there'll be too many people about for us to be able to get out without being seen. We'll stand a better chance when things on the *Chasseuse* have calmed down."

Ari was glaring at him, but at last she gave a short nod. "Fine," she hissed. "We'll give it until seven bells in the forenoon. But after that, we're getting out, sailors be damned."

Nine hours.

Common sense told him they should wait longer. But the burning impatience that had worked its way into his bones, the sick fear that they'd be too late, that the Rosette commodore would have done something irreparable, was hissing in his mind that nine more hours, after all the time that had already past, was far too long.

He gave her a small smile. "I won't argue with you on that."

She nodded and turned away, pacing up and down the small room.

Silas ran his hand through his hair and sank down on the remaining hammock, closing his eyes.

They were going to kill Gracie. He was certain that's what Matisse intended to do with her. He'd have no reason to need a pirate captain alive.

But he'd been right too—going out now was an invitation for both he and Ari to be killed, and dead they'd be no use to Gracie.

He swore under his breath and stood restlessly, then sank down again, drumming his fingers against his thigh.

Damn this to hell. He was used to waiting in the navy. He was used to forcing himself to sit still and wait orders, not thinking for himself even when he knew what they needed to do and what needed to happen, because that was his duty, and asking questions was not.

Now that he'd pledged his life and his loyalty to Mad Dog, he didn't have that to fall back on. And he hadn't realized, until he lost it, how much it would feel like the ground under his feet disappearing—and how much it would feel like finally being able to breathe, after a lifetime of holding his breath.

He stood, glancing around quickly. If they were going to get out, they'd need more than just Ari's knife.

"Ari," he said, holding out his hand. She came over and dropped the knife into it, and he began slicing carefully through the lines of rope on the hammock. He'd repaired his hammock enough times on long postings, when he was young and first starting out in the navy, that he knew well enough how they were put together, and how to take them apart to give himself as many usable lengths of rope as possible.

Ari watched him a moment, then set to work helping.

It was painstaking work, but he was grateful for it—he wasn't sure he survive the hours of waiting without something to keep his hands busy.

Every so often she'd stand restlessly and pace back across the cramped cabin. At one point, she must have got too close to Hollis's hammock, because Price cracked an eye open and mumbled, "Any closer and I'll bleed you out like a damn pig."

Silas raised an eyebrow. He could have sworn the *Verity's* first mate had been dead to the world, and his first thought on seeing them on the deck of the *Sweet Jenny* was how entirely proper of a naval officer they looked.

It seemed they were something more than they appeared.

He had half a dozen coils of thin rope beside him, and had stretched out on the floor to get a few minutes of sleep himself, when Ari crouched beside him. "Been listening at the door," she said in a low voice. "Sounds like things are quieting down out there, and figure it's been at least nine hours since we got locked in here."

He glanced up at her and nodded, pushing himself upright. "Do we have a plan, or are we just going to get out and kill as many of them as we can until we find the captain?"

She grinned, the expression tight on her face. "Figure we'll make a pirate of you yet, Sil."

He smiled without humour. "Navy trains us to kill without asking questions. Just following orders. At least here I get the choice."

Ari glanced at him, then shook her head. "Don't rightly know what's out there, but I figure we can do better than go out and die. You got any information on the layout of Rosette naval ships?"

Silas frowned, biting the inside of his cheek. "They mentioned them in the Academy," he said at last. "But it's not until you make captain or first officer that they share the briefings and specs from the navy's intelligence agents. The best I can give you is specs of a Level navy ship, and hope they're not too different."

Ari let out a short, frustrated sigh. "Suppose that's the best we can do. You'll have to get us down to the brig, I'm guessing that's where they'll have taken Gracie. Be difficult to break in there with my knife, I figure, so we'll have to kill someone who has a key. But then, don't figure as that'll be a problem, all things considered." She glanced up at him, and the look on her face made him shiver.

"And once we find her?" he asked.

He didn't say what was on both of their minds—it might be too late. They might not find Gracie in the brig, because she might already be dead.

They'd deal with that if they had to. In the meantime, he wasn't about to let himself think it.

"Once we break her out, we'll figure out what the hell they've done with the *Sweet Jenny*," said Ari curtly, pushing herself to her feet. "If they've brought her into a bay here, we'll find her. Otherwise we may have to steal a skiff. Either way, ain't going to know until we're out there. But they haven't gone into jump yet, I know that much. I'd have felt it."

Silas stood as well, slinging the coils or rope onto his shoulder. His muscles were humming with adrenaline, his whole body aching to finally do something. "Well then," he said, turning towards the door, "I suppose—"

He stopped.

Price stood in front of the door. Their face was pale under the brown of their skin and still drawn from weariness and puffy with sleep, their dark, curly hair pulling free of its regulation ponytail, but their expression was grim and businesslike. They held the shiv in one hand, and the way they held it told Silas they knew how to use it.

"I'm sorry," they said, their voice remarkably steady. "If you want to leave here, you'll be doing it over my dead body."

Ari narrowed her eyes. "Figure that can be arranged," she said. "Your dead body, and the body of your damn captain. Although that's hardly a loss. Looked dead when she walked in here."

Price's expression didn't change, but Silas could see how their fingers tightened on the shiv.

He sighed. "Price," he said, trying to keep his own voice level. "What do you want?"

Price glanced over at him. "If you leave, when the Rosette officers come back, I suspect they'll execute the captain and myself." Their voice was still steady. "However, if I were to alert them that you were trying to break out …"

"Won't need to execute you, because I ain't leaving you alive to tell anyone," Ari snapped. "And I ain't letting you stand in the way of me getting my captain out, so if that's how you want it—"

"Wait," said Silas through his teeth, stepping forward. "If we fight here, none of us are getting out." He turned back to Price. "What do you suggest, then? Do you plan on letting them take you back to the Rosette System and lock you up for the duration? You'd risk your life to protect your captain. I can respect that. But if you think that Ari and I won't do the same—"

Price blew out a long breath. "No," they said. They were, Silas noted, also speaking through their teeth. "I know Ives well enough to know that there's not a chance in hell we'll go peacefully back to the Rosette System. But if you break out, we lose our chance to do so. So—" They hesitated, clearly bracing themself. "We all get out together, or none of us do."

For a moment, Silas stared at the *Verity's* first mate.

Their expression was still calm, but he could see the iron determination under it.

"How the hell do you expect us to trust that you won't give us away the moment you're out?" Silas snapped, his patience fraying. "Your captain looks more dead than alive. For all we know, you want to leverage our escape to get yourself and Ives somewhere safe."

"You'll be able to trust us, because we'll go together." Their voice was still, somehow, calm. "All four of us. I imagine you'll want to get your captain and get back to your ship, no? So we'll go with you. You'll need us, anyway—I've been keeping up to date on the information we have on the Rosette ships. You won't be opening the airlock doors to get yourself off the ship without a code, and I'm your best chance to find you one. I doubt piracy has given you much time to keep up on the latest Level intelligence briefings. So, your choice. All together, or none of us."

For a long moment, no one moved. Silas's heart was pounding hard and fast—he and Ari could take Price easily, exhausted as the naval officer clearly was. But there was something about the grim expression on their face that told him they wouldn't go down without a fight, and he doubted their threat to alert the guards was an idle one.

"They're right, Ari," he said at last, in soto voce. "We're going to need the codes, and if Price can get them for us, that's a good thing. Besides, between Price and Hollis, they should know the layout of the ship. Hollis, at least, should be able to get us where we need to be."

"You sure that's why you're agreeing?" Ari asked, her voice matching his. "Or is it because they're navy, Sil? Is it because deep down, you don't believe naval officers shouldn't be treated the same as pirates? If the tables were turned, would you feel the same?"

He closed his eyes.

He'd been asking himself that same question.

"We need them," he said at last. "We need them, because we won't get Gracie off in time without them."

He wished he was more certain he was telling the truth.

Ari studied him for a long moment. "Fine," she said at last, voice flat. She turned to Price. "You have five minutes to get yourself and your captain ready to go, and she'd damn well better be able to stay on her feet. Either of you slow us down, and we'll shoot you."

"Very well," said Price in a clipped tone. They straightened, dropping the hand holding the shiv. "Five minutes. But don't think to double-cross us, or I'll see to it that you regret it."

3

Hollis

"Captain."

Hollis could hear the voice through the muddy water of her consciousness, and she swam toward it.

"Captain. I'm sorry, but it's rather urgent."

Foster. It was Foster, it had to be, because no one else could possibly say those words in that polite a tone.

She groaned, and heard Foster breathe out a sigh of relief. "Captain, I'm sorry to wake you, but we need to get going."

Hollis squeezed her eyes shut and tried to remember where she was and where they could possibly be going. The last thing she recalled was standing on the bridge of the *Verity* …

No.

She felt the sudden, sick drop in her stomach.

She'd surrendered to Mad Dog—her ship and her life in exchange for her crew. But not just her life, Foster's as well. Set in the balance together. But that had already happened, hadn't it? She and Foster had gone down to the *Sweet Jenny,* and she'd thought she'd watch Foster die in front of her before she died herself, and then …

Her eyes popped open, and she tried to jerk upright.

Foster's hand on her shoulder held her steady. "Easy, Captain," they murmured. "How are you feeling?"

They were bending over her, their face still pale and wan from exhaustion, but they looked as if they'd had a few hours' rest, at least.

She closed her eyes and let her head drop back, taking quick stock.

She couldn't have been sleeping overly long, if the residual weariness on her first mate's face was anything to go by, but her mind felt clearer than it had in a while—not the bright, over-sharp clarity of too much adrenaline and too little sleep, but something approaching normal. Her injury … She tried to move, and grimaced.

"Price." Her voice came out hoarse. She cleared her throat and tried again. "Price. If you would be so good as to help me sit up—"

They did as she requested, face pinched in a familiar concern.

"We're breaking out," Foster said quietly in her ear as she settled herself into a sitting position on the swaying hammock. "I don't trust the pirates, but I believe they're our only chance at the moment. They believe Mad Dog is being held here, and judging from my conversations with them, they're determined to get her out. Not, perhaps, our ideal outcome, but I believed it would be better than the alternative. But if we're going to leave, we've got to do it now. I think the *Sweet Jenny's* second mate would as happily wet her knife in our blood as work with us, so we'd best look sharp."

Hollis took a steadying breath, trying to bring her mind back into focus. "If we go with them, it will put the lives of Greene and the crew at risk."

Foster gave a short nod. "It may. But the pirates are going

regardless. It was all I could do to talk them into waiting. Speaking of which," they held out a small, sharp object that she instantly recognized. "I borrowed your shiv. I hope you don't mind."

Hollis's eyebrows shot up. "You threatened the pirates with my shiv?"

"I didn't want them to murder you in your sleep." Foster's voice was clipped, and there was a tone to it that told her they'd rather not elaborate on their familiarity with the street-brawler's weapon.

That had likely been the reason the Rosette sailors hadn't found it —no one would expect a captain in the Level navy to carry a shiv, of all things. But then, most captains in the Level navy hadn't grown up in the Stacks.

"At any rate," Foster continued, "the Rosette navy thinks those pirates are part of our crew. If they get out, it'll put Greene and the rest of the crew in danger whether or not we come along. If we go out with them, at least we have a chance to do something about it."

Hollis gritted her teeth.

But Foster was right, on every point. One glance at the two grim-faced pirates in the corner assured her of that—the pale, blonde-haired woman with her fine features and the fierce look in her startlingly blue eyes, and the grim-faced man who'd once been naval, still with blood crusted in his clothes, spattered across his brown skin and matted in his brown hair and days-old beard.

She shook her head. "We'll have to make it quick, then. With any luck, the commodore will be more focused on recapturing us than on punishing Greene, for at least a few hours. Once we're out, we can figure the rest out from there." She paused. "And we'll keep a weather eye out for a way to get back to the *Verity*. We can't overpower the pirates, at least not right now, but if we get a chance —"

Foster nodded. "Do you think you can walk?" they whispered.

"I can walk. Give me a moment, if you would. And may as well keep the shiv—I think you'll be more effective with it than I will, as things stand."

Foster frowned as she unbuttoned her jacket, trying not to wince at the movement. "Captain?"

"We don't have bandages, I imagine," she said shortly. The movement was making her gut ache again, and she didn't have the breath to spare for explanations. She stripped off her shirt as Foster quickly averted their eyes.

"God's sake, this is hardly the time for modesty," she said through her teeth. "Help me wrap this, if you please!"

Reluctantly, Foster turned back, taking the edges of the shirt she'd wrapped clumsily around her waist.

"Tight as you can," she said grimly. "I'm certain Smyth would be horrified, but this will hold me together for long enough that we can do what we need to."

Foster nodded and pulled the makeshift bandage in a tight wrap around her torso. Hollis bit her tongue hard to keep from gasping at the pain, sweat standing out on her forehead, and then it was done. She let out a short breath, head spinning a little, and shrugged back into her jacket, fastening it clumsily. The tight bandage around her stomach and lower rib cage made breathing difficult, but once the shocking agony of tightening it was done, the pressure of it made the pain more bearable.

Bracing herself, she got gingerly to her feet and paused, letting her legs remember how to hold her up.

On the far side of the room, the two pirates watched her and Foster narrowly. The woman held a slim, wicked-looking blade, and her expression told Hollis that Foster hadn't been exaggerating the danger. The man, Sil, if she remembered correctly, held several coils of what she recognized, after a moment, as rope disassembled from one of the hammocks.

"So she's alive after all, more's the pity." The pirate woman's voice was thick with scorn, but Hollis could hear the tension under it.

"I'm dreadfully sorry to disappoint you," said Hollis tartly. "Now. Do we have a plan, or are we simply going to walk out the door into the Rosette sailors' pistol fire?"

"The plan is, we're going to find Mad Dog, get her the hell off this ship, and get back to the *Sweet Jenny*." Sil's voice was as grim as his expression. "Your first mate threatened to either gut us or give us away if we left without you, so looks like you're coming with us."

Hollis shot a quick glance at Foster, who was staring straight ahead, their face its usual emotionless mask, and for a moment had to bite back a smile.

"As practical a plan as that may be," she said instead, turning back to Sil, "it seems to lack detail."

Sil sighed. "Ari can pick the lock with her knife, and if your first mate deigns to help us, between them and myself I think we can take down the guard outside the door." He gestured to the rope. "I know how to kill with a garrotte. Not the prettiest death, but it's quiet, and quick enough. And Price seems a hand with a shiv." He turned to Foster. "You'd bleed Ari out like a pig if she came a step closer to your captain, I think you phrased it?" His voice dripped irony. "I assume you can make good on that with the Rosette sailors."

Foster didn't meet Hollis's eye, just gave a short nod. "That's acceptable," they said, their voice impressively bland.

"Once we get to Gracie and get her out, we'll worry about getting the codes to get off the ship," Sil continued.

"It may be wise to do that first," Hollis began, but Sil shook his head sharply.

"I don't know what they're planning to do with Gracie, but I suspect it isn't good. We've been locked in here over nine hours already, on top of the time they held us before they locked us up. We need to get to her before they decide she's not worth the trouble and shoot her."

Hollis nodded slowly.

The only experience she had with pirates was from the wrong end of a cutlass or a ship's gun.

She'd always been told, and believed, that pirates were bloodthirsty, vicious, and inherently selfish. She hadn't, honestly, expected this level of loyalty.

But then, had the pirates been what the navy said they were, Mad Dog wouldn't have spent her last request on trying to protect her injured crewmember, or saving the two standing in front of her right now.

She wouldn't have listened to Sil when he'd negotiated the surrender that would have killed Hollis and Foster, but saved the crew of the *Verity*.

"Very well. We find your captain, and figure out the rest from there," she said. She turned to Foster. "I assume, Price, that you're up to date on the latest naval intelligence briefings?"

"Of course, Captain," said Foster. "I believe it was the latest briefing that included information about the airlock codes."

She gave them a small smile, and for just a moment, a smile flickered across their face in return.

"Well," she said at last, turning back to Sil and Ari. "I suppose there's no sense in wasting time."

Ari was still scowling at them. She turned on Sil. "Damn you, if this goes badly, it's on your damn head."

"I know." His voice was quiet. He glanced at Hollis. "Captain Ives. You don't know me, and I know you only by reputation. They say you're a woman of your word. So. Do you swear that you'll not betray us to the Rosette officers? Do you swear that you'll help us find and rescue Mad Dog, if we agree to get you off the ship with us?"

Hollis looked over at Foster, then back to Sil and Ari. "I do," she said.

Sil nodded. "Price. You still have that shiv? Because we're going to need it."

4

It was late.

It was always late, it seemed—Judith could hardly remember how it felt not to be tired, not to have exhaustion dragging at her bones like a physical weight.

She glared down at the charts and documents on her desk.

There was something wrong with the mission she'd sent to Blackrock.

At first, she'd thought it was simply the mixture of guilt and relief that she was finally going to do what she'd realized she'd have to, so many years ago—take down Blackrock, and take down Gracie Madox with it.

But it wasn't that. There was something off about this whole situation, starting with the original mission, and continuing through the assassination attempt on Hollis Ives, and the ever-increasing anti-war protests.

There was something connecting them. There was a common thread she couldn't quite see, and she was growing increasingly certain that this one thread, if she pulled on it, would unravel more than just Commodore Webb's mission to Blackrock.

It would send shudders through the Naval High Command itself.

She sighed, and let her eyes run over the documents again, forcing her tired brain to focus.

Gracie had known about the attack on Blackrock, because Judith had warned her. But there'd been another item Judith hadn't paid attention to at first, because it hadn't seemed to matter—an information leak intercepted by a pirate ship.

It wasn't impossible for that to happen on its own, but the circumstances seemed far too convenient, the coding on the leaked information something a child could have worked through.

Then the assassination attempt on Hollis Ives. Again, a matter she'd put to one side as something with an obvious enough solution —someone who'd wanted to keep Stacks captains out of the ranks. Ives and her first officers had come to the same conclusion, and it seemed to fit. But now it was nagging at the back of her mind.

Why had it happened when it did? Why directly before the attack on Blackrock? It didn't make sense.

The answer was there, she was sure of it. She just wasn't seeing it.

The mission she'd sent to Blackrock wasn't optional. It was entirely necessary. It had taken the report by Commodore Webb for her to realize what she'd known all along—as long as Gracie was alive, the navy would never be safe.

But there was something there she'd overlooked, something she wasn't seeing, and it was going to drive her mad.

She sighed, and turned back to her documents, trying to push back the weariness clouding her mind.

"Mate Usher. A moment, if you would."

Judith looked up, startled, then jumped to attention. "Commodore Lloyd."

He smiled. "At ease, Officer." He glanced around the deck of the ship. "Do you have a moment to speak with me, Mate Usher?"

"Of course, Commodore." Judith's heart was pounding too quickly, but she managed to force her face into the respectful mask that was so useful as a petty officer in the navy.

What was this about? She knew damn well that her performance as second mate of the Independence had been exemplary.

Grace caught her eye from the corner of the deck, where she was speaking to her division of sailors, and gave her a wink.

Judith caught herself blushing, and scowled, which only made Grace's infuriating grin wider.

Commodore Lloyd led her to a private corner of the captain's deck before he turned to study Judith.

She met his eye coolly.

"Usher," the commodore said at last. "I've heard nothing but good from your captain. Exceptional officer, he said you were."

Judith inclined her head. "Thank you, Commodore."

He paused a moment. "The first mate on this ship is Grace Madox, am I correct?"

Judith nodded, biting back a sigh of relief.

She knew enough about naval politics to know that Grace's parents, vice-admirals both, had their enemies, and she recognized Commodore Lloyd's name now.

"I hear word that the two of you have become quite close," he continued. "A good thing, I think—strengthens the ship, and a strong ship strengthens the navy." He paused, catching her eyes. "But I'll warn you, Usher—Mate Madox is known in the High Command as one to keep a sharp eye on. Brilliant officer, yes, but she's been on the brink of a charge of insubordination on more than one occasion."

Judith frowned. "Commodore. With respect, I'm certain Mate Madox is fully *loyal to the navy. She is at times unconventional, yes, but I've seen her risk her life for her crew on more than one occasion."*

He raised his eyebrows a little. "Ah. But risking one's life for one's crew and being loyal to the navy aren't quite the same thing, are they?" He shook his head. "You may do as you see fit, of course, Mate Usher. I merely wished to give a word to the wise. I'd hate to see her drag you down with her, if she goes."

Judith's heart was pounding again, but it wasn't fear this time, and she had a brief, disorienting moment where she realized that she was far angrier than she by rights should be for the reputation of someone who was, after all, only a fellow officer.

She drew herself up. "Commodore." Her voice was icy. "I appreciate the warning. But believe me, I know Mate Madox. She'd never do something to harm the navy."

The commodore was still watching her, his eyebrows raised. He let the silence hang for a long moment. Judith didn't drop her gaze, and neither did he. "How certain of that are you, Usher?" He asked at last, quietly. "How entirely certain are you? She'd never harm the navy, you say. How well can you know someone to be sure of that?"

She wasn't sure how long she'd been hearing the quiet footsteps in the back of her mind before they registered on her consciousness.

She frowned and sat up, glancing around. For the first time, she realized how dark it was—the night had come on so gradually, and she so absorbed in her documents, that she hadn't noticed enough to turn on the overhead light, reading the holo-notes by their own glow.

No one else should be in the Admiralty offices at this time of night. She was certain she'd been the last one to leave for the last week running, and this was late even for her.

The footsteps passed close by her door.

She shut down the cloud of notes hovering over her desk with a quick flick of her wrist, and stood silently.

By the sound of it, the footsteps were those of someone who did not want their presence known.

Had her light been on, whoever it was would have seen it through the crack under the door. But the glow of the holonotes was dim enough that they likely wouldn't have noticed it over the dim nighttime lighting of the Admiralty hallways.

She crossed to the door, walking quietly—she'd been in this office long enough to know every creaky floorboard, every uneven spot in the wood that might scuff against the sole of a boot—and paused, listening.

The footsteps had faded down the hallway, but they weren't going in the direction of the exit. They were heading back towards the offices.

She placed her hand on the door latch and swung the door cautiously open.

Away from her, down the hall, a small glow, like a torch, perhaps, was disappearing into a doorway. The door swung shut, and the light was cut off.

Judith tapped through an alert to the guards, and hesitated.

But she knew by experience it would take the guards a couple of minutes to get there. And there was something about the stealthy way the figure had moved that made her suddenly very, very certain that whatever it was they were doing, it was somehow vital that she know it.

She stepped out into the hallway on silent feet and followed.

Her heart was pounding, the old recklessness of serving shipboard stirring in her blood.

There was a chance this was just another faceless bureaucrat working late. But she knew it wasn't.

She stepped carefully, watching where she put her feet. She was older and heavier than the figure she'd seen, but she knew these halls better than she knew the apartment she called home, and it was easy enough to keep her footfalls quiet.

She reached the doorway the figure had disappeared inside, and had to bite back a quick intake of breath.

It was Admiral Moore's office. And she knew damn well what was in that office—the fleet's positional layout and weapons specifications.

She put her hand gently on the door latch.

It should have been locked, but it swung open easily under her fingers. Inside, a figure bent over the document cabinet in the corner, a pile of documents and data chips beside them on the floor, a torch held between their teeth.

The door made no sound—someone must have greased the hinges recently—but the movement as it swung open was enough to alert the intruder.

They spun, yanking out a pistol. The light of their torch shone directly into Judith's eyes as they turned, and she stumbled back, caught off guard.

There was the sharp *crack* of a projectile pistol going off, then a bright explosion of pain in her shoulder. She hissed out a curse, grabbing for her cutlass with her good arm, and lunged for her attacker.

She slashed her cutlass down as the figure scrambled to re-aim the pistol, and it went flying from their hand.

They cursed. They'd dropped the torch, as well, and the light reflected against the white wall of the office was enough to illuminate their shape. Judith lunged for them again, but the figure had pulled out their own cutlass, and the two weapons clashed with the sharp ring of metal on metal.

Whoever this was, they were a skilled hand with a cutlass. And Judith was older now, and not as used to fighting for her life. But she'd trained her whole damn life, hell, she'd spent her years at the Academy sparing with Grace Madox, who might have been the strongest swordswomen she'd ever met, and her muscles moved almost of their own accord. She caught the blow aimed for her face, parried, and struck at the figure's thigh. They leapt back to avoid the blow, and she stepped in, pressing her advantage. They swung, and she caught the blow again, but they were stronger than she was—the tip of the blade scraped down her arm, leaving a warm rush of blood in its wake. She shoved the blade back by main force, feinted a blow at their side, and when they moved to parry it, slashed down with all her might.

Her blow went true, and she felt the familiar resistance of flesh and bone as it cut through the muscles of the figure's shoulder and chest and skittered across their ribcage, then she used the momentum of the stroke to bring her blade around and slap the flat of it hard on their wrist.

The clatter of the cutlass falling to the floor was loud in the sudden silence of the deserted office.

The figure leapt for the fallen weapon, but Judith reached it first, bringing her foot down on the blade and swinging her own blade to rest at the figure's throat.

They froze.

"Who the hell are you? What are you doing here?" Judith snapped. She was breathing heavily, her heart pounding in an odd, stuttering way. Blood soaked through her shirt and jacket where she'd been shot, and from the long, shallow cutlass-gash on her arm, but the pain was distant, the way it always was in a battle.

The figure made an abortive movement, and Judith pressed the tip of her cutlass harder against their throat.

Behind her, the door burst open, and light flooded the room. "Admiral Usher?" Someone began, then swore. "Admiral, you're injured—"

Judith blinked against the sudden light, and in the momentary distraction, the figure she'd been holding at cutlass-point scrambled away.

"Detain them, for God's sake!" she snapped, and two of the guards leapt for the figure, pinning them to the ground before they could do whatever it was they'd planned.

Judith sagged in relief, grabbing for the desk against a sudden wash of dizziness.

"Admiral! Call a medic," one of the guards shouted, but Judith shook her head and straightened.

"There will be time for a medic in a moment," she said, and crossed painfully to the figure lying on the floor.

In the light, she could finally make out their features. It was a young man with light skin and bond hair, dressed in a nondescript clerk's uniform. His face was twisted with pain and hate, but she recognized him vaguely as someone she'd passed in the hallway more than once.

"What's this all about, Admiral?" one of the guards asked.

Judith stared down coldly at the man in the grip of the two guards. "What were you doing in Admiral Moore's office at this time of night?" she asked. "What were you after?"

He didn't answer.

"Watch him," Judith snapped to the guards. "If this is what I think it is, he'll likely have some means of killing himself. I'd prefer that not happen until we have opportunity to question him."

The guards nodded, and as they secured the prisoner's hands, Judith turned to the pile of documents and data chips on the floor.

Her head had begun to spin, and for a moment she wasn't sure if she'd keep her balance as she stooped awkwardly to pick them up.

But when she saw what was on them, she cursed.

"Restrain this man, please, and bring him to my office under guard," she said, turning to the guards, who were standing behind her, faces sharp with concern. "Then please call a medic and instruct them to come to the Admiralty offices at once. I won't have time to go in to the hospital, I'm afraid. I need to ask our friend here some questions."

5

Silas

Silas consciously avoided tapping his foot as Ari bent over the lock, twisting the slim blade into the narrow space.

They had to find Gracie. They had to, and he knew damn well that it could already be too late.

And it wasn't just that. Ari's words had started a niggling unease in his chest.

He'd pledged his loyalty to Gracie. But he wasn't sure, standing here with two naval officers, that he could entirely trust himself to keep his priorities straight, to go against the duty that had been engrained in him since he was younger than he could properly remember. He wasn't sure, if the naval officers betrayed them or risked their plan, that he'd not hesitate to shoot, if it came to it.

And if he did—if some unconscious part of him held him back from what he needed to do, and Ari or Gracie or one of the others was hurt by it—he wasn't sure he'd be able to forgive himself.

"There," said Ari at last, straightening. There was a grim, haunted look to her face that told Silas she was as aware as he was of the need for haste. She turned back to the two naval officers behind them. "Price. Ain't making a secret of the fact I don't like you, but we're going to need to kill people, and we're going to need to do it quick and quiet. Think you can handle that?"

Price gave a short nod, their grip tight on the shiv.

"Good," said Ari. She glanced at Silas. "You ready?"

Silas drew in a steadying breath. He looped the thin rope a few more times around his hands, leaving a shoulder's length in between, then nodded grimly. "Ready."

Ari palmed her knife, holding it at the ready, and with the other hand, cautiously pulled the door open.

The guard at the door turned. His eyes widened when he saw them. He opened his mouth, but before he could call out Silas stepped up behind him, slipping a loop of the rope around his neck and yanking it tight. The guard's eyes bugged out of his head as he scrabbled at his throat, but Silas pulled the rope tighter, shoving his knee into the man's back, until his body went limp.

In killing people, at least, his naval training did him credit.

He lowered the unconscious man to the ground and bent, relieving him of his weapons and sliding the jacket off his shoulders. Ari gestured Hollis and Price out, and Silas dragged the man back into the room the four of them had just vacated, tossing the sparker to Ari, and slit the man's throat with his own cutlass.

He'd killed plenty of times before. These were enemy sailors, and he wasn't going to waste time feeling guilty over it. But there was something about the disorientation of doing it on his own initiative, rather than on orders from a superior officer, that made that distinction harder to keep up.

He gritted his teeth.

This was to save Gracie's life, and if it was his choice, it was one he was making freely.

He shut the door quickly before the ghost, if there was one, had time to form, slipped the Rosette navy jacket over his shoulders—it was a bit small, but it would do something, at least, to cover the bloodstains on his shirt—and nodded at Ari.

She started forward, following Hollis's whispered directions.

They made their way silently down the corridors. Ari held up her hand at the corner, and the four of them flattened themselves against the wall, hardly breathing, as a uniformed company jogged past in the intersecting corridor.

Silas frowned, watching them move through the narrow hallway, the rapid precision of their steps, the way they moved as a unit unfamiliar in his memories from the navy.

Then he realized, and bit back a curse.

The uniforms should have told him, but he wasn't used to watching for the differences in Rosette System uniforms.

These weren't sailors.

These were soldiers.

Matisse's fleet wasn't just here to attack the navy. They planned to land ground troops on the Level.

The horror of the realization sent sickness churning in his stomach.

This was war, the likes of which the Level wasn't close to prepared for. The Level depended on the protection of its navy, and if these ships could slip through while the Level wasn't watching for them …

He forced the thought away. He wasn't in the navy any longer. This didn't concern him. He needed to get Gracie and get off the *Chasseuse*, and the Level be damned.

He consciously ignored the memories of his aunt and uncle who'd raised him, his childhood home with his younger cousins, boisterous games of dice with his crewmates below deck. Lawrence, hair tousled and eyes heavy with sleep, smiling up from the pillow beside him.

That had been a long time ago. Every war had its casualties.

From the way the two Level naval officers' posture stiffened, they'd seen it too. But they, too, seemed to realize there was nothing they could do about it at the moment.

"We go right here, then we'll have to get down below decks. I don't know that I'll be able to manage the ratlines, but there should be a lift." Hollis spoke in a whisper, but the tightness in her voice told Silas exactly how much it cost her to admit to weakness. "But we won't be able to keep out of sight forever. We'll want a disguise."

Ari and Silas exchanged glances, and he stepped up to stand next to Ari in the corridor.

They weren't waiting long. There were footsteps in the corridor ahead of them a minute later, and a small knot of sailors rounded the corner.

Silas tensed, and as they passed, he stepped silently out, slipping his makeshift garrotte around the neck of the last sailor in line.

The woman dropped without a sound seconds later, and Silas dragged her back into the corridor, relieved her of her weapons and jacket, and slit her throat. Ari stepped forward to disperse her ghost as Silas tossed the jacket to Hollis. "This should fit you," he said tersely. "But remember, the moment you put it on, you're no longer an enemy captain, and you're no longer covered by the rules of war. You're a spy, and you'll be shot on sight."

Hollis raised her eyebrows as she pulled off her jacket and replaced it with the one he'd thrown her. "If you recall, I was on the point of being shot when these ships appeared. I hardly see how this would be worse."

Silas huffed out a small, surprised laugh, then turned back to the hallway.

The next sailor was alone, and went down easily. The third, Silas had just slipped his garrotte around their neck when two more sailors stepped around the corner.

One of them gave a startled exclamation, then Ari shot him. He went down, but the other sailor had already pulled their energy pistol. Silas shoved himself back against the wall as the shot hissed past him. The sailor he'd been choking struggled, pulling him off-balance, and slipped their fingers through the rope around their neck, yanking it free.

Silas cursed and went for the cutlass he'd taken off the dead guard, but before he could raise it, there was a knife at his throat.

The sailor grunted out a question in a language Silas didn't understand, their voice a hoarse rasp.

And then their eyes widened, blood bubbling up around their lips, and they slipped to the ground. Price stood behind them, blood dripping off the end of their shiv.

"Thank you," Silas panted, straightening.

Price nodded, with no noticeable softening of their expression, and bent beside the body.

When Silas glanced up, Hollis stood in the entrance to the corridor, face set in a grimace of pain, energy pistol in her hand, and Ari was dispatching the ghost of the last of the fallen sailors.

The three of them pulled the bodies of the Rosette sailors into the corridor—Hollis had stepped forward to help, and then stopped at the glare from her first mate—but there wasn't anything they could do about the red smear of blood in the hallway.

"They'll figure out something happened soon enough," said Price, straightening. They'd shrugged into the jacket of the man they'd killed. There was a bloodstain on the back, but, Silas decided, it was probably still better than the alternative. "We'd best get moving."

They reached the lifts without further incident. Their stolen jackets did enough to hide them from casual glances, and Ari managed to keep them safe from anything closer than that.

Silas looked longingly at the ratlines—much faster to climb down, and there wouldn't be a record of their passing—but the tightness around Hollis's eyes made him refrain from saying anything. Whatever he knew about Hollis Ives, she clearly wasn't one to admit weakness unless there was truly no alternative. If there had been even the slightest chance that she could have made the ratlines, she'd never have suggested the lifts. Still, by the time they reached the lower decks, it had been far longer than he'd hoped.

He strode forward after Ari, footsteps loud on the silent deck. From behind him he could hear Hollis's laboured breathing as she tried to keep pace, and when he glanced over his shoulder, he could see the pallor in her face, the way her teeth were clenched. Price had dropped back beside her, and she was leaning on them heavily, but she met his gaze with narrowed eyes.

He sighed and grabbed Ari's arm. "Come on," he whispered, "no point in making Captain Ives pass out, she's the one who knows her damn way around this ship."

Ari scowled at him, but reluctantly slowed, and when he glanced back again, Price cast him a quick, grateful look.

He gritted his teeth. This didn't matter, none of it mattered. He was here to save Gracie, not these naval officers who'd happily shoot her down.

"The door ahead of us leads to the cargo room," said Hollis at last from behind them. Her voice was tight with pain. "If we get through that, we should be able to get into the brig from there."

Ari nodded without looking at the woman, and knelt in front of the door, holding up the key she'd taken from one of the sailor's bodies.

The door opened, and the four of them slipped inside.

The cargo hold was dim, and Silas barked his shins on assorted boxes of supplies more than once as they crossed the broad space, clenching his teeth to keep from cursing. Then they were through, and out the other side.

The corridor that led through the brig was narrow and dimly lit, and the doors, more solid-looking than average, were set at close intervals along the wall.

"Any idea how the hell we're going to find her in here?" Silas muttered through his teeth. "Because I'm guessing we have minutes before we lose our chance."

"Wait," said Price, holding up a hand. "Do you hear that?"

Silas paused.

Now that Price mentioned it, he could hear a faint, high-pitched whine that didn't sound like an alarm. It was coming from close by, too, and there was something about it that prickled at a memory in the back of his brain …

He swore, glancing over at Ari.

Her face had gone very pale. "They're torturing her," she whispered.

He didn't bother answering—she must have heard of the Rosette army's torture methods as much as he had.

He broke into a run, trying to track the sound and paying no attention to whether Hollis and Price were keeping pace. Ari was ahead of him, and she pulled up in front of a door. By the time Silas came to a panting halt beside her, she was already crouched, holding the key-card to the lock.

The light above the door flickered, then flashed red. Ari swore, pulling out her energy pistol. "Guess we're doing this the hard way," she muttered. "This ain't the same as the lock I picked with my knife."

"Wait." Price had come up beside them, Hollis, somehow, keeping pace. They pulled the bloody shiv out of their pocket. "Let me try with this. I've done similar a few times."

Silas frowned, trying to wrap his head around the *Verity's* proper first mate picking locks. Hollis caught his eye and gave a small, grim smile. "Don't … don't judge them on looks," she panted, a hint of humour in her voice even through the tight pain.

Price straightened, brushing off their hands, stepped back, and kicked hard at the point of the door where the fastener met the wall. It flew open with a bang, and Ari and Silas stepped quickly through.

Inside, the high-pitched whine was almost unendurable, and it seemed to wrap around him, squeezing his brain and burrowing into his eardrums. The lights overhead were bright enough that he had to blink several times as his eyes adjusted to the sudden change, and it took him a moment to make out, in the brilliant, sterile white, what was lying in the centre of the room.

Then Ari choked out a curse, and Price muttered, "My God."

Gritting his teeth, Silas looked down at Gracie's bloody form, limp on the floor.

Her face was deathly pale, and bruised so badly that she was scarcely recognizable. Dark blood dripped from the corner of her mouth and pooled around her cheek, matting in her hair, and there were matching dark stains across her shirt, her hands swollen and bloodied.

Vomit rose in his throat, and for a moment he wasn't sure if he'd be able to keep it down.

He swallowed hard, and forced his voice out. "It won't be long until they come to check on her. We'd best get her out of here and figure out what the hell we're going to do next."

6

Gracie knew well enough—she'd always known—that there was no such thing as resisting torture. Everyone broke, at some point.

But she'd been right. The Rosette sailors weren't being careful.

The worst of it was when they were done, for a few minutes or hours—when they'd throw her here in the brig.

It was almost worse than the physical pain. The sharp whining in her ears made thinking impossible, even if she'd had the ability to think through the pain that was so intense that it seemed to fill the world, so intense and so complete that she was drowning under it.

She'd had a few moments of lucidity—enough to have the grim satisfaction of knowing she'd played it right. She'd been injured enough times to be able to judge the severity of what had happened to her, and she wouldn't live through another of their torture sessions.

She wasn't sure she'd live long enough for them to drag her out of the room again.

The noise—that was the part she wasn't sure she could bear. The noise, and the light. They coated the pain that sang through her body with every breath, every movement, covering them like a blanket, sitting hot and heavy and unbearable over everything.

She tried to focus on her breathing, tried to focus on the clean pain each breath brought, but she couldn't, because the sound filled her brain, pounding into her head like a spike. It would send her mad, eventually. It would send her mad, and she'd almost welcome the pain of the torturers if it meant the sound and the light would stop.

Faintly, from the part of her brain that could still focus on anything at all but the sound, she heard the door slam open, footsteps coming inside.

Was it time already? Were they coming to bring her out to torture her again?

Every moment in this damnable place felt like an eternity, and she couldn't judge time or sanity or the evidence of her own damn senses.

Even though she knew this would be the last time, even though the thought was a bone-melting relief, she could feel the way her heart rate surged at the thought, cold fear running through her veins like blood.

You didn't get used to pain like this. And only a fool or a liar could claim not to fear it.

She was afraid—a cold, heavy fear that rose around her like a cloud and choked off her breath. But it hardly mattered, in the end, if you were afraid. It was what you did with the fear that mattered.

The footsteps stopped abruptly.

"My God," someone breathed, and a voice she knew choked out a curse.

With an effort that felt almost impossible, she cracked her swollen eyes open.

The brightness of the lights, reflected off the impossible whiteness of the room around her, sent a spike of pain through her head, but she blinked it back grimly. The room wavered around her, and then a blurred figure came into semi-focus beside her.

"Captain." Ari's voice was choked and desperate. "Sil'n me are going to lift you, OK? Got to get you the hell out of here before anyone comes in to check."

She couldn't summon the energy to mumble a response.

Arms lifted her, and she had to bite back a scream as pain jolted through her bruised body. Ari was cursing, low and steady, but Gracie was upright, somehow. And then whoever was holding her started forward, and the world went mercifully black.

Something was different. Something had changed, and it took Gracie a moment to realize what it was—the sound was gone.

For a moment, she thought she might sob with the relief.

Her entire body ached, pain lancing through her at the slightest movement, and her head pounded and throbbed, but the sound was gone. And when she cracked her eyelids open again, rather than the bright white light of her cell, the scene around her was dimly lit and quiet.

She pulled in a shallow breath. She could taste the iron tang of blood on her lips, and her face was bruised badly enough that her eyes couldn't open farther than slits, but she could make out a small huddle of figures standing a short way off, arguing in low voices.

She swallowed, the movement a sharp pain against her bruised throat, and spat the blood pooling in her mouth. "Ari?" she managed.

Her voice came out as barely a croak, but two of the figures turned abruptly at the sound.

"Captain?" Ari's voice broke on the word. "Captain, you're awake?"

Gracie tried for a wry smile, then gave up. "Ain't too happy about it, but yes," she mumbled through swollen lips.

"Captain. Thank God you're still alive." Sil crouched down beside Ari, sick relief written across his face. "I wasn't sure we'd been in time."

Gracie would have smiled at that, if she could have managed it.

If only he knew.

She'd failed, somehow, miscalculated. They'd taken less time than they should have to break out, and she was still alive, and there was no way in hell she'd talk them into leaving her.

But the way her body sagged in relief at the thought that she was out, she was away and the torturers wouldn't get her again, made it almost impossible to feel anything other than sick gratitude.

She pulled in another shallow breath and let her eyes slide past him to the room around them. "Where'd you bring me, lad?" she asked.

"We're in the cargo hold of the *Chasseuse*," Sil said. "But they'll find us soon enough, I think."

"Silas." A third figure came over to join them. In the dim light, Gracie didn't recognize the newcomer's face. "Captain Ives said she knows a place we may be able to hide for a while. Your captain can wait there while we get the key to get out."

Sil stood, his posture tight with anger and worry. "Dammit, how the hell do you think we'll get her there? I don't dare carry her far without a stretcher, not the way she looks right now. We've got minutes, maybe, before the whole damn ship's on the alert, and—" he broke off, gesturing helplessly at Gracie.

"Sil, Ari," she croaked.

They both turned towards her quickly. "Captain?"

She took another shallow breath, fighting back the pain. "I know you two, and I figure … figure one of you has some rum on you."

There was a moment where Sil and Ari looked at each other. Then, reluctantly, Ari pulled out a slim flask. "Comes in useful sometimes," she muttered. "Ain't a bad idea to have something to get someone talking when you need it."

Gracie almost smiled despite the pain. "Ain't questioning your judgement, lass," she murmured. "But I figure we're not getting out of here 'less I can move, and I'm not going to be able to walk without passing out as is. So unless you've got some damn strong painkillers in that jacket of yours, figure rum'll have to do the trick."

Sil took the flask from Ari and handed it to her, and she tipped it back with a grimace. The liquor burned its way down her throat, but the numbness that followed the burn was blessedly welcome.

Sil raised his eyebrows, watching her. "Thought you didn't drink, Captain," he said, as she took another long pull.

"Don't prefer to," she mumbled. "Don't mean I can't if there's cause for it." She tipped her head back against the wall she'd been propped against, closing her eyes a moment. "Won't be much help getting out, I'm afraid." Already, she could feel the alcohol taking effect, dulling the sharp knife-edge of the pain and blurring her thoughts. It was a familiar relief, one she'd sought far too often back when she'd first fled the Level, when everything was sharp and fresh and she'd thought the hurt of it would kill her. Rum had taken the edge off that pain, too, but never for long enough. Not any longer than it would this pain, but at least this she was doing to some purpose.

She wasn't going to make it out, not like this. She'd been hurt before, but this was … different. There was something broken inside her, and she could feel the strength seeping from her limbs like water seeping through fabric. But Ari and Sil wouldn't leave her here. She knew that to her bones—they wouldn't leave her any more than she'd have left them. And so she'd do what she had to to make sure she wouldn't keep them from getting out.

She took another long pull from the flask, fighting the urge to cough.

On an empty stomach, and exhausted as she was, this would be enough rum to set her stumbling—but then, she'd need that much if she intended to get herself back to the *Sweet Jenny* before she collapsed.

And she had to. They'd never get out trying to carry her, so she'd have to walk.

Sil was pacing back and forth, running a hand through his hair, and she smiled a little, watching him.

She hadn't been sure, when she first signed him on, if he'd make it on the *Sweet Jenny*. But it seemed she'd judged him right after all.

"Go on, Sil," she mumbled. "You take me to this place that Captain Ives here knows about, get whatever information you need from the ship. Going to need a few minutes for the rum to work, anyways, otherwise I ain't going to be walking anywhere. Then we'll get to the *Sweet Jenny*. They've not jumped yet, and I've no doubt it's because they can't figure out how to jump the *Verity* without blowing her to fragments, but that won't last forever."

"I'm not leaving you." Sil's voice was hard. "I'm not going to leave you alone, you're half dead as it is."

Gracie let her eyes fall closed again for just a moment. It was getting harder to hold onto her thoughts, and that, too, was almost a relief. "Ari'll stay with me," she murmured. "And if what I saw back on the *Sweet Jenny's* any indication, figure Captain Ives ain't going anywhere in a hurry either. Three of us can stay back, you and Price go on. Faster you get there, the faster we can get back."

"I'm not leaving my captain with Ari and Mad Dog," Price snapped.

"Mate Price," Hollis began, but Sil cut in, stepping forward to put a hand on Price's shoulder.

"I was in the navy as well," he said, his voice quiet. "I know damn well what it's like, and I know what they tell you about pirates. But if you believe nothing else, believe this: Ari and I won't do anything that would jeopardize Mad Dog's life. We don't know the ship like Ives does, and with Gracie hurt like she is, we wouldn't stand much of a chance to get away on our own anyways. Gracie's right—let's get her and Ives somewhere they'll be safe, and Ari can protect them if it comes to it, while you and I get what we need to get the hell out of here."

Gracie watched the scene with an odd detachment—Price's stiff posture, the way Ives leaned against the wall, as if she wasn't sure how much longer her legs would hold her up, Ari's hand on the butt of her pistol.

At last, Price gave a short, brusque nod. "Fine." They turned to Ives. "Captain, what do you think?"

"I think that's the best option any of us have at the moment." Ives' voice was sharp with a mix of pain and concern.

"Gracie, can you stand?" Ari was crouched next to her. Somehow, with the woman's help, Gracie managed to get herself upright. Her head spun a little, but at least now she could stand without blacking out. She nodded, and Ari slipped a gingerly arm around her waist, avoiding, at least, the worst of the bruises. "Lean on me, then," Ari whispered.

Gracie almost smiled. Even with the alcohol dulling the pain, she could scarcely have stayed upright without Ari taking most of her weight.

"Let's go," said Sil, and they started across the floor of the darkened cargo hold.

They ran across two sailors as they stepped cautiously through the exit and out into the corridor beyond. Sil and Price dispatched them with a brutal efficiency that made her raise her eyebrows, then dragged the bodies back into the cargo hold.

Ives, in front, led them down a maze of narrow corridors, until at last they reached a small door. Ari bent over it, and a moment later it swung open.

Inside were cluttered stacks of what looked like obsolete tech and broken spare parts.

"I doubt anyone will look for us here," said Ives, stepping inside. "And we're not far from where they store the life vessels, for when we make our escape." She turned to Silas, her glance taking him in quickly, and her voice went hard. "Silas. I know what you did back on the *Sweet Jenny* to negotiate my surrender. I saved your and Ari's lives in thanks, and it's the only reason I'm currently trusting you. But I warn you, if my first mate is killed or captured on your account …"

"Price and I are after the same thing," said Silas, in an even voice. "We both want to keep our captains alive and get off this damnable ship. And until that happens, I'll protect Price as if they were my own damn crew."

Hollis studied him a moment longer. "Thank you," she said at last, sinking down onto an empty crate.

Ari lowered Gracie to the ground as well, leaning her up against the wall. Gracie managed to bite back the sharp gasp at the motion, but there was a moment she wasn't certain she'd be able to hold on to consciousness.

And then at last she was settled, and she leaned her head back against the wall and closed her eyes, letting the voices fade to sound as Price and Silas took their leave.

She wasn't sure if it was the rum or the pain or simply the fact that she was dying that brought the memories crowding so thick around her.

She'd always fought them off before. But now, it hardly seemed to matter—the pain of them faded by the pain in her body, leaving only the touch of sweetness.

Gracie looked up at the tap on her cabin door. "Come in," she called, leaning back in her seat.

She didn't know who it was. But she had a guess.

The door swung open, and Jenny Usher stepped inside.

Gracie grinned, pushing back her chair. "Jenny. I was wondering if you'd stop by."

Jenny pushed the door closed behind her. Her expression was stern, but there was something in her eyes that told Gracie that the woman had been thinking about their kiss that afternoon, in the corridor by the captain's cabin, as much as Gracie had.

"Grace," Judith said. "I ... we can't do this. There are rules in the navy about ... relations between officers on the same ship."

Gracie smiled lazily, cocking her head to one side. "Relations? What sort of relations did you have in mind, Mate Usher?"

Jenny blew out a short breath, and Gracie grinned wider. Something about Jenny did that to her, the way she responded to Gracie's teasing, her quick, exasperated breaths, the way she tried so hard to pretend it didn't affect her as much as it did Gracie.

"This isn't a laughing matter," she snapped, but the tone wasn't nearly as

hard as she'd probably intended.

Gracie stood, leaning up against the desk. "It's not, at that," she said quietly. "I never figured it was."

Jenny's eyes caught hers, and even after these months they'd served together, the gravity-force of it punched the breath from Gracie's chest.

Jenny took a step closer, as if she was pulled by that same magnetic draw, unable to stop herself. "There are rules," she said again, but her voice was quieter now, a hint of breathlessness to it.

Gracie stood where she was.

She'd already fallen for Jenny. She'd long since given up trying to pretend to herself otherwise, trying to pretend she could be suave and aloof. Hell, she'd fallen so hard she wasn't sure, anymore, which way was up.

But she'd not push her. Jenny would come of her own accord, or she wouldn't. And if she didn't, perhaps that would slice the beating heart from Gracie's chest, but she'd not push. She couldn't. This was too important.

This was her whole world, and she'd never take something that important other than freely offered and given.

Jenny took another step. The cabin wasn't large, and she was close enough now that Gracie could have reached out and touched her. But she held herself back.

"Grew up in the navy, Jenny. I know the rules, and you know that," she said instead. "So what did you come here to tell me?"

Jenny closed her eyes. "It's easy enough for you, Grace." Her voice was unsteady. "Your parents are vice-admirals, both of them. You say the navy wouldn't dare throw you out—maybe it wouldn't. But my parents have no name behind them. I don't have the protection you have." There was a desperation to her words, as if she was trying to convince herself as much as Gracie.

Gracie waited until she'd opened her eyes again, waited until her gaze was locked with Gracie's.

"Jenny," she said softly. "You know me better'n that. If you don't want this, I

won't say another word. But if you do—Jenny, if they'd throw you out, they'd have to throw me out first. If they tried to punish you, they'd have to step over my body to do it."

She could see the quick rise and fall of Jenny's breath from here, the tension in her body, the desperate wanting.

Her own body was hot with a desire that was almost a physical need, enough that if her hands hadn't been holding onto the desk behind her, they'd have been trembling.

"I put my own body between my sailors and the pirates' cutlasses. I'd defy the navy itself to save their lives and bring them home, because they're mine. And I protect what's mine, Jenny. I protect it with my blood."

"Grace ..." Jenny's voice caught, and she took the final step, so close that Gracie could feel the heat of her body.

Gracie reached out, finally, letting her hand slide down Jenny's cheek, cupping her face. The air between them was so heavy with want she could feel the humming tension of it on her skin, taste it on her tongue. She leaned in, never taking her eyes from Jenny's.

"You don't want this, Jenny, just tell me," she whispered against Jenny's lips. "And I'll not do it again."

Jenny's heartbeat pulsed rapid and unsteady under her fingertips.

"Grace," Jenny said again, her voice a hoarse whisper.

She closed the breath of space between them, and the taste of her lips on Gracie's was enough to pull Gracie under completely, drown her and leave her gasping for air and praying she'd never surface. She tangled her fingers into Jenny's hair and pulled her closer, dragging their bodies together, the hunger in her kiss matched by an answering hunger in Jenny's.

Perhaps she'd known, even then, she was dooming herself.

Perhaps she'd realized, even then, she didn't care.

The door clicked shut, and the sound of Ari's footsteps crossing the floor towards her pulled her from her memories.

"Captain. How are you feeling?"

From the sound of her voice, she'd crouched next to Gracie.

Gracie lifted her head with an effort and forced her eyes open, biting back the comment that had jumped to her tongue. "Figure I'm as good as I'll be until we get back to the *Sweet Jenny,*" she mumbled instead. She wasn't sure if it was the alcohol or the injuries slurring her speech, and she wasn't sure, in the end, that it made a difference.

She'd not meant to be here. But now that she was, she'd have to figure out a way to get them off the ship and back to the *Sweet Jenny.* Ari and Sil would have to take the ship back on their own—she knew well enough she'd not last much longer than that, and she'd be no use even if she did. But getting them off the Rosette ship she would do, if she possibly could.

She'd protect what was hers with her blood. After so much that had turned out to be a lie, that, at least, was still the truth.

And Sil and Ari and the rest of her crew were hers.

She glanced over at Ives. The young naval captain was slumped against the wall as well, and there was a sharp pain in her expression that she must have been holding back, probably for her first mate's sake.

Gracie's mouth twitched a little in a smile. Not much to work with, truth be told—three uninjured out of the five of them, and they had to get themselves off a fully-crewed enemy warship.

Still, she'd worked with worse odds in her time. She knew Ari, and she knew Sil. She knew damn well she could depend on them. And this Hollis Ives and her first mate, whatever else she might say of them, were as courageous and bull-headed as she'd ever been.

"Well then," she said, raising her voice enough that Ives would hear. "Guess we'd best figure out a way off this ship for when Sil and that naval officer get back, hadn't we?"

7

Silas

When the door clicked shut behind them, Silas and Price turned to look at each other.

Silas shook his head. "Listen," he said quietly. "I know you hate me, and I can't blame you. But I assume you want to keep Hollis alive as much as I want to keep Gracie alive, so we're just going to have to damn well trust each other until we can get them both off this ship."

Price studied him for a long moment. Their expression was still that frozen calm he'd noted, the one that was so familiar from his days in the navy—you didn't show emotion in the navy, you did as you were told.

But he'd seen the way Price used a shiv, seen how they'd reacted to Ari's threat. They were clearly competent in a fight, and right now, that was all he cared about.

"Very well," they said at last. They paused. "I'm … sorry about your captain."

Silas jerked his head in a grim nod, and tried to push away the sight of Gracie lying on the floor in the brig.

Ari would keep her alive. He knew damn well that Ari would sell her soul to keep Gracie alive, if it came to it. And right now, he needed to focus on what he and Price were about to do.

"You have the directions?" he asked.

Price nodded. "Best if we both have them, I think." They sent a copy of the roughly sketched map over to his comm with a flick of their wrist. Now that they'd apparently decided to trust him, they seemed averse to wasting any more time on suspicion.

The Rosette officers hadn't bothered taking their comms, thank God, probably because their communications block the fleet had set up would have made it impossible for them to contact anyone on the *Verity* or the *Sweet Jenny* regardless, but at least he and Price would be able to contact Ari and Hollis if there was trouble.

Silas studied the map. "We're going to be seen," he said at last. "There's no way around it. We'll have to get across the main deck if we want to get to the code room."

Price glanced down at the Rosette System uniform jackets the two of them wore. "Will this be enough, do you think?"

"Not unless you know how to speak Settic," Silas muttered. "I know how to say hello and ask to use the necessary, and my accent is probably bad enough they wouldn't understand even that."

Price cracked a small smile. "I know a little. I couldn't carry on a conversation, but I can understand it well enough."

Silas nodded, biting the inside of his cheek. Then he sighed and stripped off his jacket. "Sailors before the mast dress about the same, whether they're merchant, or pirate, or navy. We'll just have to hope it's the same in the Rosette navy." He glanced down at his shirt.

His stomach still twisted at the sight of the blood—the weight of the Level naval officer pulled up against him as he slit her throat, the hot rush of blood down his arms and chest, his frantic panic at

Temple's limp body, all still far too bright in his memory.

"But I'm afraid I'm not going to pass for anything but a murderer at the moment," he added, shaking his head.

Price raised an eyebrow, but declined to comment.

Silas sighed, and reached down reluctantly to retrieve the jacket. Dressing as an officer would mean he'd likely be expected to answer when spoken to, but maybe Price could do the speaking for both of them …

Something soft hit him, and he yanked it away on instinct before he realized it was a faded white officer's shirt. He glanced up to see Price re-buttoning their jacket.

"Cut the cuffs off, they'll mark you as an officer. But if you don't tuck it in, it should do well enough to cover the bloodstain on your breeches," they said.

Silas blinked at them, then nodded and stripped off his bloody shirt, replacing it with Price's. It was too narrow in the shoulders, and the shirt-sleeves, once he'd pulled out his stolen buck-knife and hacked off the fine cuffs, came half-way between his wrist and elbow, but the ill fit and the hacked off sleeves, along with the small spatters of blood and dirt from the battle, were more than enough to disguise the officer's cut of the shirt.

He laced the shirt quickly, kicked the Rosette officer's jacket and his own blood-encrusted shirt into a corner, and turned to Price. "Let's go," he said, and the two of them started off.

They made their way cautiously along the mostly deserted corridors until they reached the ratlines leading up to the main deck. They scrambled up them quickly, jumping off at a small corridor just outside the main deck and brushing off their clothes, then stepped out onto the main deck.

Price walked purposefully ahead, and Silas followed in their wake, watching the movement on the deck from the corner of his eye. It was bustling with activity, but nothing unusual for a ship of the line. That was a good sign, at least—their escape must not yet have been discovered.

His heart pounded quick and hard.

Just get to the code room, get the information, and then he and Ari could get Gracie off this godforsaken ship and back onto the *Sweet Jenny*. And then …

He consciously refused to let himself remember the way Gracie's face had looked, the limp droop to her body, the small trickle of blood dribbling from the corner of her mouth.

Vee would be able to bring her around. Vee was good at what she did, and she'd save Gracie, she'd find a way.

A voice blared out through the amplifiers on the deck, loud enough to shock Silas out of his thoughts. He glanced up quickly. Price tensed, but continued walking, and Silas followed suit, his jaw clenched so hard it hurt.

He hadn't understood the words of the broadcast, but the urgency in them gave him a good enough guess as to what this was about.

An officer stepped in front of them, grabbing Price by the arm, and shouted something.

Price gave a terse answer and gestured to Silas. The officer nodded and pointed down a corridor. Price beckoned, and Silas stepped smartly forward, hoping he'd read the situation correctly, and followed Price at a brisk pace down the hall.

"They found the guard," Price hissed over their shoulder as they walked. "They're sending out parties to look for us."

Silas nodded and kept pace as they turned a corner.

The moment the two of them were out of sight, they looked at each other and broke into a run.

The ship was swarming with search parties, but at least it meant that no one questioned an officer and a sailor sprinting down the halls in the organized chaos.

The two of them reached the edge of the deck unhindered, vaulted the rail, and slid down the ratlines to the deck indicated on Hollis's map.

"There'll be guards when we get there," Silas panted as he ran.

Price nodded. "I doubt we'll have time to distract them. Do you have a weapon?"

Silas touched his pocket. "I picked up an energy pistol."

"I have a cutlass. Between the two of us, we should be able to keep them from getting word out, I think." Their voice was grim.

The two of them slowed when they turned down the final corridor leading to their destination. "Do you have the key?" Price whispered. Silas pulled it out of his pocket.

When they reached the door, he crouched in front of it. "You ready?" he whispered.

Price nodded. Their body was tense as a whipcord, their cutlass held ready.

Silas took a deep breath and tapped the lock. The light above the door flickered green, and he shoved the door open, pistol raised.

A handful of people were gathered around the bank of computers in the centre of the room.

Silas shot the first officer in the face as she turned towards the door, then shot two more as they started for him. Price had already stepped around him, and the sailor in front of them slumped to the ground, clutching at a bloody cutlass-wound. Price spun, catching another sailor across the throat as they pulled out their pistol.

Silas dived to the floor as an energy blast lit the air above his head. He rolled to his feet and lunged at the woman holding the pistol, wrestling it from her hands and bringing the butt of it down across her temple. She slumped, eyes fluttering closed, and he scrambled to his feet, his shot finding her just as she began to stir.

He gasped in a breath and took quick stock of the room.

Price had taken down two sailors, and was facing another, the ring of steel on steel deafeningly loud in the small room. Besides the woman on the floor, Silas's shots had killed one sailor outright, and the other was slumped back against the wall, clutching her stomach. That left one injured and three left to fight, and the blue haze of a ghost gathering around at least one of the bodies.

He half-turned towards it, reaching for his sparker on instinct, when a movement from the corner of his eye caught his attention.

A sailor was reaching for the panic button, fear clear on her face.

Silas jumped for her. She stumbled backwards, holding up her arms to protect herself, then Price's arm was around her waist and she slumped as they slit her throat.

Silas turned on the remaining two sailors. "Give up now, and we'll let you live," he panted.

They stared at him blankly, their faces sharp with terror.

Price gave him a wry glance, and repeated the words in Settic.

One of the two remaining sailors opened his mouth as if to respond.

Then his eyes went wide, and Silas glanced over his shoulder in time to see a fully-formed ghost, teeth bared, black eyes locked on the sailor.

For a moment, no one moved.

Then the last of the sailors, huddled near the door, brought his wrist up as if to call for aid.

Silas turned his head away as the ghost sprang, the sailor's shrill scream and the wet sound of ghostly claws through flesh telling him everything he needed to know. The other sailor yanked a sparker out of his pocket, his hands trembling.

He wasn't in time. Another ghost materialized behind him, one of the sailors Price had taken down. The man didn't even have time to scream.

The woman Silas had shot gave a small, brief sigh, her body going limp. The ghosts' attention sprang towards her, and they drifted closer, but a moment later a blue haze began to gather over her still form.

Silas bit back a curse.

He and Price wouldn't stand a damn chance against three ghosts.

Price caught his eye and mouthed carefully, "Get the door open, I'll keep them occupied."

Silas gave them the slightest nod in return.

The ghosts' attention was still focused on the dead woman, but the moment he moved, it would shift.

Price lit their sparker, and both ghosts spun, their hungry gaze finding the *Verity's* first mate as Price backed slowly into the corner.

Holding his breath, Silas shifted towards the door.

The ghosts were drifting closer to Price now, the glowing sparker the only reason both ghosts hadn't yet sprung, but it would only hold them back for a moment.

Across the room, the blue over the dead woman's body was beginning to coalesce into its final human-shaped form, gaze turning towards Price with the hungry, piercing interest of the dead.

Price's eyes found Silas, and there was a grim look there that told him they knew they'd put their life in Silas's hands. If he chose, he could leave them to die, and there'd be nothing they could do about it.

Silas took a deep breath, tightening his hands on his own sparker.

Then, in one swift movement, he covered the remaining distance to the door and flung it open. The ghosts spun on him, and he threw himself through the opening, landing hard on the floor, the only thought in his head to get somewhere, anywhere, defensible. The ghosts streamed after him, and in the back of his mind Silas heard Price's low curse. Then Price had grabbed him by the back of the shirt and yanked him inside, slamming the door behind the two of them with their foot.

For a few moments, he and Price lay there panting. At last, Price grimaced and rolled to their feet. Their jacket, Silas noted, was stained with blood, their face pale.

"Are you hurt?" he asked, shoving himself upright.

Price glanced down at their arm, where an expanding red stain blossomed out from a ragged cut in the fabric. "Not badly, I think. At least, nothing like Ives and Mad Dog."

Silas raised his eyebrows. "That's not saying much."

Price stared at him, then chuckled reluctantly. "I suppose it's not, at that." They paused. "Thank you. I ... wasn't sure you'd get the door in time."

He heard the words they didn't say—they hadn't been sure he'd get the door at all, before they were torn to pieces.

He smiled a little. "Thank you. I wasn't sure I'd survive after I did."

They gave him a brief smile in return, then turned to the computers. "I don't think anyone got word out, but someone will recognize those ghosts. We'd best get what we came for and get out."

Silas retrieved the energy pistol from where he'd dropped it. "Best get the coordinates of the *Sweet Jenny*, while you're in there. We won't want to waste time scanning for her."

Price nodded. Silas crossed to the door to listened for footsteps as

Price bent over the computers, and tried not to think of how easy it was to fall back into the automatic structure of command he'd known for most of his life.

He knew, logically, it couldn't have been more than a few minutes, but his entire body was humming with tension, and every second seemed to take an hour.

There was already an alarm out for them, and they still had to get back to where they'd left Hollis and Ari and Gracie, and from there to the life vessels.

"There. I think I've got what we need," Price said at last, straightening.

Silas nodded, and cautiously pulled the door open.

The ghosts, it appeared, had moved on to look for easier prey, and he stepped out into the corridor, Price at his heels. He pulled up the map on his comm, oriented himself, and started forward at a brisk pace.

They'd barely made it to the end of the hallway when they were spotted. An officer, walking in the other direction, pulled up sharply. They gestured at Price's bloody arm and snapped out something that must have been a question.

Price shook their head, clearly trying to defuse the situation. The officer stepped closer, raising their wrist to their mouth.

Price caught Silas's eye, and Silas lunged for the Rosette officer. Before he could get the loop of rope over their head, though, they'd raised their wrist and called something over the comm line.

Price swore and stepped forward, laying the officer out on the floor with a swift uppercut. "Come on," they snapped, "They'll be on their feet in a moment."

Silas followed them as they took off down the corridors at a sprint towards the room where Gracie and Ari and Hollis waited.

"We're not going to make it down there," Silas muttered as the two of them pounded around another corridor. The corridors behind them were filling with shouting sailors. "We'll have to meet them near the life vessels." He tapped his comm, opening a line through to Ari. "Ari," he snapped when she answered. "We're on our way, but we've got company. Can you get to the life vessels and meet us there?"

There was a moment's pause. Then Ari said, her voice grim, "Don't sound like we have much choice. Call in when you get there." Then the line went dead.

8

Gracie

"Captain?" Ari's voice made Gracie turn, and she winced at the movement.

Ives had come over, lowering herself painfully to the ground beside them, and she was watching Gracie with sharp suspicion.

Gracie smiled.

The rum had dulled the pain by now, enough that it was bearable, but in exchange it had left her thoughts muddy, her head spinning a little when she tried to move.

"Ives," she managed. The word slurred in her mouth, but she found it difficult to care. "Pull us up a map, there's a good lass. Don't figure Sil and your Mate Price'll have the leisure to come back'n fetch us, so we'd best figure a way to get all of us off this damn ship for when they do come back."

Hollis pulled up a note and set it to hover in front of the three of them, enlarging it enough to make it legible. It was a quick and dirty sketch, and between the rum and the torture, Gracie's vision was less than certain, but if she focused, she could make the drawing make sense.

"This is the life-vessel airlock I think will be our best chance," said Hollis, pointing. "We should be able to get there from here unseen. It won't be quick, but if Ari can fight, I can handle a pistol, at least." Her voice was grim, and Gracie heard in it what she wasn't saying—Ari could fight, but Gracie would be a liability.

Lass wasn't wrong—Gracie knew well enough she'd be the one they'd be dragging out.

It would be so easy to lie back, let her eyes fall closed, let Ari and Hollis between them figure out a strategy to get them off the ship.

But Hollis was navy. She'd have been trained to take officers prisoners if possible, trained that people in positions of authority didn't deserve to die. She'd have been trained to minimize casualties, and Gracie knew damn well that would get them killed. And Ari—the woman was ruthless enough, but she'd be worried about Sil and worried about Gracie.

Gracie studied the map, squinting as it blurred and wavered before her eyes.

Then she leaned back again, smiling just a little.

They called her ruthless, back on Blackrock. They called her heartless and vicious, and she knew damn well she'd become that over the years. That had been what she'd needed to survive, and she didn't regret it.

But there was a reason she didn't drink much anymore, other than cold sweet tea.

Ruthless as she'd been, vicious and cunning and heartless as she'd needed to be to keep herself and her crew alive, there was always something, some part of her, that held her back from her most vicious impulses.

When she drank, that part of her went away.

Even she had been shocked, sometimes, at the plans she'd made when she was drunk, and there was nothing that kept her from the worst of herself. She'd looked at what she'd done, or what she'd planned to do, and a cold pit would open in her stomach at the horror of it.

She wondered, sometimes, if after everything she'd done, everything the Level had done to her, she was really any different from the vicious, bloodthirsty ghosts—turned by her pain and trauma into something not entirely human, a vessel of vengeance and fury.

She could hold it back when she was sober.

But now … well, now, perhaps, it was exactly what was needed.

"Those compartments, lass. Next to the life vessel airlock. Those're crew bunks?"

Hollis glanced down at her map, and her eyes narrowed a little, formed into tight lines of worry. "Yes," she said shortly. "They're crew bunks, but there's too many of them. Between that and what we saw on our way to find you, I suspect they're carrying soldiers for a ground assault on the Level."

Gracie nodded. She'd guessed as much herself. "Those ground troops," she said. "They'd not have traveled at FTL before this, no? I doubt they've seen much action. Rosette System hasn't been in a ground war since I've been alive. And they'd need to pack them in tight to have room. Figure they may have skimped on the ghost-doors between the compartments."

Hollis was watching her, the worry in her gaze turned to calculation. "It's possible," she said slowly.

The tone in her voice told Gracie that she was humouring someone too drunk or delirious to make sense.

Just as well, likely.

"One last question, Ives, then we can go," she said. Her head was spinning in earnest now, and she had to fight back nausea when she tried to focus her eyes. "Level ships of the line, they'll have an emergency door between the crew bunks and the life vessels. You figure they have them on the Rosette ships as well?"

Hollis nodded again, glancing up to catch Ari's eyes. "Yes, I believe they do. It's standard design." She paused. "We'd best get moving, I think. Do you think you can walk?"

"Aye," Gracie slurred.

She wasn't entirely sure she could walk, wasn't sure her legs would obey her.

But she had to. There wasn't another choice, if she wanted to save her crew.

From outside, there was the sudden, shrill sound of an alarm going off. Hollis's head jerked up, expression sharp with worry, and she could see the worry on Ari's face.

Sil and Price must have been seen.

She'd been expecting it—they'd hardly make their way through a ship full of enemy sailors and soldiers searching for them without someone noticing.

With luck, they'd at least got what they went for. If they hadn't, she wasn't sure she could think of another plan quick enough to save them.

But she'd worry about that when it came.

"Ari, if you'll help me up, lass? Sounds of it, we'd best be on our way."

Ari crouched next to her, slipping an arm around her back.

Even that movement jolted pain through her whole body. She gasped with it, and felt Ari flinch.

"'S alright, lass, just get me up," she mumbled, and somehow, between the two of them, she staggered to her feet.

For few moments she had to concentrate hard not to vomit, and she was leaning on Ari so heavily that the woman was practically carrying her.

But she was upright, and for now, it was enough.

She was upright, and she'd get Sil and Ari off this ship in one piece. The rest would be up to them.

Hollis

Hollis grimaced.

Every part of her hurt, and the exhaustion that she'd managed to push down while they were making their escape was creeping back, now that her body had a chance to stop for long enough to take stock. The makeshift bandage cinched tight around her middle was enough to keep her upright, and stop the probably irrational fear that her innards would spill out if she wasn't careful, but damnation, it hurt.

She pulled the stolen pistol from her belt and checked it, then crossed to the door to listen before pushing it open. The corridor outside should be deserted. Even with the alarm, she couldn't imagine anyone would think to search where she'd hidden them.

"Ari!" Silas's voice through Ari's comm was enough to make Hollis jump. "We're on our way, but we've got company. Can you get to the life vessels and meet us there?"

"Don't sound like we have much choice," said Ari grimly. "Call in when you get there."

Hollis tapped her own comm. "Price? Are you alright?"

"Fine, Captain." Foster's voice was sharp with worry. "But they've spotted us, I'm afraid."

"I'll send through the coordinates to the life vessels," Hollis snapped. She tapped the airlock's location through her comm. "Can you get there?"

"I believe so," said Foster at last. "But the airlocks will be guarded."

"We'll deal with that when we get to it," Hollis muttered, tapping off her comm. When she turned, Mad Dog was on her feet, face pinched and pale with pain, leaning heavily against Ari.

"Well, Captain Ives, shall we go?" she rasped.

Hollis nodded, and pushed the door open.

She'd guessed correctly, thank God—the path she'd marked for them was all but deserted, and there were few enough sailors that crossed their path that they were able to stay hidden in the shadows. Mad Dog was clearly doing her best not to hold them back, but Hollis could hear the laboured rasp of her breathing,

Finally, Hollis opened the door to the cargo hold carefully, and they peered out down the corridor to the entrance to the life vessels.

Hollis swore under her breath.

"What is it?" hissed Ari from behind her.

She shook her head tightly. "They've set a guard. There's no way we get through there without them sending up an alarm, I'm afraid."

Ari cursed, her voice hard and strained. "Guess we wait for Sil and Price to show up, then kill as many of the damn bastards as we can. Still possible we can get out before they kill us."

"Ain't ... ain't such a bad thing if they send out an alarm." Mad Dog's voice was thick with pain and barely audible.

Ari turned to look at her. "Captain?"

With an obvious effort, Mad Dog turned her head to look at the pirate woman. "Ari. Need you to do something for me, lass."

Ari frowned. "Aye, Captain?"

Mad Dog's lips pulled up into an expression that was more a grimace than a smile. "Need you to get over there and kill a couple of those sailors." She turned to Hollis. "You got another of those keys, don't you?"

Hollis nodded, frowning.

"Good. You're going to get in there and open that door. Let them send up their damn alarm, then Ari, you kill a handful of those bastards." She paused, calculating. "As many as it'd take to get three, four ghosts, I think. Slit their throats, shove them through the door, lock it."

For a moment Hollis stared at her, mind ticking through the options—Mad Dog was too injured or drunk to think straight. She was trying to cause enough of a distraction that Foster and Silas could get back. She was …

Ari sucked in a breath, a quick, horrified little gasp, and it was that that made Hollis suddenly realize.

She felt her blood turn to ice.

"They'll send out the alarm, and it will open the doors between the life vessels and the crew's quarters," she said in a low voice.

"Not just the one, either," Ari said, her own voice barely more than a whisper. "They'll open all of them, because that's the whole damn reason the crew quarters empty onto the life vessels."

"And it'll clear the way a treat," said Mad Dog. Her words were still slurred, but Hollis could hear the sharp intelligence under them, the unnerving calculation that had almost sent her to her death twice now. "Figure once the ghosts see there's warm bodies to be had on the other side of those doors, won't need to do much to get them out of the airlock."

For a moment, Hollis and Ari stared at each other, and Hollis saw her own horror reflected in Ari's eyes.

How many sleepy, bleary-eyed Rosette sailors and soldiers would the ghosts rip apart before they were stopped? A hundred? More?

Mad Dog was watching her. "This is war, Captain Ives," she mumbled. "And I figure you've done worse in your time, when it was pirates on the other side of your guns." She turned to Ari, her voice still mild. "That was a damn order, lass."

Ari sucked in another quick breath. "Aye, Captain," she said. She turned to Hollis. "You got the stomach for it, Ives, or are you going to hand the damn key to me?"

Hollis pulled in a long breath, the pain of it against her injury steadying.

Mad Dog was right. This was war. And even if she herself wouldn't have dreamed up a revenge this vicious—she realized, suddenly, that as much as she'd always been fighting from the bottom up, clawing and desperate to survive in a world that didn't want her, she'd never known, really, the kind of desperation that would drive someone to dream up something like this. The kind of desperation that didn't end in an honourable duel, and the risk of being thrown out of the Academy if you were found out, but in a frantic, brutal battle for survival, where you ripped someone's throat out with your damn teeth or you let them do it to you.

That was Mad Dog's world. Ari's world.

And, sympathize with the pirates or despise them, she'd had a hand in making it.

She nodded brusquely. "We'd best do it quick-time, then. Silas and Mate Price will be here shortly, unless I miss my guess."

9

Silas

Silas and Price pounded down the ship's corridors towards the coordinates Hollis had sent, shouts and the sound of footsteps following. Silas had his energy pistol out, and Price, running beside him, did as well.

Price hissed a curse, and Silas glanced over his shoulder in time to see them send an energy blast at one of their pursuers who'd rounded the corner.

Silas swore as well, anxiety humming through his muscles and throbbing in his brain.

The two of them would make it to the airlock, probably, but they'd bring far too many sailors and soldiers on their heels, and he had no idea how long it would take to break into the airlock and onto one of the life vessels.

He gritted his teeth and tried to think. They could try to lose their pursuers, but chances were they'd only manage to gain more. And there was no way he and Price could stop and fight—there were simply too many after them.

Then he frowned.

The footsteps behind the two of them were growing fainter.

He glanced over at Price.

They shrugged. "Nothing we can do about it, whatever it is," they said shortly.

"Ari?" he hissed through his comm as he ran. "Are you alright?"

"Yeah, we're fine." There was an odd note to her voice. "You on your way?"

"Be there in a minute. Be ready to move." He tapped off his comm and glanced at Price again. "It's not them in trouble, at least," he panted.

Price nodded, and they sprinted on.

By the time they approached the coordinates Hollis had given them as a meeting place, the sound of footsteps after them still hadn't returned. The realization sent a pang of unease through Silas, but … well, they had problems enough to worry them at the moment.

Ari and Hollis were waiting in a small corridor outside the airlock. Gracie was upright, but slumped against Ari, and she looked more dead than alive.

"We got the codes," Price panted as the two of them came to a halt in front of the others.

"Good," Hollis snapped. "Let's go!" She stepped out towards the empty airlock door, an abortive movement that told Silas she was used to striding, and the fact that every step was now a calculation was not something she was accustomed to.

"What the hell's going on?" Silas whispered to Ari, stepping up beside her to take some of Gracie's weight.

"Ghosts," she said shortly. "Ives and I showed ourselves, let the guards sound an alarm, then killed the guards at the door, shoved them into the airlock. Airlock emergency door connects to the crew's quarters."

He frowned at her for a moment, adjusting Gracie's arm over his shoulder as the three of them stumbled forward. "You …"

Then he realized, and felt his entire body go cold with horror.

Ari smiled grimly. "Like Gracie said, Sil—this is war."

He nodded. He couldn't exactly argue against that.

But the thought of what must have happened to the sailors, as vicious, hungry ghosts, their numbers growing with every group of sailors hunted and slaughtered, swept over them, was enough, almost, to make him sick to his stomach. No wonder his and Price's pursuers had stopped following them—this had been a bloody massacre.

Ahead of him, Hollis and Price must have been having a similar conversation, because he saw Price stiffen, then, at last, nod.

Despite the horror of it, the strategy had worked—the airlock was unguarded, and when he bent and tapped the key that Ari had stolen against it, it swung wide. He glanced at Ari, then slipped Gracie's arm from his shoulder, easing her against Ari, and pulled the sparker from his pocket. "Let me check that it's clear before anyone steps in," he said over his shoulder to the two naval officers, then gingerly, he stepped inside.

The floor was a mess of blood and shredded bodies. Corpses lay crumpled where they'd fallen, eyes wide and blank, face twisted with terror. There were four in a heap by the door, left unmarred except for the pistol and cutlass wounds that had killed them, but the others were torn with the vicious, unmistakable mark of ghost-deaths. Blood spattered the walls and pooled on the floor, and looking at the place, he could all but hear the sailors' agonized screams as they'd run to the place where they thought they'd find safety, only to discover the trap.

The ghosts themselves, though, were gone.

"It's safe," he whispered over his shoulder, but he kept his sparker out and ignited as the others stepped cautiously inside.

Price bit back a curse as they stepped in, Hollis leaning on their arm. But they drew in a long breath and kept walking.

Price must have served in the navy long enough to have seen worse than this. Hell, Silas has seen worse than this. But somehow, it didn't make it less horrifying.

Getting into the life vessels was easy enough, and with the code Price had copied, Ari was able to release the airlock.

"Wait, lad."

He turned in surprise to see that Gracie had raised her head. "Don't go just yet. May as well make it hard for them to follow, no?" She gestured weakly at the projectile pistol he'd shoved into his belt.

He raised his eyebrows, then nodded grimly.

She was right. If they were going to leave, they'd best leave the airlock as nonfunctional as possible.

"Get ready to go, I'm going to see what I can do to keep them off our tail for a while," he muttered to Ari. She nodded and slipped into the pilot's seat as Price helped Hollis to sit, and Silas strode quickly down the gangplank. He pulled out the projectile pistol, took careful aim, and fired until the gun was empty.

The airlock was reinforced, but even a reinforced airlock could be damaged by a projectile pistol, if you knew where to aim and were stupid enough to try it. When he shoved the pistol back into his belt and strode back on board, he could already hear the sharp hiss of pressure escaping.

"Good lad," Gracie mumbled. Ari had set her down on one of the seats, and she'd slumped back, eyes closed.

"Strap in," Ari called. "I'm opening the airlock."

Silas took his seat, and a moment later there came the familiar clanking of a ship's airlock opening.

The small life vessel rose gently, then lurched forward out the opening.

Silas glanced over his shoulder out the vessel's porthole as they accelerated away from the Rosette ship.

If they'd been seen, it would be a simple thing for the *Chasseuse* to shoot them down. But with the panic of ghosts tearing through the crew quarters and leaving blood and destruction in their wake, no one had time to spare to notice the tiny dot of a life vessel pulling away from the ship.

He blew out a short breath and ran his fingers through his hair, trying to block the picture from his mind.

Ghost deaths were brutal, perhaps the most brutal way for a sailor to go.

Except, of course, for what had happened in the Starfire disaster. What had happened to his parents. That, perhaps, was worse.

"Here's the coordinates of the *Sweet Jenny*, last they marked them," Silas said, straightening at last and stepping forward to crouch beside Ari. He tapped the information through to her, and she nodded and set it into the vessel's controls.

He watched her a moment before he stood again. He was still shaky with adrenaline, every muscle in his body tight, his brain buzzing.

There were bound to be Rosette sailors on the *Sweet Jenny*, but at least for the moment they were free, and off the *Chasseuse*.

He turned back to his seat.

Then he frowned, his eye catching on Gracie, slumped in the corner. She was leaned up against the back of the seat, head lolled back, but there was something about the slump of her body, the greyish pallor of her face …

He strode over and crouched in front of her.

Her eyes were closed, and she didn't respond to his presence.

He hesitated, then reached out, shaking her shoulder gently.

Her body moved limply at his touch.

"Gracie," he whispered. "Captain, we're on our way back to the *Sweet Jenny.* Can you hear me?"

Again, there was no response.

Blood trickled in a steady stream from the corner of her mouth, and when he leaned close to listen, his body cold with sudden panic, he could hear the faint rasp of her breathing, harsh and shallow and far too quick.

Price came over a moment later, and crouched beside him. "How is she?" they whispered.

He shook his head, swallowing back bile.

He'd been around dying sailors enough to know how it sounded to listen to someone die.

"Tell Ari to get us there quick-time," he said in a low voice. "Then bring me a first aid kit, anything the damn vessel has on board."

Price nodded and rose, and carefully, trying not to jostle her, Silas laid Gracie out on the bench.

When he pulled back her coat, her shirt underneath was stiff with blood.

Price returned a moment later with a first aid kit, and carefully, Silas cut away the cloth of Gracie's shirt. He was no medic, and he didn't stand a chance of curing her, but he knew how to stop bleeding, at least.

When he pulled the torn fabric back, though, he stopped, acid rising in his throat.

His hands were shaking, and he felt oddly weak.

There were cuts all along her chest and stomach, in a brutal, evenly spaced pattern. That should have been enough. But it wasn't. Beneath the cuts, he could see the bruises, bright reddish-purple flowering garishly out across her bloodied skin.

"There's nothing in this kit that'll help her," said Price quietly over his shoulder. "That's enough internal bleeding it's a wonder she made it as far as she did."

Silas nodded without looking up. He picked up a sterile rag from the kit and mopped up the worst of the blood, because he had to do something, he couldn't let Gracie die without at least doing *something*, but most of it was crusted and dried over the cuts, and he didn't want to scrape it off and risk reopening the wounds.

"Thank God she's unconscious, at least," Price murmured.

He glanced up at them, and they shook their head. There was still that trace of hostility in their gaze, but he could see the pity under it. They must have seen as much death as he had, being in the navy.

"Captain Ives?" he asked at last, forcing his mind away.

Price gave a grim snort of amusement. "She should probably be unconscious as well, but I've never met someone so damn stubborn. She's been doing this for ... three days now? The *Verity's* chief medical officer will probably skin her alive, but if she survives the dressing-down he gives her and gets some actual rest, I imagine she'll recover. It's an older wound, she just won't sit still long enough to let it heal."

Silas glanced over his shoulder at the naval captain. She'd tipped her head back against the wall of the life vessel. Her eyes were closed, her face pale and pinched with pain, but her breath was coming steady and even, and he could tell from the grimace on her face that she was conscious, at least.

He stood and crossed to Ari. "Gracie isn't doing well," he said quietly. "I don't know how we'll get her in through the airlock—there's no way they aren't guarding it."

Ari glanced up at him, smiling tightly. "Wasn't planning on going through the main airlock. Wouldn't be much of a pirate ship if she didn't have another couple entrances such as the boarders wouldn't know about, would she?" She tapped the screen. "Got the shielding up, so as long as they don't have word yet that we're off the *Chasseuse*, figure they won't be using any anti-cloaking scans to look for us. Airlock I'm using is on the opposite side of the ship as the one they'll be guarding, so they won't see us coming. And it'll put us in right near the med bay, you can get to it through a trapdoor. So as long as those bastards kept to their bargain with Gracie and left Vee and Temple be, we should be able to get her through to the med bay, even. The rest we can figure out when it comes to it." Her whole body was tight, he could see it in the strain of her posture, the white of her knuckles as she grasped the controls.

He nodded. "How long before we get there?"

She glanced at the screen. "Going as fast as she'll take us, but it'll be another ten minutes at least." She turned to look up at him, and he was almost shocked at the anguish on her face. "Don't you damn well let her die, Sil, not like this. Get her back to Vee, Vee'll know what to do. But don't you damn well let her die."

He closed his eyes. "I'll do my best," he said quietly.

Then he turned and crossed back over to Gracie.

The ten minutes passed like ten hours. No one spoke—Ari was focused fully on piloting, and Price had crossed back over to their captain, their posture tense, their jaw clenched. Silas knelt beside Gracie, dabbing at the blood from the wounds and praying to God and Our Lady of the Ghosts to grant the pirate captain mercy, this one more time.

His sparker lay beside him, ready to ignite.

He wasn't sure Ari would be able to handle dispersing Gracie's ghost if it came to it, and he wasn't planning to make her if he could help it.

And then, at last, there was the faint scrape of metal on metal that signified a ship hooking onto an airlock, and the life vessel hissed gently to a halt.

Ari was out of her seat almost before they'd locked on, striding over to kneel beside Silas. She cursed when she saw Gracie, then shook her head grimly and turned to Price. "You'n your captain best step out first, see if we're clear," she said. "Figure it's going to take Sil'n me both to get Gracie on board."

Price nodded and stood, pulling out an energy pistol. "I'll go first. Don't say a damn word, Captain."

Hollis nodded. "Very well. But I'll be behind you."

Price stepped to the airlock and tapped the button, and it opened with a gentle hiss. Silas stiffened as Price stepped out, his own hand on his pistol, but there was no sound of a battle from inside.

"It's clear, I think" said Price a moment later, their voice floating back through the open airlock door.

Ari glanced at Silas and nodded, and between them they lifted the unconscious Gracie as carefully as they could. Silas looked away, focusing on the floor of the life vessel. He told himself it was to keep from tripping and possibly jostling Gracie, but he knew it was because he couldn't bear to look at her any longer.

Price and Hollis were waiting for them in the airlock outside the life vessel—a small, dark room that immediately put Silas in mind of a smuggling compartment.

"Up there," Ari whispered, gesturing with her chin. Above them was a trapdoor, and a rickety ladder leading up, with a small metal lift attached, just big enough for one person.

"Go on, it'll be unlocked," said Ari as she and Silas brought the unconscious Gracie over to the lift.

Price climbed up with one hand, still holding their pistol in the other, and carefully cracked the door open. They peered out, then glanced down and nodded. "Clear," they whispered.

"I'll help support her, you control the lift," Silas said to Ari in a low voice. She nodded, and he started up the ladder one-handed as well, keeping pace with the lift and holding Gracie's limp body steady as it rose. Price had already pulled back the trap door and climbed out, and they helped Silas pull Gracie up, then he sent the lift back down for Hollis as Ari scrambled up the ladder after them. When they were all through and the trap door closed, Silas glanced around.

They were in the med bay, in one of the smaller rooms meant for those who were in danger of turning ghost, or as a quick escape for the medic or other patients if someone turned in the main room.

"Get the door," Ari snapped in a low voice, and Price pulled it open as Silas and Ari lifted Gracie.

Then Price froze.

"Put the damn pistol down, or I shoot you through the throat." Vee's voice, from the other side of the door, was hard.

Ari grinned. "Vee, it's alright, they're with us at the moment," she called.

"Ari?" Vee's voice was sharp with incredulity, but from the way Price's posture relaxed, Vee must have lowered whatever weapon she'd had pointing at them.

"Come on, then," she said, her voice not noticeably thawing. "Ari, what the hell—"

Price stepped back so that Silas and Ari could step through, the unconscious Gracie between them.

Vee took one look at the three of them, then swore, low and harsh. "What happened to her? No, don't tell me now, get her onto a cot. Don't figure I have much time if I want to keep her alive, from the look of it."

They maneuvered Gracie onto a cot beside Temple. Silas glanced at the man as he worked. Temple's eyes were closed, and there was an unhealthy greyish tinge to his skin, tubes and wires hooked up to his body, but at least his chest still rose and fell gently.

"Don't get distracted, lad," Vee snapped. "'Less you want to be lifting a dead body. Come on, get her up."

At last, Gracie was lying on the cot. Vee bent over her, cursing quietly as she pulled back the torn fabric of Gracie's shirt. When she looked up, her face was grim. "Torture?" she asked.

Silas nodded wordlessly.

Vee shook her head, turning back to Gracie. She straightened, and strode quickly across the room, rummaging in the small cooler for a moment before coming back with an armful of supplies. "Ari, hook this up above the cot," she snapped, handing Ari a plastic bag of dark red blood, a long tube coming off the end of it. Ari did as she asked, and Vee slid an IV into one of Gracie's forearms, then shook a small vial and injected the contents into Gracie's other arm. She pulled a breathing mask from the head of the bed and clipped it over the captain's mouth and nose, and tapped two sensors across her chest. She watched the readout a moment, and then straightened, turning to Ari and Silas.

"What the hell'd you do to her?" she hissed. "She should have been brought out in a damn stretcher. What the hell made you think it was a good idea to bring her like this? Broke her up worse than she already was, and that's saying something." There was a sharp worry under the anger in Vee's tone that kept Silas from bristling at the accusation.

"She walked most of the way herself," he said quietly. "I didn't realize it was this bad until we were in the life vessel and on our way here."

"She walked?" Vee glared at him in disbelief.

"She insisted. Ari had some rum on her, and she drank enough to knock down a sailor, and insisted on walking out."

Vee narrowed her eyes at him, then glanced back at Gracie's limp form and cursed again. "'Course she did. Knew she was dying, and knew you wouldn't leave her, so she drank enough to kill the pain and walked out before she collapsed. Damn her eyes." She shook her head, lips pressed tightly together. "She's hurt bad, Sil. We don't get her to a hospital back in the Stacks, and quick-time, she ain't going to pull through."

Silas clenched his teeth. He could hear Ari's quick intake of breath, and picture her face, but he couldn't bear to look at her, not right now.

Even if they cleared the *Sweet Jenny* of the Rosette sailors, they'd have no chance of making it to the Stacks. The Rosette ships were arranged to make a jump out almost impossible, and after what they'd almost pulled back on Blackrock, the Level navy would be holding a blockade on the Stacks and the Level both, almost certainly.

He almost didn't hear the click of the door. "Sailor? We heard voices …" The man's heavily accented voice trailed off.

Silas glanced up into the shocked face of a Rosette officer, just as Price yanked up their pistol.

"Stand down!" the Rosette officer shouted, pulling out his own pistol.

Price shot. Their aim was good, and the man dropped where he was, but there were three others behind him. Silas leapt forward with his cutlass as one of them lunged for Vee, catching the man across the chest. The man staggered back, and Silas followed, finishing him off, then turned.

The last of the sailors had fled, running out the door and slamming it behind them.

There was a moment of silence in the med bay.

"Well," said Hollis weakly, "I suppose this is where we see if we can take back a ship."

10

Silas

They left Vee with as many weapons as they could spare, and helped her drag a heavy table over to the door.

"It'll be locked, but if they do manage to break in, they'll come in one at a time," said Vee grimly. "Figure I can make them regret trying, if it comes to it."

Then Silas, Ari, Price, and Hollis slipped out the door.

Silas had seen, from the corner of his eye, the quiet, furious argument between the naval captain and her first mate, and it was clear Hollis had won it. Despite the obvious pain in her movements and the pallor of her face, he was glad of it—he had no idea how many Rosette sailors were posted on the ship, and they'd need every last set of hands.

"Alright, Sil," Ari whispered as they made their cautious way across the *Sweet Jenny's* lower deck. "Ain't going to manage all these sailors ourselves, I don't think, not now that they know we're coming. Get to the brig, let the others out, and meet us in the cockpit. Figure they'll have holed up there if they're planning to fight. And figure they're planning to fight."

Silas hesitated, then nodded.

He was the best choice for the job—Hollis and Price didn't know their way around the *Sweet Jenny*, and Ari wasn't likely to give up command on her own ship. But the thought of sending the three of them into battle without him rankled nonetheless.

Ari must have seen his hesitation, because she gave a quick, strained grin. "Don't worry, Level boy, I'll make sure to save you some sailors, if you're so worried about it."

He glared at her on instinct, then pulled up the key she'd sent through to his wrist comm, turned, and took the few steps to the ratlines at a sprint. He slid down them quickly, going hand-over-hand across the ropes almost without conscious thought, and jumped the last few metres, landing on the balls of his feet. He checked his pistol and cutlass, then started down the dark corridor that led to the brig.

He could hear the sailors ahead of him long before he reached it—voices taking in harsh, alarmed whispers. He quieted his footsteps and swore under his breath.

They'd be expecting him, then.

Silently, he drew his pistol and stepped around the corner that led to the cells.

In the dimness, it took him a moment to make out the sailors on guard—there were four of them, and they'd extinguished the lights, presumably not to make themselves a target.

On the bright side, it meant there were no stray beams of light to reveal him.

Staying close to the wall to hide his silhouette, Silas crept closer. He could hear the rest of the *Sweet Jenny's* crew behind the bars— Toothpick coughed loudly, and there was the clang of metal on metal that must be Freddie's hover-chair tapping against the bars.

"Shut up, the lot of you," one of the guards hissed, and it wasn't until then that Silas realized they must be making the sound on purpose, in case the alarm meant Gracie had made it back somehow.

The thought of Gracie sent a stab of worry through his chest, and he moved a little faster.

He was being as quiet as he was able, but even with the help of the prisoners, the sound of his boots on the bare metal floor was terrifyingly loud in the stillness.

"Who goes there?" one of the sailors called, her accent so strong Silas could scarcely understand the words. "Stop, or we shoot the prisoners."

Silas froze, cursing under his breath.

"That's right," the guard said. "Turn in your weapon and come forward."

Silas sighed. "Alright," he said loudly. "I'm coming out. Turn on the light, would you?"

A light flickered on. He had to squint and blink against the sudden brightness, but he stepped forward, holding his hands, with the pistol and the cutlass, up in the air.

"Put down the weapons," the guard snapped, and Silas nodded, making a move as if to lower the weapons to the ground.

Then he turned, tossing the pistol through the bars in a low underhand to Freddie, and lunged forward with his cutlass, counting on the fact the guards' eyes wouldn't have adjusted to the light any faster than his would have.

His cutlass caught the first guard across the shoulder, and as she fell back he pressed the attack.

"Drop it!" someone else screamed, and there was the shock of an energy blast so close to his ear that he flinched. But they'd not risk shooting him, not so close to the other guard.

She'd pulled her own cutlass now, but he pushed her against the bars, and a hand reached out, catching her by the shirt and dragging her backwards. Silas ducked another shot, then jammed his cutlass through the flesh below her collarbone. She screamed in pain, and behind him he heard Freddie's muffled grunt as she fired, the hiss of an energy pistol, the sound of a body falling.

There were footsteps behind him, and he yanked at his cutlass desperately, trying to free it. The guard screamed again, and then a sharp, hot pain sliced across the back of Silas's ribcage. He let go his cutlass and turned, grabbing his attacker by the front of the shirt and dragging him in close. Freddie shot again, and the man dropped.

He turned for the last guard, but she was gone, running footsteps fading down the corridor, and he drew in a shaky breath of relief.

"Finish her off, lad," came Toothpick's impatient voice. "Ain't going to be able to hold her forever."

He turned. The guard he'd backed against the bars of Toothpick's cell had managed to yank his cutlass free of her shoulder, and she swung it clumsily as he stepped forward. He caught her wrist and twisted, and when the blade dropped from her nerveless fingers, he snatched it up and finished her off.

Toothpick let go of her as her body slumped to the ground, and Silas ignited his sparker, looking around quickly.

A blue haze was forming around one of the guards Freddie had shot, and he stepped forward, dispersing it, then he sagged, bracing his hands on his knees a moment while he caught his breath. He straightened, fumbling for the key set into his comm.

"We have to go," he hissed. "Ari's up there with the Level naval captain and her first mate, and I don't know how long they'll hold out without help."

"Won't ask about the naval captain, figure Ari knows what she's doing," said Toothpick, stepping free of the cell. He bent to retrieve weapons from the fallen guards as Silas loosed Freddie and Jumper. "Gracie?"

"Vee's got her," Silas said grimly.

Toothpick glanced quickly over at him, then shook his head. "We'll spin yarns later. Let's go find Ari."

Freddie tossed Silas back his pistol and grabbed the one Toothpick handed her, and Jumper scooped up a cutlass and a short knife, a grim expression on his face.

"You going to be alright, lad?" Freddie asked, frowning at Silas, and it wasn't until then that he remembered the cut along his back.

He grimaced and tried to peer over his shoulder, the pain suddenly reasserting itself across his consciousness.

"Bleeding, but long as you can still fight, take off your shirt and wrap it. Don't figure we got time to go visit Vee at the moment, and it'll be easier to take back the ship if you ain't about to pass out from loss of blood."

He gritted his teeth at the delay, but did as Freddie asked, then the group of them sprinted for the ratlines.

When they reached the captain's deck, Silas pulled himself up over the rail. His back and arms were aching, and he tried to shake the tension from his shoulders as he ran. Up ahead, there was the sound of a struggle, and be breathed a quick sigh of relief—at least that meant that someone was still alive from the small group that had started out.

He glanced over his shoulder at the others. Toothpick gave him a quick not, and Silas took the few steps across to the cockpit, shoved the door open, and stepped through into the middle of a battle.

Ari, cutlass out and teeth bared, was backed against a wall fighting three sailors at once. Blood streamed down her arm, and she was fighting left-handed, but at the moment she seemed to be holding her own. Hollis and Price fought back-to-back, Hollis firing steadily, the shots loud in the tiny space, Price with their cutlass out.

Silas yanked out his own cutlass and lunged at one of the sailors facing Ari. The man turned in time to catch the blade across his face, and he howled in pain, dropping his cutlass. Silas finished him off and stepped over the body, barely catching the downstroke of another cutlass on his blade and turning it at the last moment. It cut a long, shallow scrape along his forearm, and then Ari stabbed the woman through the back, her cutlass protruding through the sailor's ribcage. Silas turned to the remaining sailor as Ari braced her foot on the dead woman's hip and pulled her blade free. "You always fight half-naked, Sil?" she asked, grinning. Then she cursed, "Ghost," she snapped, and from the corner of his eye he saw her yank out her sparker, stepping past him to thrust it into the blue haze forming over one of the bodies.

The sailor he was fighting was good with a blade, and the strain of the past few hours was catching up with Silas. He blocked and parried, but the sailor pushed him back step by step. He was concentrating on her cutlass, and almost didn't notice when her hand slipped into her pocket.

He only saw the pistol at Ari's alarmed shout. He dropped to the ground as the pistol fired, grabbing at the woman's ankle and pulling her down with him. She fell on top of him, then her hands were scrambling at his face, thumbs aimed for his eyes. He grabbed for her wrists, and she kneed him in the stomach, knocking the breath from him. He managed to roll, pinning her to the ground, and swung his elbow around in a move one of the older sailors had taught him as a boy, slamming it against her temple. Her grip loosened for a moment, and he snatched up his cutlass, slamming the butt of it into her face, then jumped to his feet as Ari scooped up the pistol and shot her through the head.

Silas staggered, catching himself against the wall, and blinked to clear his vision. Toothpick was in one corner, cutlass out, but the sailor he was fighting looked on the verge of collapse. Jumper and Freddie were finishing off another sailor, and Hollis and Price …

He swore, grabbing for his sparker.

Price was also finishing off their opponent, but Hollis was backed against a wall, sparker out, ghost hovering half a metre away. Its teeth were bared, and it was clearly about to spring.

Silas jumped forward just as the ghost did, his sparker and Hollis's both catching the thing at once.

He wasn't sure which one of their sparker tips caught it, but it hardly mattered. The ghost dissolved, blue mist dissipating across the floor.

Hollis's eyes rolled back in her head.

Silas stepped forward, barely catching her as she slumped.

He caught Price's quick, alarmed exclamation from the corner of his mind, and they stepped forward, yanking out their pistol. Silas looked down and realized, belatedly, how this must look—if they hadn't seen the ghost, and they wouldn't have from that angle, all they would have seen was him lunging towards Hollis, something in his hand, and Hollis collapsing. But he couldn't duck, and he didn't have time to shout an explanation—

The pistol went off, and Silas flinched instinctively, waiting for the burning pain.

There was the muffled thud of a body on the deck behind him, and Price holstered their pistol. "One of the bastards wasn't quite dead," they said shortly.

He turned to see a Rosette sailor lying where they'd fallen, eyes wide in surprise, a long knife in their limp hand.

He breathed out a shaky sigh of relief and turned back to Price. "Thank you," he said.

They'd already crossed over and were crouched beside Hollis, feeling for a pulse, but she was alive—Silas could feel the quick rise and fall of her back against his arms.

He glanced around quickly.

Toothpick had finished off his opponent, and Freddy was holstering her pistol, a grim expression on her face. Ari and Jumper huddled over the controls.

Jumper looked up and signed something quickly. Silas frowned, trying to parse the signs he didn't understand.

Then he swore.

"What is it?" Price asked, looking up.

Silas shook his head. "Ari was quick enough to disable the comm before they could get word out, but looks like they have instructions to check in every two hours. There's an hour left before the next check-in. Then the *Chasseuse* will know exactly what we've done, and shoot us out of the damn sky."

11

Judith

The group of admirals and vice-admirals gathered around the small Admiralty conference room desk at three in the morning did not look happy to be there.

Judith quite frankly could not have cared less.

"What the hell is this about, Usher," Admiral Savoy grumbled. "Knocking us out of bed in the middle of the night. I hope it's something urgent."

"I'm afraid it's urgent enough." Judith's voice was clipped. She gestured to the peacekeepers in the back of the room, and they dragged their prisoner forward.

The man was restrained with his hands cuffed behind his back. His injury from the fight hours before was neatly bandaged, but there was a red stain seeping through the fabric.

Judith couldn't bring herself to feel sorry for him.

"This man," she said, keeping her eyes fixed on the assembled admirals, "was a clerk in the admiralty offices. I say was—he's currently a prisoner, being held on my orders on charges of espionage."

She could hear the sharp intake of breath from one or two of the admirals.

"That's a weighty charge, Usher," said Admiral York.

Judith turned on her. "It is indeed. However, it is also true. And when I looked deeper into this, I found there are at least three other clerks in the Admiralty with connections to this man. One of them, it appears, has been spreading naval briefings to civilian organizations. Have you not wondered about the protests? How it is that they know so much about the navy's plans?" She shook her head. "It has become clear to me that our High Command, and perhaps Parliament itself, has been infiltrated. None of the people who were arrested were willing to talk. I don't know how far this has gone, but it has already gone much too far. Our society, and our navy itself, is at risk."

"Do we know what they were after?" Savoy asked sharply. "Surely we have officers who know how to get information out of people."

Judith bit her lip.

She didn't want to admit, even to herself, how tempted she'd been by that option.

"Information gathered under torture is notoriously unreliable. Besides being against our international agreements," she snapped instead. "Believe me, I wish to God it were otherwise, but if we torture their spies, we'll have no immunity for our own agents who are captured, and the information we gain will be suspect. With luck, the threat of the executioner's noose will be enough when it comes closer. But in the meantime, we're on our own."

Savoy snorted in disgust. "Very well. We'll treat our spy with kid gloves." He leaned forward, placing his elbows on the table. "But I assume that's not the only reason you called us in in the middle of the night. That information could have waited until tomorrow."

Judith nodded slowly. "I'm afraid that's not the worst of the news," she said, lowing her voice. "Some of the documents I found on the spy included information that was used to justify the initial attack on Blackrock, led by Commodore Webb. Why, Admirals, do you think that someone from the Rosette System would want a fleet of our naval ships posted at Blackrock?"

There was a moment of stunned silence. Then Vice-Admiral Stirling cursed. "Either they wanted to weaken us for a future attack, or …"

"Or they're planning an attack while the fleet's away," Judith finished, her voice hard.

York stared at her. "Admiral. You've just ordered three fleets to Blackrock. They should be there within a few hours."

Judith drew in a long breath. "I know. If they planned an attack, we won't get those ships back in time. They're two day's travel away, at the fastest, and we won't get through to them even on the emergency channels until they're out of FTL." Her jaw was clenched, the tension in the pit of her stomach enough to make her sick.

"What are you going to do?" Vice-Admiral Wright's voice was quiet, but she heard the dread under it.

She sighed wearily. "I've put all the remaining ships on alert. But it's not enough, if they come at us with a fleet. If they take down our defences, and are able to land soldiers …"

There was a moment of silence, as the others realized, abruptly, what she'd realized, the moment she'd put the pieces together.

"We don't have a ground defence force that would be able to stop an invasion," York said, voice soft with horror. "At best, we could mobilize the peacekeepers, but they're not trained for war."

"We have the reserve army, but it won't be enough. They'll take time to mobilize, and they've never been more than a defensive force to use against the Ghost Army in the Stacks."

"The Ghost Army ..." began Savoy.

Judith cut him off with an impatient gesture. "Will just as soon spit on our corpses as help us. You can hardly blame them. It's an open secret that the government knows full well about the ghosts that are vented down to the Stacks, along with the oxygen, and they do nothing to stop it. No, the Ghost Army will turn on us in a moment, if given the chance."

"What, then?" Savoy snapped. "What the hell do you suggest? We sit here and let them take the Level and the government, slaughter anyone who resists?"

"No." Judith's voice was hard. "Our only option is to keep them from getting past our defenses and landing ships. We don't have a backup."

York swore, her voice loud in the quiet. "So tell me, Admiral Usher," she said. "How in the hell are we going to do that?"

Judith drew in another long breath. "If we can figure out where they're planning to strike, and when ..." she began. She stopped abruptly.

"Usher? What is it?"

"There's something else," she said slowly. Her mind was spinning with the implications. "They passed on information to the pirates, pressured Parliament into approving an attack on Blackrock, but that wasn't all." She looked up. "You remember Hollis Ives."

The raised eyebrows around the table were answer enough.

Some of the Admirals gathered here had been as opposed to Ives' promotion as any of her political enemies. She hadn't called them here because they agreed with her politically.

"There was an attempt on her life a few days before the mission.

She assumed, as did I, that the point of killing her was to weaken my ability to promote more Stacks captains and officers. But what if it wasn't? What if they'd been trying to weaken me, instead?" She glanced around the table. "If Ives had been killed, that would have been a statement on my judgement in promoting someone who engendered so much hatred in the ranks. And if Ives had been taken off her ship at the last minute, I suspect Parliament would not have tasked me to find her replacement, as they would have with any other captain. I suspect that would have given whoever's infiltrated our government the opportunity to influence that decision."

There was silence around the table, but Judith hardly noticed it.

How had she not seen this? How had she not connected the pieces?

"They wanted the *Verity*," York said slowly. "Why?"

Judith closed her eyes and tipped her head back. "God help me, I don't know. They have no reason to want Blackrock, not that I know of, and even if the *Verity* turned on the other ships, she's one ship of seventeen. She'd be shot down."

"And the crew. They'd not have followed the orders of a captain who was ordering treason, not without a fight. What would one captain do against a crew and officers who were determined to stand against them?" York added.

"Unless … unless they didn't plan on going up against the fleet." Judith could feel the blood drain from her face. "Unless they simply needed a Level naval ship, with all the naval passcodes and clearances." She stood abruptly. "Admirals. The last I heard, the *Verity* had requested permission to go after Mad Dog. Commodore Webb granted his permission. And the *Verity* wasn't shot down, we'd have received an alert."

"Is Mad Dog working with the Rosette System?" Savoy asked, his voice tight with horror.

Judith shook her head impatiently. "That's not Mad Dog's style. She wouldn't join up with another navy, even if it meant taking us down. Pirate she may be, but she's Level born and bred. She'll happily watch the Level burn, but it'll be her own doing, not some other system's."

She ignored the questioning looks at her certainty.

She was certain, she knew it in her bones that no matter how much Gracie hated the Level, working with the Rosette navy, who didn't have any cleaner views on pirates than the Level had, wouldn't be something she'd choose on her own accord.

If the Rosette navy had tried to take the *Verity*, they'd have had Mad Dog and the *Sweet Jenny* to deal with first. Because Mad Dog wasn't one to give up her prize.

Nor, if she recalled correctly, was Hollis Ives.

For the first time since she'd found the man crouched in the dark in Admiral Moore's office, Judith felt the faintest stirrings of hope.

"Pull me up a map, if you please," she snapped.

One of the admirals did, and she scanned it rapidly, her heart pounding. At last, she looked up. "This is what we shall do, admirals: we will get every goddamned ship within a twelve hour's FTL jump back here at once, get them fully crewed, and set them on patrol around the Level. We will commandeer every merchant ship large enough to have weapons for self defence, and we'll pull the third-year Academy officer candidates to command them. I want every sailor—naval, merchant or otherwise—drafted into service. I will institute goddamn press-gangs if necessary."

"Parliament—" Savoy began.

"Parliament be hanged, this is the survival of the goddamn Level. They can make their formal complaints once we live through this," she snapped.

"And the fleets at Blackrock?" York asked.

Judith drew in a deep breath. "I shall call in to the fleet at Blackrock, as soon as they are out of jump and able to receive emergency broadcasts," she said. "I shall instruct them to be prepared to engage Rosette warships in battle."

The other admirals stared at her.

"We were just discussing the fact that the Rosette System would have no reason to go after Blackrock," said Savoy at last.

Judith turned on him. "From the information we have, I believe we can assume the Rosette warships have attempted to capture both Mad Dog and Hollis Ives. I'm not sure they'll be able to do that without one or the other of them escaping. And if either Mad Dog or Ives escapes, the Rosette navy will move heaven and hell to get them back. They'll not risk the *Verity* or the *Sweet Jenny* getting away and betraying their plans. Their strategy depends on us not finding out in time to get our own fleets back in position."

"Why in the hell would Mad Dog or Captain Ives run to Blackrock, rather than the Level or the Stacks?" Savoy asked.

"Ives won't jump back to the Level, because she'd die of torture before she led them back here," said Judith grimly. "And Mad Dog's smart enough to know we'll be on the lookout for her here, after the stunt she pulled on Blackrock. So we'll give them reason to jump to Blackrock, instead." She chewed on the inside of her cheek for a moment, then looked up. "We'll send out a broadcast, where it'll be picked up easily. I want broadcasts going out on all the general channels that we're sending ships to Blackrock. We can use the pretence that we're seeking the pirates' surrender, but we must ensure the broadcasts are easily interceptable."

"Won't that risk alerting the Rosette navy that the Level is unguarded?"

"For God's sake, they already know every move we've made since the beginning," she snapped. "I'm certain they have a precise count of which ships we've sent out, and how long it would take us to recall them. I could pull the ships back, yes, but they'd only be in time to bear witness to the destruction. We don't have the ships here to last a two-day battle. We'll win or lose this before the fleets return, regardless."

York shook her head. "I don't like this, Admiral. We're depending almost entirely on chance. Even assuming that you're right, and the Rosette navy has come after the *Verity*, we have no reason to believe that either Ives or Mad Dog are still alive, let alone that they'll get away and hear the broadcast. Isn't this putting too much of our plan on that hope?"

Judith drew in a long breath. "You're right," she said flatly. "But I don't believe there's a better option. Even if we called in the moment the ships at Blackrock were in position to receive an emergency broadcast, it would do us no good. As I said, the Level will be won or lost before they can return. We shall mobilize the army, and we shall commandeer every ship we can find to defend the Level. That's all we can do, and I don't know that it will be enough. This, at least, is a chance."

She could see, by the looks on the faces around the table, that they knew how slim of a chance it was.

But they also knew, as well as she did, that they didn't have another viable option.

When the other Admirals had finally left, Judith sat for a moment, almost too weary to push herself to her feet and stumble home to her apartment.

The pain in her shoulder was a persistent ache that throbbed through her despite the bandages and the painkillers the medic had given her. The shot had only grazed the muscle, not gone through bone, but it hurt damnably, and she was tired enough that her eyes were almost too heavy to stay open.

For a moment, she contemplated simply laying her head in her arms on her desk and sleeping here.

She shook her head wryly.

She'd go home. She'd rest better at home, and she needed a clear mind for what was coming.

But it wouldn't hurt to rest her eyes, just for a moment …

"Grace." Judith could see the tension in Grace's shoulders from across the room, the utter stillness that only came when she was beyond fury.

Anyone else, perhaps, wouldn't have dared enter, would have stepped out, closing the door behind them, and waited for a better time.

Grace could be volatile, angry, furious, but Judith knew in her bones that Grace would never hurt her. Grace would die before she'd hurt her.

She didn't turn, just stared out the window, but she didn't tell Judith to leave.

Judith stepped up behind her, laying a hand on her shoulder. "Grace," she said in a quiet voice.

She could feel the tightness of Grace's muscles, the way they relaxed a little at her touch, the way her shoulder lifted as Grace drew in a steadying breath.

"If you're going to scold me for what I did, Jenny—don't." Her voice was low with warning, and Judith sighed.

"I spoke to the captain. I spent half an hour with him, but I think I've convinced him to drop the charges of insubordination. You won't get the lash, this time," she said. "I assured him that whatever else you might be, you're loyal to the navy."

Grace turned, so abruptly that Jenny's hand dropped from Grace's shoulder to fall to her side. "I'm loyal to the navy? No, Jenny. I'm loyal to my damn sailors. He gave me an order that would have killed them. And I took them in anyway, and then he ordered me to leave them behind." Her words were sharp and hard, and Judith could feel the pain under them. "He'd have me flogged for holding that damn skiff until they were back on board with me, those that were still alive? Then here's my back, and he's welcome to it."

Judith closed her eyes.

She'd thought, once, before she'd met Grace, that the woman had gained her position because of her family—both parents vice-admirals, how could their only daughter not gain every promotion?

She'd revised her position over the two years she'd known Grace, served with her, fought beside her, slept with her. Grace had earned her way to the position of first mate just as much as any officer in the navy had earned theirs. Grace was Grace, bull-headed and stubborn and utterly certain she was right, and she'd have been Grace, whatever position her parents did or did not hold.

Her parents were only the reason Grace's back wasn't laced and scarred thick with lash-stripes. Because Jenny knew well enough lashes wouldn't stop her.

Even with her parentage, she had lash-stripes—Jenny had traced them often enough with her fingers, when they were lying together in the close, warm intimacy of the dark, although she'd never asked what Grace had done to earn them.

There was something small and fragile inside her that didn't want to know. Something that didn't want to hear the words Grace spoke when she was angry like this.

"You're loyal to the navy, Grace," she said instead, keeping her voice steady, holding Grace's eyes when she looked up to meet Judith's. "We both are. We swore our lives to it."

Even like this, crackling with anger and sharp with pain, Grace's eyes caught hers and held them, pulled the breath from her.

She'd never believed you could love someone so much it hurt, but it hurt, the way she loved Grace.

It hurt, how afraid she was when Grace spoke like this, hurt like a dagger twisting in her chest.

Judith had spent a great deal of her life trying to exorcise her fear. And she'd done it, for the most part. There was very little that frightened Judith Usher, and she hadn't realized how falling in love with Grace would cut that away from her.

"I'm loyal to those who are loyal to me, Jenny. What's the navy, if it doesn't protect the ones who serve in it?"

Judith closed her eyes. "It's not perfect. I know it's not perfect. People die who shouldn't, maybe, but more people survive because we protect them. The Level protects them, the navy protects them. It's not perfect, but it's better than nothing."

"And for those it doesn't protect?" Grace's voice was still sharp with hurt and fury. "For those it kills, it's still better than nothing? If I'm loyal to the navy, Jenny, it's because of what it should be, not regardless of what it is. I can't be loyal to a lie."

Judith sucked in a quick breath. "And if you're not loyal to the navy, Grace, then what? Where does it end? You refuse to follow an order to save a sailor's life, and the next officer refuses because they disagree with the order, and then the next because they can. Where does it end?"

Grace studied her a long moment. At last she reached out, running her hand along Judith's cheek. "My Jenny," she whispered. "If the navy asks me to give up those who trust me … the navy can go to damnation."

Judith closed her eyes and leaned her face into the warmth of Grace's palm, and tried not to feel the ice cold the words had sent down her spine and slipped into her chest.

Judith jerked her head up with a start, disoriented.

Even in her sleep, she couldn't escape the unease.

Even in her sleep, she couldn't escape Grace Madox.

But Gracie might be their salvation yet. If she heard about a naval attack on Blackrock, she'd do everything in her power to prevent it.

That, Judith knew with certainty.

And she tried to push from her mind the possibility that at this moment, it very well may be that neither Hollis Ives or Gracie were alive enough to do anything about it.

12

Hollis

The first thing Hollis was aware of was arms lifting her.

"May as well get her down to the med bay. We'll want Vee's take on things anyways, and wouldn't hurt to get the rest of us bandaged up."

Vaguely, she recognized the sharp voice as belonging to Ari.

She jerked her head up. Foster cursed, and she felt them stumble, almost dropping her.

"Price," she managed, blinking her eyes open.

Foster and Silas had linked arms to carry her. She could see Ari ahead of them, her pistol in one hand, sparker in the other, and beside her a woman she didn't recognize in a hover chair, with light brown skin and black hair, her arms and shoulders heavy with muscle. Another man strode along beside them, taller than either Silas or Foster, a grim expression on his dark face, his black hair going to grey, and with him a younger man, light skinned, slim, and nervous-looking, who didn't meet her gaze.

Her memories were coming back now—the fight, the ghost. The faces around her were the pirate crew Silas had released from the brig.

And she realized, with a sudden chill, that she and Foster were now entirely at the pirates' mercy.

"Lie still, Captain," Foster said. There was a grim note to their voice that told her arguing would be futile. And besides ... well, honestly, the thought of trying to walk right now, with the way the pain in her gut was setting her head to spinning, was almost more than she could bear.

She closed her eyes and dropped her head back on the rest made of Silas's and Foster's clasped arms, and let herself be carried.

When she blinked open her eyes again, they were in the small med bay. Silas and Foster were lowering her onto a narrow cot, and the pirates' medic—Vee, they'd called her, a slight woman with dark, short-cropped hair, cold green eyes, and a forbidding expression—scowled down at her. "What's wrong with this one?" she snapped. "And Sil, don't you try to duck out, I can see the blood on your shirt." She snorted. "Fighting bare-chested, were you? Well, I suppose there were one or two happy enough about that." She shot a glance at Ari, who smirked.

"Now then," she said, turning back to Hollis.

"I'm fine," Hollis tried, leaning back.

"It's a three-week-old wound that she's ... broken open. Again," Foster said grimly.

Vee raised her eyebrows, unbuttoning Hollis's stolen Rosette navy jacket. "A three-week-old wound? What happened to her? Did she ..."

She stopped short.

"She got her stomach ripped open by ghosts," said Foster, their tone frigid.

Gently, Vee sliced through the makeshift bandage of Hollis's bloody shirt, and looked over the injury. "It's a damn wonder you're still on your feet, lass," she said at last, glancing up at Hollis's face. She tossed her a blanket, and Hollis pulled it around her shoulders. "Now, lie back and don't make a fuss. You'll keep, and I have those here as won't."

"Vee. We ain't got time for this, you can look at them later," Ari snapped, stepping forward. "We've got less than an hour before the whole damn fleet starts shooting at us."

Hollis gave a choked exclamation, trying to push herself upright again, but Foster lay a hand on her shoulder and shot her a quick, cautioning glance.

They must have realized, too, the position the two of them were in.

Vee turned to glare at Ari. "And why didn't you tell me this sooner?"

Ari closed her eyes, and Hollis could see the strain and weariness on the woman's face. "Because that's the thing—we can jump the *Sweet Jenny*, maybe, but we ain't jumping back to Blackrock—the naval ships'll still be camped out there. And we ain't jumping back to the Stacks, neither—don't figure they'll have left it unguarded, after word of what happened to the fleet gets out."

Vee was silent a moment. "If we get to a resource planet as'll have us, it's possible I pull Temple through," she said at last. "But the captain …"

"You are damn well going to save Gracie, Vee. That ain't a question." Ari's voice was flat and hard.

Vee sighed. "You get me somewhere with the right equipment, I'll do my best. But …" She gestured at the cot.

Hollis followed her gesture.

Mad Dog's bruises had darkened and spread, her eyes closed, her face slack. If it hadn't been for the monitors hooked to her chest, the lines writing themselves across the screens above her head, Hollis would have assumed she was already dead.

"It's not going to get better by us sitting here talking about it," Silas snapped. He'd been pacing back and forth by the door, agitation in every line of his body. "Ari, come on. Let's get moving, see if we can even jump out of here in the first place."

"Wait," Hollis gasped.

They all turned to look at her.

She sucked in a slow breath, trying to steady her heartbeat. "Wait, please."

"If you think I'm going to risk Gracie's life getting you bastards back to your ship—" Ari began in a low voice, face vicious with anger.

Silas put a restraining hand on her shoulder. "We don't have time to wait, Captain Ives. What do you have to say?"

"Don't jump out. You won't make it, not past the whole Rosette fleet."

"Oh, so we should just let them shoot us down? You'd like that, wouldn't you?" Ari snapped.

"No." Hollis was speaking through her teeth. "Get us to the *Verity*. Help me take her back. With two ships, we'll stand a better chance of breaking through their blockade."

"You heard Vee," said Silas, his voice still, somehow, measured. "By the time we take back the *Verity*, it may well be too late for Gracie. I understand your position, Ives, but we're not going to—"

"The *Verity's* a three-hundred-and-fifty crewed naval ship," she snapped. "Our med bay is equipped with everything you'd find in an emergency room in a Level hospital. It's better than you'd find on most resource planets, and a hell of a lot closer. You help me take my ship back, I'll instruct my chief medical officer to give you free run of the med bay for your captain."

Silas and Ari both turned to look at Vee.

Hollis could feel her first mate's eyes on her, but she didn't meet their gaze.

Perhaps they were right, and trusting the pirates was a mistake. But it was work with them, or lose her ship and her crew both.

At last, Vee gave a short nod. "If the *Verity's* med bay is what the lass says, it's our best chance. Ain't a resource planet close by that'd let us land who'd have tech to match that. Ain't perfect, but I may be able to keep our captain alive yet."

The pirates spoke among themselves quietly for a moment.

"That's all very good, Captain Ives," said Toothpick at last, turning to her. "But it still leaves the fact that the *Chasseuse* is going to start shooting at us in under an hour."

Hollis closed her eyes.

She was so damn tired, and her head was spinning, and she wasn't sure how much longer she'd be able to hold herself up, and she wanted, with all her soul, to lay back on the cot and let the pirates jump them to wherever the hell they wanted.

But she was a naval captain, God damn it, and she wasn't going to abandon her ship.

"I think I've a way to solve that," she said, forcing her eyes open again.

The pirate crew was watching her, sharp interest mingling with the hostility in their combined gaze, and she could feel Foster's eyes on her as well.

"My second mate, Greene, is currently on the *Verity*," she continued. "As I said, it's a three-hundred-and-fifty-crewed ship of the line. The only reason the Rosette officers could take her so easily is that he offered his surrender. They'll need our sailors still to crew her, they'll not have enough spare sailors to crew her out without them. If the sailors were to turn on them—and they would, if Greene ordered them to, I know my crew—it would take a hell of a lot of effort to secure the ship."

"And a lot of deaths," Silas put in, his voice grim.

Hollis nodded sharply. "Sacrificing my sailors is the last thing I want. But it's the last thing the *Chasseuse's* captain will want either. And Greene's loyal enough to the Level that they must know I'm the only thing holding him back from giving that very command." She turned to Toothpick. "Get me up to the cockpit, and broadcast a message to the *Chasseuse*. Let them know that you've captured me, and you'll release me onto the *Verity* when they give you a jump path out."

The pirates glanced at each other, and again conferred in low tones.

Foster leaned down next to her. "Captain." Their voice was low. "Are you sure you know what you're doing?"

Hollis gestured at the pirate crew with a flick of her eyes. "If you have any better ideas, Price, please tell me. This is the only thing I could come up with."

"And if they simply take you at your word, make themselves a jump path, and jump out?" Foster asked.

She sighed. "You heard them. This is their best chance to save their captain's life. I don't know these pirates any better than you do, but from what I've seen of them, that's the one thing they'll sacrifice their escape for."

Foster nodded slowly. "I suppose you're right," they said, straightening, but she could hear the worry in their tone.

At last, Ari turned to glare at Hollis and Foster. "Alright," she said in a low voice. "You got what you wanted, Captain. We'll help you take your ship back. But I swear to Our Blessed Lady of the Ghosts, if Gracie dies, I'll hunt you down and carve your damn heart out with my buck-knife. So best hope you're telling the truth about your med bay." She turned on her heel and stalked out the med bay door, presumably towards the cockpit. "And that's assuming we make it out of here alive," she muttered, as the door slammed behind her.

"Ari's on the controls," said Toothpick, in his mild voice. "Jumper on the guns, quick-time. Sil, you're with Ari, after you and the naval officer there get Ives up to the cockpit. Vee, do what you need to so she don't die on the way up there, that'd lower our bargaining position. Freddie, go help Jumper."

The crew scattered to their assigned duties with surprising alacrity, and Toothpick turned to Hollis. There was sharp mistrust in his face, but he gave her a short nod. "I'll expect you on the deck. You and the officer here will have to be restrained, and you'd damn better play your part."

Hollis nodded and glanced at Foster.

They sighed, worry clear in their face. "Very well. Captain, for God's sake let Silas and myself carry you up there, at least. I'm certain there will be plenty enough for you to do when we try to take back the ship, and I'm equally certain you'll not agree to sit quietly while we do it. So at least rest for long enough to get your strength up."

Vee had come up behind Foster, and she nodded curtly. "Don't like agreeing with a naval officer, but they're right. Ain't going to stay on your feet much longer, and Sil ain't hurt bad enough that he can't help." She turned and gestured Silas over impatiently. "Come on, lad, got enough to do here without babysitting you. But I'll expect you back here when everything's done, get that cutlass scratch looked at."

Silas nodded and crossed over to Hollis. He and Foster exchanged glances.

"Captain?" Foster asked.

She nodded stiffly, and bit back the burning humiliation of being lifted like an invalid.

When they reached the cockpit, Ari and Toothpick were waiting. Toothpick gestured to a chair, and Foster and Silas set Hollis down gently. Then Foster stepped back, their posture noticeably stiff, as Silas tied her legs to the chair and her arms behind her back, and pushed a gag into her mouth, securing it with a strip of cloth.

When he'd finished, Silas turned to her first mate. "Price?"

Foster nodded and sat down in the chair Toothpick had provided, and Silas restrained them, as well. Then he stood. "Alright," he said, turning to Toothpick. "I think we're ready."

Toothpick nodded and strode over to the ship's comm. He tapped it on, broadcasting the scene; she and Foster restrained, Silas standing a pace away, his face hidden to avoid recognition—as far as the *Chasseuse* was concerned, Silas was still naval—with a pistol aimed at their heads.

"This is the *Sweet Jenny*, paging the *Chasseuse*," Toothpick said. There was something cold under his calm tone. "Got a bargain I think you might be interested in making."

13

Hollis

"This is the *Chasseuse*." The voice through the *Sweet Jenny's* comm line was sharp. "We know you've taken back the ship. What do you have to say before we shoot you down?"

Toothpick's smile was chilling enough that Hollis shivered at it. "We have Captain Ives and her first mate here on board," he said. "Captain Mad Dog got off your ship, and she ain't happy about the way she was treated. So here's her bargain: We can shoot Ives and her first mate, broadcast it through to the *Verity*. Figure that will make things a little excitable on board. Or, we can make a trade. You open us up a jump path out of here, and we release these two into an airlock on the *Verity*."

There was a long moment of silence. Then the visuals flickered on, and Commodore Matisse's face appeared over the screen.

He looked furious.

"Let me see that you're telling the truth," he snapped in his heavy accent.

Toothpick tapped the comm screen to display the visuals.

Silas stepped forward, head still lowered, and yanked the gag off

Hollis's mouth disdainfully. "Go ahead, talk to your officer friends," he grunted.

"Commodore," said Hollis. She didn't have to fake the hoarseness in her voice. "I am, as you can see, alive, and as well as can be expected in the circumstances."

The man was silent a moment. At last he said gruffly, "Captain Ives. I am sorry for the indignity visited upon you. I ask you to please, in the circumstances, request that your crew and second mate remain calm."

"You may inform my crew that I am alive, and aware of my duty to them and the navy," said Hollis. "Tell them I shall do my best to live up to that, despite the circumstances I find myself in, and I expect them to do the same."

"Very well," said Matisse at last. He turned to Toothpick, and his face took on an expression of disgust. "And you, pirate. We will acquiesce to your conditions. But be warned—if you harm the captain or her first mate, all our agreements are off."

"Of course." Toothpick's voice was still cold. "We'll bring her to the aft airlock on the port side of the *Verity*. You'll leave it empty, because if me or my crew see a single damn Rosette sailor, we'll kill them, and then we'll kill the captain and her first mate and dump the bodies. Moment you have a jump path that's acceptable, we drop them there, and we jump out."

Matisse gave a brusque nod, and Toothpick cut off the communication.

There was a moment's silence in the *Sweet Jenny's* cockpit.

"You think they'll hold to their word?" Silas asked quietly.

"Ain't going to give them a chance to re-think it," said Toothpick. He turned to Ari. "Take us in, Ari. Once we're in close to the *Verity*, they won't be able to hurt us without risking their prize."

Silas turned to Hollis, reaching into his pocket. His hand emerged with a pistol, and for an instant, looking at the grimness in his face, she wondered if Foster had been right—she'd miscalculated, and the pirates intended to shoot her here on their deck. Then he dropped the pistol in her lap and sliced through her restraints with a quick slash of his knife.

"Captain? Can you do this?" Foster asked quietly, standing and coming over to her once they, too, had been released.

"I'll be fine, Price," she whispered back, steel in her tone. She paused. "You were right. I brought this crew here. I led them into this. And I will be damned if I don't do everything in my power, down to my last breath, to get you and them out of this alive. If that's not enough to keep me on my feet, then I'm in much worse shape than I ever imagined."

Foster opened their mouth as if to reply, then closed it again, shaking their head.

It was only minutes later that the jolt and scrape of the *Sweet Jenny* hooking on to the *Verity's* airlock echoed through the cockpit.

Ari settled the ship, then pushed back from the controls and stood. "Go on, get moving," she said, coming up beside Hollis. "Vee's going to stay here, keep the bastards talking, but I figure the quicker we get started, the more likely it is we don't end up bleeding out on the *Verity's* deck."

Hollis nodded and pushed herself carefully to her feet. Foster held out an arm, but she ignored it—best to look, at least, like she was able to support herself on her own two feet.

At the moment, what she wanted and what the pirates wanted were one and the same. And as long as Gracie lay dying in the *Sweet Jenny's* med bay, it was likely to remain that way. But if the situation should change, in any way … she was very conscious of exactly how vulnerable she and Foster were.

Best not make herself appear weaker than absolutely necessary.

She couldn't help but notice, as they made their cautious way to the airlock, how the pirates hemmed them in on all sides, Silas and Ari in front, Toothpick, Jumper, and Freddie behind.

The sound of the *Sweet Jenny's* airlock door opening was loud in the silence.

Silas poked his head out first, then stepped out cautiously. A moment later, he leaned back inside. "All clear," he whispered.

The group of them stepped out into the *Verity's* familiar airlock.

Hollis hadn't realized, until that moment, how stepping back on her ship would send a surge of relief through her so strong she staggered with it. And she hadn't realized, until she had to blink away the traitorous tears welling in her eyes, how thoroughly she'd believed, when she'd stepped onto the skiff headed to the *Sweet Jenny*, that she'd never set foot on the *Verity* again.

The pirates spread out around them, checking the airlock carefully for signs of recording devices or hidden Rosette sailors, and Hollis and Foster waited by the *Sweet Jenny's* airlock.

Hollis's muscles were so tense that her entire body ached.

Ari glanced over her shoulder and nodded, and the *Sweet Jenny's* crew formed up again around Hollis and Foster.

"Stun pistols for now, don't want to be dealing with ghosts until we have the numbers to manage it," said Toothpick in a low voice. "Figure we'll have plenty of chances to kill later."

The pirates took up their positions without speaking, as if they'd fought together long enough that speaking wasn't required. Ari nodded to Freddie, who'd maneuvered her hover chair next to the controls.

The pirate woman tapped the doors control, and the doors slid silently open. Hollis felt a quick jolt of pride at their noiselessness—her crew had kept them maintained perfectly, even though airlock doors were an easy task to slack off on.

The guards at the door were tense, their hands on their weapons, but they were watching into the ship, and they didn't notice the intruders until three of them were lying stunned on the floor. A woman brought up her comm, alarm spreading across her face, and Hollis shot her with the stun pistol Toothpick had handed her. She dropped without a groan. Foster, beside her, was firing off stun-shots in quick succession, and then it was over, the airlock guards reduced to slumped bodies.

Toothpick gestured, and the pirate crew bound and gagged them with uncomfortable efficiency. Then Toothpick tapped through his comm to the *Sweet Jenny's* line.

Faintly, they heard Vee's sharp voice through the comm: "… far as I can see, that ain't nearly enough space for us to jump through. You figure you can set a bargain with us, then close off our escape before we make it out? Don't know what you heard about Mad Dog and her crew, but we ain't such fools as all that."

He tapped the comm line off and turned to Hollis. "Alright," he said. "She'll be able to hold them for another few minutes at best. Get us to your crew, Ives."

Hollis nodded. "I suspect they're keeping the petty officers in the brig, and the crew they don't need to keep the ship running locked up in the crew quarters," she whispered. "Best get the officers first, it'll be easier to organize the crew if there's a chain of command."

Toothpick raised his eyebrows, but Silas nodded. "She's probably right," he said shortly. "It'll take less explaining if the sailors are getting commands from their appointed petty officer."

"Lead the way, then, Captain," said Ari. She wore a dangerous grin, and Hollis bristled at the sarcasm in her tone, but taking offence at the moment would be beyond foolish. So she simply nodded and stepped forward, Foster beside her, and the pirates fell in around them, weapons drawn.

The tense uncertainty of the whole endeavour reminded her of their escape from the *Chasseuse*, hours earlier. But this was the *Verity*. This was her ship, and she knew every corridor, every locked door, every one of the ship's idiosyncrasies.

The ship was eerily silent, the only sounds the sharp footfalls of the occupying sailors.

To run a ship of the line of this size properly, with gun ports crewed and regular watches, took the full three-hundred-and-fifty crew. But to run it on a skeleton crew, and with the captain and officers surrendered, they could likely get away with around a hundred.

That would mean most of those would be the *Verity's* own crew— she couldn't imagine the *Chasseuse* being able to spare more than a few dozen of its own. And considering the speed with which their captain had acquiesced to the pirates' demands, she assumed the number of Rosette sailors on board was closer to twenty than a hundred. If they'd had enough sailors on board to keep down an uprising, they'd have no reason to negotiate with the *Sweet Jenny*. But they wouldn't know for certain until it was too late to turn back.

They made it down to the lower decks without incident. Outside the narrow corridor that led through to the brig, Hollis held up her hand.

"There'll be guards posted at the entrances to both hallways," she whispered. "We'll need two or three of you to go through the storage compartment and come in from the other side, otherwise there'll be no chance we take them down before they sound the alarm."

Ari glanced at Toothpick, then jerked her head at Silas and Jumper, and the three of them slipped around through the storage compartment. A moment later, there was a soft tapping through Toothpick's comm. "They're in place," he said quietly.

Hollis took a deep breath as Toothpick pulled the door open.

From the other side of the hallway, there was the *thud* of falling bodies. Someone shouted, and the guards who were still upright started towards them at a run. Hollis stepped out in front of the pirates, took careful aim, and sent the first two guards down. Freddie took down two more, and Foster finished off the last.

Hollis paused a moment, listening for the sound of the *Verity's* alarms. None came, and she breathed out a quick sigh of relief. She holstered her pistol and started forward as the pirates stepped back to let her through.

"Captain?" Emmett's voice cracked with disbelief when he saw her. "What the devil—"

She shook her head. "No time for explanations. What's the situation on board?"

Emmett paused a moment, and she studied him covertly. His face was grim, and there were dark circles under his eyes, but he didn't seem hurt, thank God.

"I'm not entirely sure," he said at last. "They locked up all the officers here in the brig, and a handful of the crew. I believe they took a skeleton crew to keep the ship running."

She nodded. "And the crew? How are they taking it?"

He shook his head wearily. "I did my best to keep order, Captain. They went peacefully, most of them. But ..." He shrugged helplessly. "I don't know more than that."

She nodded, chewing the inside of her cheek. "Alright," she said at last, turning to the pirate crew. "We'll release the officers, and then some of us will release the crew who are locked up, while the rest mingle with the skeleton crew running the ship."

Ari grinned. "Then we'll kill every last one of the Rosette System bastards."

Hollis gave a sharp shake of her head. "I'll not endanger my crew any more than I have to. The Rosette officers are only to be killed if they resist and we're unable to restrain them any other way. I suspect they'll surrender when they realize they're outnumbered. We will accept their surrender. Do I make myself clear?"

Toothpick studied her. There was something dangerous in his gaze that made her want to look away.

She met his eyes stubbornly.

At last, Silas stepped forward. "Listen," he said in a low voice. "We can't afford to argue—Gracie doesn't have the time left to waste." He turned to Hollis. "Ives. You swear, on your honour and your life, that you'll not betray us?"

"May Our Lady drink my lifeblood if I go back on my word."

Foster and Emmett turned to look at her oddly, but the Stacks oath seemed to have had the desired effect on the pirates. Toothpick nodded abruptly and turned.

"We'll do this the navy's way, then," he said to the others, sharp sarcasm in his voice. "Death is only for those of us who don't merit naval-officer status. Come on, lad's right. We don't have time to waste."

Whatever Hollis might say of the pirate crew, they were as efficient as any group of naval officers. In a bare few moments, Toothpick had organized them into two groups, one under him and one under Ari.

"Captain," said Emmett, stepping closer and lowering his voice. "You don't mean to tell me we're working with the pirates. They tried to execute you."

Hollis sighed. Her head ached, and her body ached, and she was so damn tired that she could have fallen asleep standing, and she wasn't even close to being finished whatever the hell they were doing here. "But they didn't. Ari and Silas and Gracie saved my and Price's life more than once in our escape. I have no sympathy for the pirates. But right now, they have a dying captain desperate for medical aid, and we have a ship that's been taken over by the Rosette System navy, and if either of us turns on the other, we both die. We're fighting a common enemy at the moment, and that's enough for me."

"You've offered to use our med bay to save Mad Dog's life?" Emmett's voice was sharp with incredulity.

"She saved mine," Hollis snapped. "Come, Greene, our duty is to the Level navy, and I believe a fleet of Rosette warships poses more of a danger to our navy than a single pirate captain."

Even as she said it, she was caught with the sudden, uncomfortable brush of a memory—those frantic, horrifying minutes back at Blackrock when she'd realized what Mad Dog had done to the nav systems, what she was about to do, what was going to happen to the entire seventeen-ship fleet if Hollis couldn't get her warning through in time—a second Starfire disaster that would leave thousands dead, frozen bodies and the wreckage of ships drifting through space …

She pushed the thought away, and started after her officers.

She'd been right—once her own sailors were freed, taking back the ship was a bloodless affair. Hollis accepted the surrender of the highest-ranked Rosette officer, and locked him and the remainder of the officers in the brig.

And at last, she stood on the bridge of her own damn ship again.

She closed her eyes for just a moment, revelling in the feeling, and then had to put out a hand quickly to grab the side of the control desk.

"Captain."

She blinked her eyes open at Foster's voice.

Their face told her exactly what they'd been about to say.

And, as much as she hated it, they were likely correct—now that the excitement had died down, her head was spinning, and she was finding it harder and harder to push back against the pain.

"Alright," she said, turning to Emmett. "Mate Greene, you will instruct the sailors back to their places. Have our mechanics check the guns and shields to figure out what the hell the Rosette spy did to them. And for God's sake, don't let anyone touch the damned navigation system—I don't want to end up with our own personal Starfire disaster."

"Aye, Captain," said Emmett. "And what are we going to do next? It won't take long before they realize we've taken back the ship, even if no one managed to get off an alert."

Hollis grimaced. "I am afraid I shall need to go down to the med bay. I shall discuss our options with you via holoscreen."

Somehow, saying the words reminded her body of what she'd put it through, and she almost staggered at the sudden wave of dizziness. Foster stepped up beside her, discretely catching her arm like they had so many times, and she realized, with a start, that she'd almost come to depend on them doing so.

She turned and gave them a wan smile. "If you'd be so kind as to accompany me, Mate Price, I believe it wouldn't hurt for them to take a look at you, as well."

"Aye, Captain," Foster murmured, and Hollis found herself

suddenly wondering if they'd just realized how long it had been since they'd last slept as much as she had.

Her legs were embarrassingly weak, and she had to stop and rest more frequently than she really liked to think about. By the time she and Foster made their way down the lifts and over to the med bay, the pirates and Archibald were in a standoff in front of the doors.

She blew out a quick breath. At least no one seemed to have pulled their weapons yet, thank God.

"Officer Smyth," she called, loud enough to be heard over the arguing. "I promised the crew of the *Sweet Jenny* our care of their injured in exchange for their help freeing the ship."

All the heads swung towards her, and Archibald's expression turned quickly from one of irritation to one of alarm. "Captain?" he snapped, taking a quick step towards her.

She shook her head. "The pirates, I believe, are in worse shape than myself at this time. Get them stabilized, and then there will be time to see to myself and Mate Price."

For a moment, Archibald looked like he wanted to protest. But at last, reluctantly, he nodded. "Aye, Captain," he said, and turned back to where Vee was glowering at him. "Go ahead then, bring them in," he muttered with bad grace.

To Archibald's credit, when the two injured pirates were brought on board, his irritation turned instantly to a sharp, professional concern, and soon he and Vee were working side by side over the two cots.

Hollis closed her eyes a moment. The room was spinning around her now, and she realized, suddenly, that she was going to be sick. She bit down hard, trying to hold back the vomit. Archibald must have glanced over at her, because she heard his voice, wavering and distant, snapping at one of the junior medical officers. "Get the captain lying down, for God's sake, and see what the hell she's managed to do to herself since she left the ship. Price too, they look like they're about to fall over. Go on, quick-time!"

And then, finally, mercifully, she was lying down on a cot, and she could close her eyes against the world spinning without worrying about falling over. The noises around her were fading in and out like a comm line with a bad connection, and she felt, vaguely, the cold of a disinfectant wipe on the inside of her arm, then a sharp prick.

It couldn't have been more than a few minutes before the painkiller took effect. When it finally did, though, the lifting of the cloud of pain around her mind was shocking and unexpected enough that it took her a few moments to adjust.

Now that the world was clearing, her mind could translate the voices around her into words, and she blinked her eyes back open.

Archibald and Vee were still hovering over the two cots, speaking to each other in curt, businesslike tones that told her that, whatever animosity they had towards each other, it would be put to one side until the crisis was past.

"Hollis?"

She looked up to see Silas standing near her cot, Ari next to him.

"We got you your ship back, Captain, and to your credit, you kept your word about Gracie and Temple. But we have hours at most before we're under attack. If I understand things correctly, you have no guns, no shields, and no functioning nav system for your jumps, and the *Sweet Jenny* just gave up her jump-path out. So. What the hell is your plan?"

14

Gracie

Gracie felt the pain first, throbbing through her consciousness, whining through her nerves and crawling under her skin.

She knew pain, though. She was familiar with pain. And she'd lived on the knife-edge of survival for long enough that she could push past it, force her brain to translate the sounds of voices on the edges of her consciousness into words.

"… best I can do for her, and we can only hope it's enough."

It was a man's voice she didn't recognize, with a crisp Level accent, sharp with concern.

"Vitals are coming back, so that's a good sign, leastways." That voice, she did recognize. Vee. "Mad Dog ain't one to stop fighting, not her. She'll pull through, I reckon. Although," she added reluctantly, "wouldn't have done without your ship's tech. So I thank you for that."

"Thank the captain," said the man curtly. "I'm doing as ordered, although God knows I have little enough cause to love pirates."

"And Our Blessed Lady knows Mad Dog and our Ari and Sil had little enough cause to rescue your captain and bring her back here rather'n shoot her through the head," came Vee's tart response. "So it's a damn good thing she, at least, understands a bit of that honour you naval bastards go on about."

"Vee?" Gracie croaked. Her voice came out hoarse and barely audible. One of her eyes was swollen shut, but she managed to open the other a crack.

"Captain?" Vee's voice was sharp with a mixture of worry and relief. "You're awake?"

Gracie tried to smile reflexively, then stopped, wincing. "Afraid I'm too stubborn to die just yet," she managed.

"Thank Our Blessed Lady of Mercy," Vee breathed. Gracie couldn't see her as any more than a vague form in her blurry vision, but the relief in her voice was utter and unmistakable. "Thank Our Blessed Lady."

For a few moments, Gracie breathed through the pain, trying to bring her mind into focus.

"Tell me what we have, Vee," she said at last, her voice a low rasp. "What're we working with here? Or have the Rosette bastards taken us again already? And how's Temple?"

Vee glanced around quickly, and leaned in. "We took both ships back, Captain. You're on the *Verity* now, and thank Our Lady for that —couldn't have kept you alive much longer'n this with the equipment we have on the *Sweet Jenny*, but the *Verity's* carrying a goddamn hospital on board. Temple's going to pull through as well, got him past the worst of it. But the rest ain't good. Got you here by telling the Rosette commodore that you'd captured Ives and we'd kill her if they didn't open us a jump path. Figure we have a couple of minutes at most before they figure out they've been had, and the *Verity* ain't got shields or guns on her."

Gracie let out a breath. "Don't sound good, do it?"

Vee shook her head. "It don't, truth be told." She hesitated, and that more than anything told Gracie that whatever she'd say next, it wasn't good news.

"Captain, that ain't all." She leaned in closer. "Haven't told the rest of the crew yet, seeing as there ain't much we can do about it. But got word over the *Sweet Jenny's* comm from Captain Holdfast—Rosette fleet has a communications block up, but it ain't enough to block the *Sweet Jenny's* communications, what with the mods we have on her. Anyway, the damn Level navy decided to take Blackrock out once and for all, after what we did. Three fleets they sent, practically the entire damn navy. Don't figure the pirates'll hold out long without you there. Hell, three fleets, not sure they'd hold out either way."

Gracie closed her eyes, pulling in a long breath. "What the hell we going to do, Vee?" she said, without opening them.

"I don't know," said Vee grimly. "But I'll tell you, it don't look good. Without you there, doubt the rest of the pirate captains'll stop bickering long enough to figure out a defence. There's a couple of the traps we set from before that they didn't trigger last time. That'll hold 'em off for a bit. But it ain't going to hold them long. If we do get out of this mess, don't figure we'll have a berth to take the *Sweet Jenny* back to, or many allies left alive out of it."

Gracie managed a small nod.

Not just her crew, then. The Admiral had decided to take everything—her allies, her home, her berth, her friends.

At least the pain clouding her mind and thickening in her throat numbed the horror of it.

From the corner of her mind that was still paying attention, she could hear low voices arguing behind her—Sil, it sounded like, and Ari, and Ives and Price.

"I have every damned mechanic on my ship looking into the guns," Hollis snapped. "And every damned one of them tells me it'll take hours, if not days, to get them back online. We may have a few of the light precision guns that were taken out by your damned electromagnetic pulse, they won't have been taken out by the spy, most likely. I have my sailors working on that, and they'll do the best they can. But that's not going to hold off a dozen fully crewed Rosette naval ships."

"Well, Captain," Silas's voice was dripping with irony. "I do hope we can come up with something, considering we're stuck here on your account." He paused. "Ari. What are the chances the *Sweet Jenny* can fight her way out?"

"Not good," said Ari grimly. "There's a chance we get them looking at the *Verity* and we take ourselves off. Might be they don't bother coming after a pirate ship. But it's a slim chance, and it'd leave us in the same position we were in before—Gracie and Temple both need the med tech on this damn ship until we have a better option."

"Even if the *Verity* had full use of her guns and her shields and her nav tech—what then?" Ives said. "We couldn't stand up to that many Rosette ships—no matter how good my crew, we're simply too far outnumbered. We could possibly clear a jump path, but where would we go? I won't lead them back to the Level, not without alerting the Level navy first, and I can't get through to them—I've tried. The Rosette ships have blocked off communication. And they'll follow the *Verity*, wherever we decide to jump to. At best, it would give us a choice in what sector we die."

Gracie closed her eyes. The combination of the pain and the rum had left her head floating, her thoughts oddly disconnected.

She shifted on the cot, trying to force her mind to think.

Blackrock. Judith had sent ships to Blackrock, three fleets.

What Gracie had almost done had frightened her. And just like back when they were lovers, Gracie knew how Judith had reacted, as clearly as if she'd been in the room with her—she'd decided, rather than admit her oversight, to take down Gracie and the pirate settlement together.

But it was odd, really, that word had reached the *Sweet Jenny* so quickly.

"Vee?" she mumbled.

"Captain?"

"Vee, Holdfast didn't tell you how they got word the ships were coming, did they?"

She could picture Vee frowning, trying to parse her words for their meaning. "Yes," the woman said at last. "Said the navy'd been broadcasting the attack across all the general channels. Wasn't even encoded, they said."

Gracie nodded slowly, something settling across her mind that she wasn't sure whether was fondness, or fury.

So that was Judith's game.

"Grace!"

She'd spun, her cutlass already in motion. The sailor Jenny'd been fighting didn't have time to turn, Grace's cutlass shoving through his back and out his stomach. She jerked it free, turning in time to catch another cutlass-blow on her blade, and from the corner of her eye saw Jenny's sparker glowing as she dispersed the man's ghost.

A few months ago, she'd never have turned her back on a forming ghost. But she knew Jenny like she knew her own self, and they fought together like they could read each other's thoughts.

Later that night, after the battle, after the boarding party had been repelled,

Jenny had pushed herself up on one elbow in the cot. The faint light of the lamp set her blonde hair glowing, a halo around her face. "You could have been killed, Grace." She said the words quietly. "If I'd not been in time with the sparker—"

Grace rolled up on her elbow as well, watching her. She'd never tire of watching Jenny, reading her thoughts in the small quirk of her lips or the twitch of an eyebrow.

"You could have been killed too, if I wasn't in time with my cutlass," she said at last, running her fingers through the gold halo of hair around Jenny's face.

God, Jenny was beautiful.

"You'd never have let that happen." There was no question in Jenny's voice.

Grace smiled. "No, I'd not, at that." She paused, running her hand down Jenny's bare throat, resting the backs of her fingers on the soft skin just under her collarbone. "Jenny, if I have a heart at all, it's here. Beating in your chest. I trust you like I trust my own life. And I'd sooner let my own self die than let you get hurt." She pressed a kiss to the underside of Jenny's jaw. "I'd not turn my back on a ghost unless I knew, without thinking of it, that whoever had my back knew me like my heart beat in their chest. That I knew them so well that their hand might as well be my own, and my sword might as well be theirs. But that person? I'd trust her with my life. I'd trust her with the world."

Even after all these years, she and Jenny could read each other's thoughts, time and distance be damned.

And she'd play into Judith's hands, because she didn't have another choice.

"Ari?" Gracie's voice was still so hoarse she wasn't sure if the woman would hear her. But Ari jerked around at the sound, her eyes going wide.

"Captain?" She crossed over to Gracie in two steps, her face gone deathly white. "Captain, thank God …" Her voice cracked, and she dropped her face into her hands.

"Gracie." Sil sounded almost as desperate as Ari. "Captain, are you—" he turned to Vee. "Vee, how is she?"

"Better'n she has any right to be," Vee muttered.

Gracie swallowed, wincing. Her head still felt foggy from the rum, her thoughts fragmented, but the benefit, she supposed, of having been tortured half to death was that a hangover would hardly weigh on the scale.

"Ari," she managed. "I'm fine, lass." That was stretching the truth to breaking, perhaps, but she needed the woman to focus. "Need to talk to you and Ives, though."

Ari pulled in a long breath, then nodded, stepping away. "I'll get her for you, Captain."

Gracie let her eyes fall closed again for a moment, too tired to try to keep them open.

She was aware of someone, probably Sil, speaking with Vee in a low voice, then coming to crouch beside her. "Captain?" he asked quietly. "Is there anything I can do?"

She managed a small smile, without opening her eyes. "Figure there will be, lad," she mumbled. "Let's wait to see what Ives has to say."

When she blinked her eyes open again, Ives was seated in front of her in one of the med bay hover chairs, Price standing over her shoulder and glowering at Gracie. Ari stood next to them, and the hostility between the two was enough to raise sparks.

"Captain Ives," Gracie rasped. "Vee here tells me we've taken your ship back, but you don't have a way out. That true?"

Ives paused a moment, then gave a brusque nod. "Yes. That seems to be our situation currently."

Gracie nodded as well. "Don't reckon as you've heard about

what's happening in Blackrock," she continued at last. "Vee here got word from some of the pirate captains back there. Looks like your friend Admiral Usher sent three more fleets out that direction."

Ives sucked in a quick breath. "Dammit!" she hissed, turning to Price. "Devil take all of this. We can't jump back to the Level even if we do manage to get our message through, they're practically undefended."

Price didn't look any more happy than Ives at the news, but they just nodded. "We'll have to come up with another solution, then," they said in a low voice.

Ari and Sil had both stiffened, and Gracie could see by their faces that they knew exactly the implications of that large a fleet posted off Blackrock.

"Can't say as I much like the thought of the *Sweet Jenny's* berth being turned to smooth glass either," Gracie continued at last. "So I figure I may have come up with something that'll solve this for both of us."

"And what might that be?" Ives snapped, turning back to her. The strain of the last few days was evident in every line of her posture, and Gracie got the distinct impression that she was only sitting down, rather than pacing the room, because her first mate and chief medical officer had both threatened mutiny if she didn't.

"Well, Commodore Mattise may not follow the *Sweet Jenny*, if we got her away," said Gracie. "But I reckon he'll take his fleet and follow the *Verity* into the depths of hell. Pirates ain't exactly known for being loyal to the Level, so they don't see much danger from us, but the Rosette navy ain't going to risk a Level naval ship getting past them, sending out a warning." She managed a small shrug. "Way I figure is this: you need the Level navy to know about our friends here, and they ain't taking your calls. I need the Level navy to stop bombing my goddamn home. So. You jump the *Verity* back to Blackrock. The Rosette fleet follows you, and lands right in the damn middle of your three Level fleets. Your navy stops bombing the *Sweet Jenny's* berth, on account of they're in a full-out war, and you don't lead the Rosette fleet back to the Level. Figure we both win."

There was a moment of silence.

"We wouldn't be able to warn them what was coming, not until we were there," said Hollis slowly, glancing at Foster.

Foster gave a tight shrug. "She's right, though. The fleets at Blackrock will be armed for a fight, at the least. It's better than any alternative we've come up with so far."

There was another moment of silence. Gracie let her eyes fall closed again, and focused on remaining conscious.

This whole damn thing would have been easier if her mind was clear, but then, she didn't often get to choose an ideal circumstance to fight for her life.

Ives would take her suggestion, she wasn't worried about that. There wasn't another viable option, and the woman was clever enough to see it. It was still possible she'd save Blackrock.

And the rest, she could deal with as it came.

"Very well, Captain Mad Dog." Hollis's voice was cold, and Gracie almost smiled. "Suppose I agree with your reasoning. That still leaves us here, without guns or shields, and without the ability to calculate a jump, thanks to you."

Gracie pulled in a shallow breath, and coughed painfully. It was a moment before she was recovered enough to speak, and she could see the stark fear on Ari's face.

She breathed through the agony for a moment.

"I figure I may have a solution for that, as well," she managed at last, the words rasping painfully in her throat. "But I ain't sure you or your first mate there will like it."

15

Hollis

"Captain. I understand we don't have a lot of options, but this is madness." Foster's voice was low, but Hollis could hear the strain under it.

Emmett, who'd come down from the bridge to join the two of them, didn't look any happier.

Foster was right. Foster was absolutely right. Mad Dog's plan was the perfect setup for a betrayal.

On its face, the suggestion was an intelligent one—the pirates would take the *Sweet Jenny* and make a run for it, make themselves a jump-path and jump out, letting the Rosette fleet see that the *Verity* was unguarded. Their jump, however, would only be a few light-minutes. They'd wait long enough for the Rosette fleet to break formation to take back the *Verity*, knowing that the *Verity* was in no shape to jump out herself. Then they'd jump back, send through jump-coordinates for the *Verity* to follow so the *Verity* wouldn't be depending on her own rigged nav computer to do the calculations, and both ships would jump for Blackrock, leading the Rosette ships after them into an ambush.

But Mad Dog was notorious for luring naval captains into complacency, and then destroying them. She was notorious for sacrificing every person who stood in the way of safety for her crew, her own life be damned. And Hollis knew damn well that between safety and Mad Dog's crew was exactly where she'd positioned herself.

It wouldn't even be difficult—the *Sweet Jenny* could simply jump and not look back, or even just wait a few extra minutes, until the *Verity* had been shot to pieces, then swoop back in through the Rosette ships and collect their prize.

She'd have no way to protect her ship, or to protect her own crew.

But … Mad Dog was right as well. They hardly had another option.

"I don't like it either," she said, her tone matching her first mate's. "But I don't intend to leave us entirely at their mercy. I'll insist on conditions that will do something, at least, to protect us. And they haven't turned on us yet."

"That's only because they had something to gain," Foster hissed.

"They still do. Mad Dog, at least, seemed interested in saving Blackrock. I think her previous actions back that up. And as for the rest, as long as Mad Dog can't survive without our medical tech, we still have a hold on them."

The pirates, to their credit, had allowed Hollis and Foster their privacy for the conversation.

In the end, though, there was hardly need for them to pressure her. They probably knew as well as Hollis did how scant their current options were.

Foster was silent for long enough that she wasn't sure they were going to respond. At last, though, they jerked their head in a quick nod. "I can't disagree with you there. I'll follow your lead, Captain, you know that. But I don't like this."

"Greene?" asked Hollis, turning to him.

"I agree with Price," he said, his voice grim.

Hollis nodded without speaking, unease twisting in her gut.

But they didn't have the time to spare agonizing over the decision.

She went to stand automatically, but Foster's hand on her shoulder stopped her. "Captain," they said, a note of warning in their voice.

Hollis sighed heavily.

The painkillers had taken enough of the edge off the pain that she had to remind herself to be careful, but Foster was right—if the last few days had taught her anything, it was how devilishly difficult it was to captain a ship when you were constantly one wrong move away from passing out.

"If you'd be so kind," she said, her tone stiff, and Foster nodded, leaning down to engage the hover-controls on the med bay chair.

She maneuvered her seat carefully back over to where Mad Dog lay on her cot.

There was a woman on the pirate's crew, Freddie, if she recalled correctly, who used a hover chair, maneuvering around her ship with the ease of long practice. The *Verity* was as much set up for sailors who used a hover chair as the *Sweet Jenny* was, but Hollis lacked the skills and practice the pirate had, and her movements were jerky and unsteady.

She studied the pirate captain surreptitiously as she approached.

Mad Dog still looked more dead than alive—her eyes closed, face bruised and swollen, bandages covering her body and tubes and monitors hooked up to her arms and chest. Hollis could almost have convinced herself that the woman couldn't possibly pose them a danger, not like this.

But she remembered, all too well, the horrifying screams from inside the emergency airlock back on the *Chasseuse,* the grisly scene afterwards—the torn corpses, the blood-spattered walls.

That had been Mad Dog's plan. It had saved all their lives, but she wasn't sure she'd ever get the sight of it out of her head. And that had been before—when Gracie was stumbling drunk on rum and without the benefit of any of the medical treatments and painkillers Vee and Archibald were pumping into her now.

No, Mad Dog was not someone she could afford to underestimate, not even like this.

"Captain," she said, when at last she'd fumbled with the hover chair controls and brought the thing to sit on the deck.

Mad Dog's eyes fluttered open, and she glanced around without moving her head. Even after the painkillers, Hollis could see the lines of agony in her face at even the slightest movement.

Ari and Silas, who'd been talking in one corner with Vee and Toothpick, glanced over, and a moment later, the four pirates had come to join them.

"You make up your mind yet, Captain Ives?" Mad Dog's voice was a hoarse, barely audible rasp.

Hollis drew in a steadying breath. "Price and I have talked it over. I believe the plan you put forward is our best option. However, I must insist on terms to protect myself and my crew."

Mad Dog raised her eyebrows just a little. "What terms, then?"

"You'll stay on the *Verity*." She held up a hand as Ari opened her mouth to protest. "Ask Vee or Officer Smyth—I hardly think it wise to transfer her to another ship with the state she's in now."

Ari glanced at Vee, who gave a reluctant nod. "She ain't lying," the pirate medic said. "Gracie'll do better if we don't move her." She turned back to Hollis. "But I'm warning you, Ives—you harm one hair on her head, and I'll give you and your crew cause to regret it."

The tone of her voice told Hollis the threat was not an idle one.

"The hope, I believe, is to keep your captain from dying of her injuries," Hollis said sharply. "However, it will also offer my crew some assurance that you won't take the *Sweet Jenny* and leave the rest of us here stranded."

"Vee. Lass has the right to ask for security, I figure," said Gracie mildly.

Vee narrowed her eyes at Hollis, but jerked her head in a short nod.

"And my second condition is, Silas will be captaining the *Sweet Jenny*," Hollis continued.

This time, it was Silas who opened his mouth to respond. She cut him off before he could speak. "If I understand correctly, Silas is the one who negotiated the surrender of the *Verity*, before the Rosette Navy arrived," she said. "Of all of you, he's the only one I'm willing to entrust with the possible survival of my ship and my crew. You may agree with my conditions or dispute them. But without both in place, I will not agree to this plan."

"And what's your alternate plan, then, Captain?" rasped Gracie.

Hollis met her gaze stubbornly. "I shall continue to make what repairs on my guns and shields I can, and I'll go down fighting," she said. "If the *Verity* goes down, that will trigger an alert on the Level that a ship was lost. Perhaps they'll believe it was you that took it down, but either way, they'll send a scout ship to find out what happened. There should be enough evidence here of the Rosette ships, even if they've left, that the navy will figure out what happened."

Gracie was still watching her, and now she raised her eyebrows. "Still willing to sacrifice yourself and your crew for the greater good," she said at last.

Hollis narrowed her eyes and didn't respond.

Gracie closed her eyes a moment, then, with an effort, turned her head a little to look at Ari and Toothpick. "Toothpick. Ship's yours while I'm incapacitated, so I figure it's your call. But for what it's worth, I believe Captain Ives ain't asking for anything unreasonable." She paused. "That said, figure if she gets security, wouldn't hurt to ask for security for our ownselves. I'd say Mate Price there'd make a good sailor before the mast on the *Sweet Jenny*, in a pinch."

Hollis sucked in a quick breath that set her coughing.

Gracie was watching her, gaze sharp, and she could feel Silas and Ari's sudden attention.

She tried not to curse.

She'd insisted on having a hostage on board the *Verity*. She could hardly have expected less. But damn this to hell …

Price stepped forward. "I'm willing, Captain, if that's what they need for security from us," they said, their voice steady.

Toothpick glanced up at Hollis, his gaze cool and more perceptive than Hollis had expected.

Still, Gracie had chosen Toothpick as her first mate. Whatever else he was, he'd have the intelligence and ruthlessness that Mad Dog needed if she wasn't able to command her ship.

"If you think it's a fair deal, Captain, that's good enough for me," he said at last, turning back to Gracie. He looked up at Hollis. "I'll agree to your terms, Ives, if you agree to the Captain's." He glanced at Silas. "You figure you can handle the *Sweet Jenny*, Sil?"

Silas's jaw was clenched, but he gave a quick, short nod. "Aye. But you or Ari would—"

Toothpick shook his head. "Ain't a question of who'd do a better job of it. Question is, can you do it." He paused. "Gracie trusts you, and figure I do too."

Silas drew in a long breath. "Very well. I'll do it, then." He turned to Hollis, and there was something in his face that told her that whatever he had been before, he was now as much a member of Mad Dog's crew as any of the others. "You'll damn well keep the captain safe, Ives," he said in a low voice. "You'll keep her alive, and you'll keep her safe, and if you for one moment consider taking your revenge on her, or stabbing us in the back, remember that the *Sweet Jenny* has the guns to take out the *Verity* even if she were running her full shields. The Rosette ships won't get in fast enough to kill you before I take you down." He turned on his heel and started for the airlock.

"You go with him, lass," said Toothpick, gesturing at Ari. "With Gracie and Temple down, and Vee here with the captain, he don't have a full crew even with Mate Price." He glanced back up at Hollis. "And I ain't leaving Vee and Temple and Gracie here without someone else here to make sure the Level navy holds to its bargain and don't try to kill them the moment they're left alone."

Ari nodded and strode out after Silas, and Jumper and Freddie went after her. Foster hesitated the barest moment, then followed, their posture as straight and proper as always.

The click of the door closing behind them was loud in the silence.

"Captain," said Emmett at last. "What are your orders?"

Hollis closed her eyes.

She was tempted to insist that she go back to the bridge. But her body was on the verge of collapse, and Emmett would have enough to do without worrying about her.

"Mate Greene. Ready the ship, and prepare the crew for jump." She paused, and added in an undertone that only he could hear. "And let's pray to God or Our Lady or whatever you pray to that this works."

16

Silas

When they reached the *Sweet Jenny*, Silas hesitated before turning for the cockpit.

"Go on, ain't got all day," Ari snapped from behind him.

He knew damn well her snappishness was from the mixture of strain and exhaustion that they'd all been drowning in since they'd started for the Level, however many hours or days ago that had been. Still, he had to bite his tongue to keep from snapping back. Instead, he drew a deep breath, nodded, and tapped the cockpit door open.

Even having just seen her lying in the *Verity's* med bay, Silas's brain half-way expected to see Gracie seated in the captain's chair, her stained oilcloth jacket thrown over the back of it, her mild expression and sharp gaze turned on him. And the jolt at seeing the empty chair instead set a pit of nausea in his stomach.

"Well, Sil, your ship," said Ari, gesturing.

He sighed again, the tension singing through his muscles, and stepped over to the controls.

He'd piloted a ship before—captained a few temporarily, if they'd taken a prize and his captain needed someone to bring her in. But the *Sweet Jenny* was so much Gracie's ship that he could practically see her at the controls, smell the scent of her—oilcloth and sweet tea and old tobacco—permeating the air.

He closed his eyes, collecting himself. When he opened them, Ari was standing next to him, and he was surprised at the hint of compassion in her face. "Crew'll take your orders, Sil," she said quietly. "Ain't one of us here who don't trust you."

That was exactly the problem. He still wasn't sure why they trusted him, still wasn't sure he was trustworthy.

He blew out his breath. "It should be you doing this."

She grinned just a bit. "Figure I'd do a better job of it, yeah. But it ain't me, so may as well stop moping and get to work."

He nodded grimly and turned back to the controls.

When he pulled up the scanners, he could see the Rosette naval ships in their loose formation around the *Sweet Jenny* and the *Verity*. He frowned, examining them.

They were in the standard formation he'd expect if they were trying to cut a ship off. But that formation worked better against ships flying together than it did against independent ships.

Which may just save their lives. He could already see, even through the sensors, the small shifts in the Rosette fleet's formation as the ships turned, preparing to fire on them. The line they'd had through to the *Chasseuse* had been cut off, and by now the commodore would certainly have figured out that Hollis and Gracie had played him. But the fleet was braced for a counter-attack, not for a small, heavily armed ship trying to break out, and the chaos they'd caused on the *Chasseuse* while making their escape meant the flagship had drifted a little, not quite in formation with the rest.

Price had stepped in behind him and Ari, standing quietly against the wall, their face a bland mask. Silas had only known the naval officer a few hours, but he could already tell how they'd gained their position. They had the bearing of a model naval first officer—there when they were needed, fading gently into the background when they weren't.

He drew in a long breath.

He was captaining the *Sweet Jenny*.

That was one thing he'd learned in the navy, he could damn well give orders with the best of them. And if he couldn't drive the navy out of himself, he could at least by God use it to save Gracie and his crew.

He pushed the screen to one side and tapped the comm. "We'll run out past the *Chasseuse*. Jumper, I want you on the guns and shields. It's going to get hot in here quick enough, so keep a weather eye out. Freddie, can you keep us running singlehanded?"

"Long as you don't do anything to her that'll need me holding things together in the engine room, figure I will," she said through the comm line. "But you'll owe me a hell of a lot of greasing and polishing to make up for it, lad."

He smiled a little, despite himself, and turned to Ari. "You're piloting," he said. "I'll chart you a course. Price, you're here until I need you somewhere else."

Price nodded and took the copilot's seat, and Ari slid into the pilot's seat.

Price would be best used on the guns, but the *Verity's* first mate would almost certainly be lost at Jumper's sign language and code tapped through the comm, so Silas would have to find another way to make use of them.

He turned back to the screens, frowning in concentration, then tapped in a course and sent it through to Ari.

She scanned it and nodded, then tapped the comm line. "Strap in, lifting off in five. Four. Three. Two. One." She hit the controls, and the *Sweet Jenny* detached from the *Verity's* airlock, lifting up and away as delicately as a butterfly taking flight.

There were a total of twelve Rosette ships now. A small fleet, but a fleet—more must have arrived while he and Ari were locked away on the *Chasseuse*. But they hung back, holding close to their flagship, and the *Chasseuse* was still moving sluggishly.

He glanced at Ari and Price, and knew the two of them were seeing in their heads the same thing as he was—the airlock smeared and spattered with blood, the torn bodies, the bloody trail leading up through the crew quarters, the echoes of screams from farther in.

It would be some time before the *Chasseuse* would be able to muster what was left of its sailors. Besides, Gracie was right—the Rosette navy should have no reason to come after pirates. It was unlikely that a pirate ship would take word of an upcoming invasion back to the Level, and if they did, unlikelier still they'd be believed.

A series of rapid taps through the comm told him that Jumper had set the shields. He was almost surprised at how naturally his brain had translated the response—not every word, but enough that he could understand the message without having to think about it.

It had only been … what, weeks, since he'd have been staring helplessly at the comm, or waiting for Ari or one of the others to translate for him?

"Acknowledged," he said, without taking his eyes off the screens.

The *Chasseuse* had caught sight of them by now, and it was turning, albeit lethargically, into position to deliver a broadside.

"Sight in on their shields, give them a warning," he snapped through the comm. "Don't need to take their shields out, just let them know we can."

Jumper tapped out a quick acknowledgement through the comm.

"Sil," Ari hissed. "They ain't the only ones, look."

He glanced back at the screens and cursed.

Two other Rosette ships had swung around, moving in to firing position.

"Freddie, get the engines up to full power," he said through the comm line. "We'll have to run her past quick-time if we're going to make it out."

"Aye, lad," came Freddie's terse tones.

One of the ships fired off a volley, and Silas swore as they impacted off the *Sweet Jenny's* shields.

"Get up to the gun room and help Jumper, keep the ships too busy defending themselves to put up a good offence," he said, turning to Ari. "I'll pilot. Price, you're on the charts."

Ari nodded and slid out of the seat, and Silas crossed over quickly, taking Ari's place as she turned for the gun room. Price bent over the charts, and Silas rested his hands on the controls for a moment, waiting.

"We're on full power," came Freddie's terse voice.

"Acknowledged." He jammed the throttle, and the *Sweet Jenny* leapt forward, her engines responsive under his touch.

"I'm pulling her in close to the *Chasseuse*," he said over the comm. "I'll take us in too close for her heavies to get a clear shot. Get all the shields forward and hit her hard, you'll only have a few seconds."

Jumper tapped an acknowledgement.

Another volley of shots exploded from the *Chasseuse*, and Silas barely had time to shout, "Brace!" through the line before they hit— but these were the close-range light guns. The *Sweet Jenny* shook, but her shields held. On his screen, a barrage of shots burst out from the *Sweet Jenny*, and he found he'd unconsciously braced for the jolt of the broadside, already accustomed to the *Sweet Jenny's* quirks.

Price had to grab for the arms of their chair, and Silas bit back a grin.

Then they were passed the bigger ship and through the blockade, and there was only open space in front of them.

Silas sent the *Sweet Jenny* into a quick spin, trying to shake off the missiles that were following them. Jumper had clearly seen them, because another volley of shots from the *Sweet Jenny's* long-range precision weapons lit up his screen, and the missiles exploded one by one as the shots impacted.

Silas blew out a long breath of relief and expanded the screen.

As they'd hoped, the *Chasseuse* was making no attempt to come after them, instead turning back towards the defenceless *Verity*.

"Price," he said. "Get an exact reading on the *Verity's* position and set it into the controls, then get me a jump path ten light-minutes out."

Ten minute's jump out, a five minute wait, and then a ten minute jump back would give the Rosette ships enough time to break formation, but not enough to get in close enough to damage the *Verity*. Once the Rosette ships were no longer in blockade formation, it should be a simple enough matter to clear a path out for both of them.

Price pushed the jump path through to his controls, and he scanned it quickly.

"Going into jump," he said through the comm. "Jumping in three. Two. One. Jumping."

Carefully, he pulled back on the jump controls, closing his eyes at the familiar jolt of the ship passing into FTL speeds.

Even here, though, in the space between jumps, where neither he nor anyone else could do anything to change what would happen next, he found his fingers tapping restlessly against the controls, his foot bouncing against the leg of his chair.

Price was bent over the charts, their expression stoic, their posture proper.

Silas shook his head. That would have been him, once. Although he doubted he'd ever been able to match Price's ability to deadpan.

"Coming out of jump," he said at last, sitting up straight and tapping the comm. "In three. Two. One. Coming out."

Again, there was that familiar jolt that always threatened to send his stomach rebelling, no matter how many times he'd experienced it, and the screens fuzzed and steadied as the ship came back into sub-light speed.

He watched them from the corner of his eye as he tapped in the coordinates Price had sent him for a return jump. They couldn't contact the *Verity*, but Hollis was a good captain—she'd be able to keep the *Verity* out of harm's way for fifteen more minutes, even damaged as the ship was.

Price sucked in a sharp breath, and Silas turned quickly back to the screens.

Then he swore.

At the edges of the screen, two Rosette ships flickered into view.

"Well. Your Captain Mad Dog must have frightened them more than we thought," Price said, voice grim.

"Jumper, get on the shields," Silas snapped through the comm. "We've got company."

There was a tapping through the comm that he instantly recognized as profanity.

"What's going on, Sil?" Freddie's voice was sharp with concern.

"Two of the Rosette ships followed us through," he said.

Freddie added her own profanity to the comm line as he turned back to the screens.

"They're both two-hundred-and-fifty-crewed, from the looks of it," said Price, glancing up at him. "They'll have weapons comparable to our two-hundred-and-fifty-crewed ships, but the Rosette ships sacrifice heavy power for stronger precision weapons. Their heavies will still do plenty of damage, but they take longer than ours to recharge. At least, longer than our ships of the line. I don't know how long your weapons will take, but my guess is they're quicker than what we have in the navy."

Silas glanced over at Price in surprise, but they'd already turned back to the screens.

"Sil? What're your orders?" Ari's voice through the comm sounded grim.

He closed his eyes a moment. "They're blocking us from jumping back the way we came, and we don't have time to run out around them and jump from there," he said through the general line. "That would take a solid hour at least, I'm guessing, plus jump time, and the *Verity* doesn't have that long. So we fight our way out."

He could feel Price's eyes on him, but he didn't look over at them.

This was bad, and both of them knew it.

"Get back on the guns," he said grimly. "Jumper, shields to full power. Freddie, I want every bit of power we can spare to the shields and the guns, pull back on the jump engines for now. We're not jumping until we disable them."

"Aye, lad," came Freddie's voice. She sounded just as grim as he felt.

He turned back to his screen, making quick calculations in his head.

This was just like back in the Academy, an exam question on strategy—one smaller ship, armed with heavy weapons and a quicker run-speed, against two larger ships with more guns and more sailors. Your jump path is blocked. How do you get out?

He closed his eyes a moment.

Then he opened them again, smiling to himself.

Price knew these ships' specs, but the Rosette captains would have no idea of the *Sweet Jenny's* capabilities—hell, no one but her crew had any idea of her capabilities after the new weapons Freddie and Jumper had installed. And Silas had studied Rosette System tactics for two and a half years in the Academy. He might not know what they'd do, but he knew what strategies they'd been trained on.

"Ari, hit them with the precision weapons, but only the light ones," he said through the comm. "I'm going to bring us in close, like we're trying to break out between them. The moment we're in too close for their long-range precision weapons, hit them with our heavies on half-power."

"Aye," snapped Ari.

He leaned over the controls. He wouldn't think about the fact that this was Gracie's life in the balance, and the lives of Hollis Ives and the *Verity's* crew, and possibly the fate of Blackrock and the entire Level. This was an Academy exam, and he'd be damned if he'd fail it.

He swung the *Sweet Jenny* in a wide arc, and headed back towards the Rosette ships.

They were positioned to block his jump back to the *Verity*, but a brief glance at his nav screen told him they were also blocking any attempt to jump back towards the Level.

Which meant they didn't know, exactly, what the *Sweet Jenny* had been planning to do. That was a strike in their favour.

He turned the ship two points to starboard. "Ari," he snapped. "Fire on their port sides. We want it to look like we're looking to break through back to Blackrock and the Level."

"Aye," she said, and through his screen, he could see the *Sweet Jenny's* weapons slowly turning to follow his arc, levelling in on the port side of the Rosette ships.

The Rosette ships were in range now, and their weapons sparked against the edge of the *Sweet Jenny's* shields.

"Freddie, how are we going?" he asked brusquely. "How long are we going to hold up?"

"We can take this for a bit," she said. "Ain't going to last long when we're in full range, though, and if we get hit by a broadside, we ain't coming out of it without some heavy damage."

He murmured a quick confirmation, studying his screens.

"Hold tight," he said. "Jumper, do what you can on the shields to deflect the shots, I'll take us through them as quick as I can."

They were in full range now. The *Sweet Jenny's* precision weapons were still impacting against the Rosette ships' shields, but she no longer had the advantage of distance, and the Rosette ships' heavier weapons were taking their toll.

He pushed the throttle harder, and he could feel the *Sweet Jenny* straining to obey, most of her power diverted to the shields and guns.

The ship shook at a direct hit. Sparks popped from the lighting above him, and Freddie's cursing through the comm was a steady background noise.

"We're close enough for the heavies, even at half-power, but we're in too close for their long-range weapons to hit us," said Ari.

"Acknowledged. Start firing with the heavies, but keep them at half-power only. I want them to miscalculate our range."

Another direct hit sent the *Sweet Jenny* shuddering, and he had to grab for the controls to keep her steady.

"We ain't going to take too many more like that," said Freddie quietly through his private line.

"I know, dammit," he snapped back. "Do whatever you need to to keep us moving, but we're damn well going to have to take it a little while longer."

Another direct hit. Price hissed out a quiet curse.

Then the *Sweet Jenny* jolted with a broadside of her own, her heavies, on only half-power, impacting against the very edge of the Rosette ship's shields.

The Rosette ships were coming in close, turning so that both ships would be able to rake the *Sweet Jenny* with their broadsides on her way past them.

He smiled grimly to himself. They'd put themselves directly in front of the jump path he'd need to take to get back to either Blackrock or the Level—but if he could get between them, the jump path back to the *Verity* would be wide open. It meant, of course, exposing the *Sweet Jenny* to punishing fire, and with the heavies on half-power, Jumper and Ari wouldn't even be able to hit back.

But it would give him an excuse to come in closer, which, right now, was all he needed.

The first of the Rosette ships fired. "Brace!" he shouted, and then the broadside hit.

The shields sparked, and he felt the power cut as the ship strained to stay together.

"Lad, what the hell you doing?" Freddie snapped. "Told you we wouldn't last through broadsides."

"We're going to have to last through at least one more," he said through his teeth. "Do whatever the hell you need to do, but leave me some running power." He tapped the line through to the gunner room. "Ari, Jumper, get ready. They're going to hit us again, and they'll hit us in close. All power to the shields, and then as soon as we take the second broadside, switch power to the guns. We'll only have a minute or two to rake them, and I want to damn well make it count."

Jumper tapped an acknowledgement through the comm, and Silas could hear the tension in the short, quick taps.

"Price, I want a jump path, now. Take us in right outside the Rosette fleet formation, we don't have time to jump farther back and run in."

"Aye." Price's voice was brusque, but he could hear the worry in it.

The broadside from the second ship hit as Silas turned the *Sweet Jenny*, trying to take the shots on her bow to give the shields a smaller area to protect. The ship shuddered and lurched as the shots impacted, and Silas had to grab for the arms of his seat to keep from being thrown forward into the control panel.

He was vaguely aware of Freddie's cursing, Jumper's frantic taps through the line—the shields were out, another broadside like that and they'd go down—but he was in close enough now.

He shoved the controls sideways. The *Sweet Jenny* was foundering, her movements sluggish and imprecise … but it was enough.

She swung around at his urging.

"Freddie, give me full power to the running engines," he snapped through the lines. "Jumper, pull all power from the shields, Ari, switch the heavies over to full. We're going out between them."

"Aye, Sil." There was a dangerous excitement in Ari's voice, and he knew she'd seen exactly what he'd seen. The two ships were in close, the second brought in just out of range of the *Sweet Jenny* with her heavies on half-power—but well within range of the heavies on full power, and if Price was correct, they still had a few moments before the guns on the first ship would be able to recharge enough to hit them with another broadside.

He shoved the throttle forward.

The ships ahead of him had seen the trick, too late, their bows moving as they tried to get out of the way—and then he was between them.

"Fire at will!" he snapped through the comm. The *Sweet Jenny's* guns barked as her broadsides raked the enemy ships, their guns still not ready to fire. Their shields were up, but the feint had worked— they'd underestimated her power, and the shots cut through the shields like a knife through butter. He heard Ari's whoop of triumph through the comm, and through the screens he could see the compartments of the nearest ship going, one by one, small bursts of flame licking out, then instantly extinguished.

The second ship had reacted a little quicker, and their light weapons flickered out after the *Sweet Jenny* in a quick starburst, but Jumper had seen it too, and he had the light shields up seconds before they hit, impacting and sparking out.

Ari was firing broadside after broadside, the *Sweet Jenny* shaking with it, but they had only seconds before the first Rosette ship's guns would be ready.

"Freddie, I need more power!" he snapped, and an instant later the *Sweet Jenny* jumped forward under his fingers.

Ahead of him, there was nothing but clear space, and the calculations Price had tapped into the controls blinked on the nav system.

Another burst of light weapons from the second ship, then they were through, and out, the *Sweet Jenny's* bow pointed towards clear empty space.

The first Rosette ship had turned clumsily, facing them with its broadside.

"Going into jump," Silas snapped. "In three. Two."

There was the flicker of guns firing, the brilliant sunburst of a full Rosette naval ship broadside arcing out towards them.

"One."

The shots would impact momentarily, and the *Sweet Jenny's* shields were all but down, all power fed through to the running engines.

He gritted his teeth and eased back on the FTL control.

"Jumping!"

The ship lurched, and his stomach rolled … and they were in jump.

Freddie's cursing over the comm was loud in the sudden silence, and Silas closed his eyes in relief. He could hear, in the back of his mind, Jumper's taps through the comm that he knew, if he focused on them, would be new, elegant, and creative methods of swearing at him, but he could hear the grin in Ari's voice.

"Well, Sil, Freddie might never speak to you again, and Jumper might want to knife you on sight, but I'll bet those damn Rosette ships ain't going to underestimate Blackrock pirates again. Hell, from the looks of it before we jumped, one of them's on her way down, and the other'll be busy picking up the life vessels for at least an hour or two."

He was too weak with relief to respond.

"That was … well done."

He glanced up in surprise to see Price watching him. To his shock, there was a small, reluctant grin on their face, and he found he was grinning as well.

At last, though, he grimaced and sat up. They'd be ready to come out of jump in a minute or two.

He glanced at his screen and bit back a curse of his own.

They'd been gone far, far longer than he'd agreed on with Hollis. Even with the two ships that had followed him, the *Verity* was alone and defenceless against ten fully powered Rosette naval ships.

He pulled in a steadying breath and tapped the comm. "Freddie, Jumper, Ari, do what you need to to get us in fighting shape. We don't have time to run in like we planned, so we're jumping right into the middle of it."

"That ain't going to give us time to take stock of what we're up against." Freddie's voice was grim.

"I know," he said. "But if we don't, we might not have anyone left alive to pull out."

17

Hollis

For the hundredth time in the last five minutes, Hollis resisted the urge to shove herself to her feet and start pacing.

Instead, she pulled up a screen on the comm equipment Archibald had brought for her. "Greene," she said, trying to keep her tone calm. "How are the repairs coming?"

"I have people working on them, Captain." Greene's voice was thick with worry. "We still haven't figured out what our saboteur did to the guns, and until we find it, we won't be able to fix them. But our mechanics are doing their best on the guns and shields that were taken out in the electromagnetic blast back on Blackrock. It's just a matter of replacing components, and it shouldn't take them more than another half hour."

Half an hour. She held back a groan. In half an hour, they could very well be space dust, or damaged so badly that there was no coming back from it.

From the corner of her eye, she could see the pirate captain watching her. Mad Dog was laid out on the cot, and still looked more dead than alive, but her gaze, even through bruise-swollen eyes, was far too penetrating for comfort.

"Very good," Hollis said, fighting to keep her voice calm. "Tell them to work quick-time. I need something to point at the Rosette ships when they start in our direction. In the meantime, I'll need you on the bridge. I want the bridge crew ready for action and monitoring the Rosette ships. I want someone tracking their movements at all times and passing the information on to me. I don't expect the *Sweet Jenny* back for just under twenty minutes, and I won't put my ship at risk in that time." She paused. "I believe it prudent that I remain in the med bay for the time being," she added, hating the stiffness in her tone. "But I'll keep my screen up. Please broadcast it to the bridge crew."

"Aye, Captain." There was relief in Emmett's tone.

Hollis slumped back in her seat as Archibald came over. "Captain?" His voice was still thick with concern. "How are you feeling?"

She felt, quite honestly, terrible—her muscles so weak that had she tried to insist on going back to the bridge to captain her ship, she wasn't sure she'd have had the strength to stand from her chair.

"I'm as well as can be expected, thank you," she said tartly.

He must have heard the exhaustion in her voice, because he came closer, frowning. "I'd like to take your vitals, Captain."

She sighed. "I am doing as you requested, and captaining my ship from the med bay," she said, trying to keep the sharpness from her tone. "You may do what you need to do, but I will draw the line at speaking to my crew with sensors attached to my goddamn arms." She drew in a steadying breath and lowered her voice. "I understand you're trying to keep me healthy, and I appreciate your concern. But I am walking a very fine line at this moment. We're out of contact with the navy and surrounded by enemy ships, and our escape plan depends on the loyalty of pirates. I cannot afford to let them believe that I'm on the verge of death. Speaking from the med bay is bad enough as it is, I can't afford more." Her words sounded much too close to pleading for her entire comfort, but Archibald deserved an explanation, at the very least.

He hesitated, then nodded. "I understand, Captain," he said, his voice matching hers. "But at the least let me take your vitals while we're waiting for Greene to patch you through."

She nodded grudgingly, and he stepped forward, tapping his medical scanner against her chest and the side of her neck, pulling back her shirt just enough to examine the bandage one of the medical officers had set across the injury. "I'll have to redo the stitches," he muttered, pulling her shirt closed again. "But the bandage should hold, as long as you don't overdo it too badly." He sighed, shaking his head. "I suppose considering you escaped an enemy ship, helped a pirate crew take back the *Sweet Jenny*, and then stormed the bridge and took back the *Verity*, it's better than I'd expect. But I'm telling you, whether or not you'll listen to it—your body won't hold up to much more. You're on the verge of collapse. Stubborn you may be, but if you push yourself too hard, your body will give out, and Greene will be captaining the ship without you."

Hollis nodded, biting back the sharp retort she wanted to make.

He was right, and both of them knew it. Greene had known it without Archibald telling him, she'd heard it in the relief in his voice over the comm—relief that she'd for once done as instructed by her medical officers, rather than put herself and everyone around her at risk.

But even so, it was a fight to keep her exhausted body in the chair, rather than shove herself to her feet and make her way to the bridge, passing out be damned.

"Captain, I'm broadcasting you through to the bridge," came Emmett's voice through her private line.

She straightened. "Thank you, Mate Greene."

On the screen ahead of her, the bridge flickered into view. The faces of her officers, she noted quickly, were pale and strained, but they weren't panicking, not yet.

"Officers," she said brusquely. "We will be facing Rosette ships of the line. I need each one of you at your stations and ready for action. I'm hopeful that we will not be facing them long, but we must prepare as if we were."

If they were—if the *Sweet Jenny* didn't make it back on time, if Silas betrayed her, or if, God forbid, he was shot down, the *Verity* and every soul aboard was already doomed. With full guns and shields, it would have been possible, although unlikely, that they could shoot a passage out. As it was, there wasn't a hope in hell.

"Pull up the screens, if you would, Greene," she said. Emmett nodded, and a moment later the ship's screens appeared in the corner of her own screen. She tapped to enlarge them, frowning down at the Rosette ships' formation.

She swore and tapped through to Emmett's private line. "There are only ten ships out there," she said in a low voice. "They must have sent the other two after the *Sweet Jenny*."

"I know, Captain. I just saw that." Emmett's voice was as grim as her own. "What are your orders?"

She gritted her teeth, swallowing back the sick dread in her stomach. "We go ahead with the plan as discussed. And we hope like hell Silas Hunt was recommended to the Academy for a reason."

"Aye, Captain."

She turned back to the screen.

The *Chasseuse* was still clearly recovering from the mess they'd made in the course of their escape—it was moving, but not with the sharp precision she'd have expected from a fully crewed naval ship. The others, though, were suffering under no such constraints—already the Rosette ships had formed a loose star formation around the *Verity*, close enough that she'd not be able to jump even if she had the capacity to. And the Rosette captains would know damn well she didn't have the capacity, considering that was likely the only reason the entire Rosette fleet hadn't jumped for the Level before she and the pirates had made their escape from the *Chasseuse*

Despite everything, there was a grim satisfaction in the knowledge that the *Verity's* jump on dead reckoning had impressed them enough that they were taking precautions regardless.

"They're going to close formation around us, I think," she said quietly. "They're not going to want us to be able to run out past them. Keep us facing the head of the formation, that's where they'll put their most powerful guns."

It wouldn't help much—the ships were coming in from all sides, and the *Verity* would unavoidably have to present her broadside to Rosette ships' volleys. But at least she could do her best to minimize the damage.

"Aye, Captain." Emmett turned, and she could hear him calling out orders to the bridge crew.

She glanced down at her timepiece.

It had been fifteen minutes since the *Sweet Jenny* had left.

"Captain. The bridge officers are doing as you requested, and the crew are at their battle stations," Emmett said through the comm. "The mechanics tell me they'll have our light shields up within minutes, and one set of precision weapons online around the same time. The rest will take longer, but I'm hopeful it won't be too much longer."

"Acknowledged. Make sure they have whatever they need—supplies, crew members, resources. Getting our guns and shields online is our utmost priority right now."

"Aye, Captain," said Greene, but she could hear in his voice that it wouldn't make a difference. He knew as well as she did what they were about to be facing, and he'd certainly have already given the mechanic crew every assistance he could.

She turned back to the screens. The ships would be in firing range within minutes, and she doubted they'd give the *Verity* another chance to negotiate.

The seconds ticked by, every moment crawling beneath her skin, stinging her raw nerves, until she had to force herself to sit still, force her face to remain impassive. Her screen was still broadcasting to the bridge, and she refused to let her crew see her anything other than calm. She was their captain, damn it, and she wasn't about to harm morale by her own impatience.

She glanced down at her timepiece again.

Thirty-two minutes.

The *Sweet Jenny* should be visible on her screens already—shielded, yes, but Hollis was running the defraction scanners, and she knew where to look.

There was no sign of her.

Her stomach sank.

Seven minutes past what they'd agreed on.

The Rosette ships were in close enough now that they could begin firing at any second. Silas knew, as well as she did, what their time constraints were.

She closed her eyes against the despair tightening her chest.

She'd trusted Silas—at least, as much as she could trust a traitor to the navy and the Level. And perhaps he'd meant to come back, and been detained by the pursuing Rosette ships. But … she glanced over at Gracie.

The woman was lying still, eyes closed, body limp with exhaustion.

Gracie had shown herself willing to die for her crew on more than one occasion. The first mate, Ari, wouldn't have voluntarily left her, orders or no, but Silas—if Mad Dog had given him private orders to leave her behind, told him it was the only way to save Ari and the ship and the remainder of the crew—it was possible he'd have done it. He was naval trained, after all, and wasn't that what they were taught in the navy? Sacrifice the one for the good of the many?

She turned back to the charts numbly. She felt like an automaton, her body moving because she demanded it, with no feelings or emotions left.

"Greene," she said through the comm. "Instruct Officer Davis to begin evasive maneuvers. We need to keep the Rosette ships from pinning us down."

There was a moment's pause as Emmett relayed the command. "Captain," he said quietly through her private line. "I thought the plan was to let them pin us down, and give the *Sweet Jenny* a concentrated target so she could cut us free."

"It was. But the *Sweet Jenny's* not where she's supposed to be," she said, keeping her voice low.

Emmett cursed. "We don't stand a chance of getting out without her."

"I know," said Hollis grimly. "We'll simply have to hope she'll come when she can. And we'll have to do what we can to stay alive in the meantime."

"Aye, Captain." Hollis could hear the worry under her second mate's stoic tone.

She drew in a deep breath, trying to push back the sick horror tugging at her own brain.

"Captain! We have our light shields, and two of the precision weapons ready to fire." Her weapons master's sharp voice through her comm pulled her out of her despair.

"Thank God," she snapped. "Get the shields up, and get our best gunners on the guns. We won't have much opportunity to shoot, so we need to make it count. Call in when they're ready."

"Aye, Captain."

She tapped through quickly to Emmett. "We have guns," she said. "Not many, but they're long-range precision guns, and they may be enough to get the Rosette ships to back off for long enough." She didn't finish the thought—long enough for the *Sweet Jenny* to arrive. And if she didn't arrive …

"We could try to make a run for it," said Emmett quietly. "We'll get shot to hell, but we may be able to get past the blockade. Our running engines are quick enough that we may be able to keep ahead of them, and it's possible we could try another jump on dead reckoning."

Hollis closed her eyes.

Emmett was right. They could try to make a break for it. And this may be their last chance to do so. She'd lose crew, but it would be a chance to save some of them, at least.

She turned abruptly to Mad Dog's sickbed. Gritting her teeth, she maneuvered her chair over to where the pirate captain was lying.

"Captain Mad Dog," she said in a low voice.

For a moment, she thought the pirate wouldn't answer, unconscious or perhaps simply unwilling.

But at last, her eyes blinked open, thin slits in the gruesome bruising of her face. "What is it, lass?" she asked, her voice a weak rasp.

Hollis leaned in, close enough that no one of her crew would overhear. "Captain Mad Dog. Your crew is away in the *Sweet Jenny*, and we're hemmed in by Rosette ships. So if you were lying to me before, there's no point in keeping up the lie." She paused a moment. "Are they coming back? Is the *Sweet Jenny* coming back, or are we in this fight on our own?"

Mad Dog watched her for a moment, and with the swelling and bruising distorting her features, Hollis couldn't read the woman's face. At last she closed her eyes, as if gathering the strength to speak.

"They ain't going to leave you here, Captain Ives," she said in her weak whisper. "Sil'll bring the *Sweet Jenny* back here, or he'll die trying. And I'd not have agreed to let him captain my ship, with the rest of my crew on board, if I thought he'd die trying." She paused, as if the effort of forming words was too great. At last, though, she blinked her eyes open and caught Hollis's gaze, and once more, Hollis was almost shocked at the perception in her eyes. "We ain't the navy, lass. Figure you know that. But you were surprised, weren't you, that Sil and Ari risked everything to save me? It weren't because I was their captain. They'd have done the same for any of the crew. My crew don't sacrifice each other for the greater good, not on the *Sweet Jenny*. Sil promised he'd bring her back, he'll bring her back."

The woman lapsed into silence again, and Hollis watched her, jaw clenched. Even with the bruises and swelling, she could see the hint of amusement in the captain's face. There was sharp intelligence in her eyes as she watched Hollis, and a spark of challenge, and Hollis wasn't sure if the woman was daring her to trust her, or daring her not to.

She pulled in a long breath.

Silas had negotiated a surrender that would have allowed her to save her crew. He would have killed her for it, of course, but in the grand scheme of things, that hardly counted. Hollis knew enough of Mad Dog to know Silas had put his position and possibly his life on the line to do it.

And now, she'd simply have to hope that his sense of honour, twisted as it might be, would be enough to bring him back here.

She pushed her chair awkwardly back from Mad Dog's cot, and tapped through a line to Emmett. "We'll hold here and wait for them," she said in a low voice. "We know two of the Rosette ships went after them—it may be that's delayed them. But I believe that's still our best option."

There was a pause from the other end of the line. "Aye, Captain," said Emmett at last. "But best hope they get here quick-time. Because once we start firing—"

"I know," she said.

"Gunners ready on the guns," came the weapons master's voice through the line.

She took a deep breath. "Greene. Please point us towards the *Chasseuse*, and instruct the gunners to fire at will once we're in range."

She'd turned back to the screen by the time the first two shots hummed out from the *Verity's* bow.

The impact of the guns against the *Chasseuse's* shields was visible on the screens. More shots followed the first, and the rest of the Rosette ships pulled out and around, moving in to fire on the *Verity* to protect their flagship.

"Steady on," she said through the comm. "Hold us steady. Shift all power to the port shields, but be ready to move to starboard shields as soon as we take a hit."

They were in close enough now that there was no chance, any

longer, of pulling back. She'd put herself completely at the pirates' mercy. But if the *Verity* was going down, Hollis was damn well taking the enemy's flagship with her.

The first broadside arced towards them, from the port side, as she'd anticipated. The ship that had fired pulled back to make room for another while its guns recharged, and then the broadside hit. The *Verity* trembled at the onslaught, and she could hear the screams and shouts from over her comm. She had to hold herself back from jumping to her feet, striding out onto the bridge.

She could trust Emmett to keep order on the bridge, and in the crew. She knew it well enough, but it wasn't that that made her muscles ache to move.

Her ship was in danger, and she was confined to the goddamned sick bay, and she wasn't certain she'd ever felt so damned helpless in her life.

"Take us hard to port," she snapped through the comm. Emmett relayed the command, and Hollis braced herself, watching on the screen as the *Verity* turned ponderously towards her attackers.

If they got in close enough to the ship whose guns were still recharging, it might buy them a few more precious minutes while the ships to starboard adjusted their positions to shoot without risk of hitting their fellows with friendly fire.

"All gunners, continuous fire," she called through the line, and she could hear in the background Emmett relaying her command.

The *Verity* shuddered again as another broadside hit.

"Captain. Shields are down," Emmett snapped through the line.

"Get the mechanics working on them then, for God's sake," she snapped back.

"Aye, Captain, but it won't be in time. The ships are already targeting in."

She glanced back down at the screen, swearing under her breath. She could feel Mad Dog's eyes on her, but she refused to give the woman the satisfaction of acknowledgement.

"All power to the guns, then, and keep firing," she said.

It would only hold them off for minutes at best, but they were counting seconds at this point.

She closed her eyes, clenching her teeth so hard they hurt. The words of the death prayer to Our Lady, the one she'd learned as a child, were floating unbidden in her mind.

Lady of the Ghosts, take my body, join my soul to Yours, make it a vessel of Your vengeance …

She shoved them away.

She wasn't dying here, not like this, dammit.

She turned back to the screen, not wanting to look.

The space at the edge of the screen, the coordinates where they'd agreed the *Sweet Jenny* would jump to, was empty.

She swallowed against the pit of despair in her stomach, and turned, woodenly, to hit the comm. If they were going to die, they could at least concentrate their fire on the *Chasseuse*, inflict maximum damage before they went down.

Then there was a flicker on the screen—not in the corner where she'd been watching, but right on the edge of the Rosette formation, a fraction of a light-second out.

She stared as the vis-tags popped up on her screen.

It was the *Sweet Jenny*.

She'd come after all.

18

Silas

The screens fuzzed and blurred, then came into focus as the *Sweet Jenny* came out of jump.

Silas squinted down at the screens, his heart pounding.

He'd instructed Price to bring them in as close as he dared, and it was entirely possible he'd dropped them into the middle of a trap.

"What are we dealing with, Sil?" came Ari's sharp voice through the comm.

He blew out a breath, suddenly weak with relief, and heard Price's soft exclamation beside him.

The *Verity* was still in one piece, and from the looks of her, she was still fighting.

And whatever else he might say of the *Verity's* first mate, they were precise—their calculations had brought the *Sweet Jenny* in on the very edges of the battle.

"Freddie, give me full power to our running engines," he said through the comm. "We don't have anything but light shields left, so we're just going to have to make damn sure they don't have time to hit us. Ari, Jumper, I want you firing the moment we have a target."

"You have an idea what target we're fixing to be firing on?" Ari sounded worried, and he couldn't entirely blame her.

He shoved the throttle forward, and the *Sweet Jenny* pushed him back in his seat with the acceleration. Then turned back to the screens, studying the layout of the battle quickly.

Hollis hadn't held to their original plan—thank God for that, at least, the *Verity* would have been torn to pieces by now if she had—which meant he needed a new strategy. The Rosette ships had hemmed the *Verity* in, but they were hanging back. Hollis must have regained some of her weapons, at least. And she was facing the *Chasseuse*, her bow pointed towards the Rosette flagship as if she were determined to break her way through.

"Price," he said, not looking up from the screen. "Tell me what Hollis is doing."

Price studied the screen for a moment, then shook their head. "She's waiting for us," they said, and he couldn't read the tone in their voice. "And it looks like she decided that if we didn't come in time, she'd take the *Chasseuse* down with her."

Silas studied the screen for a moment longer, then glanced up at Price. He was grinning—he couldn't actually help himself.

"Maybe she has the right of it," he said. He tapped through the comm. "New strategy. We're going to go after the damn flagship."

There was a moment of silence. "That ain't going to open us a jump path now, will it, lad?" said Freddie.

"It won't. But the other ships aren't going to let the *Chasseuse* go down without a fight. The *Verity* is heading straight for her, and if we come in firing from the other side, they'll have to either come around to stop us, or watch her taken out," he said.

"Might work," said Freddie at last. "But we ain't going to get much time if it does."

"I know." He paused. "Freddie, I need you on the guns. Ari, you're in the cockpit."

"Lad?" Freddie's voice was tight with concern. "Ship ain't going to keep herself running."

"I know," he snapped. "But it'll only be for a few minutes. You're right, we won't have much time. I'll have my hands full piloting, and Price won't have the time to calculate a jump path for us and the *Verity* both. Jumper can't be expected to handle the guns and shields on his own, not if we want to convince them that we're a threat."

"Aye, lad," said Freddie at last. He could hear the worry in her tone.

"On my way, Sil," came Ari's curt voice.

A moment later, she appeared in the cockpit.

He was almost shocked at the drawn look on her face, the tension in every line of her posture.

"You figure they've left the captain alive?" she asked in a low voice as she slid into the pilot seat.

He hesitated, then gave a quick nod. "I don't know. But everything I've heard of Hollis says she's not one to go back on her word."

"She'd damn better not," muttered Ari. "Because if she touches one hair of Gracie's head, or Vee or Temple or Toothpick—"

"Then we'll shoot the *Verity* down without stopping to ask questions," he said grimly, ignoring the way Price's head jerked up at the words. "Believe me, Ari, you'll get no argument from me. But in the meantime, best keep all of us from being shot down ourselves, no?"

She nodded and turned to the screen. "I'll get us a jump path through to Blackrock." She hesitated, reluctance clear in her tone. "Price, you calculate one for the *Verity*. You have her specs?"

"I've got them." Price's tone was cool and measured, the way it always was when they addressed Ari.

She turned to her work, and Silas turned back to the controls.

They were coming up on the *Chasseuse* fast. The *Sweet Jenny* was running her shielding, but it would be easy enough to see through if they were looking. At the moment, though, it seemed they were focused on the *Verity*.

He smiled grimly. "Jumper, Freddie, hold fire until we're up close. I want to make this count." He turned to Price. "Let me know as soon as you have the jump paths calculated. We'll need to open up a channel and send them through to the *Verity*, but I don't want to do that before the Rosette ships know we're here."

"Aye," they said without looking up, and he pulled on the controls, easing the *Sweet Jenny* around into position. She responded sluggishly, nothing like the sharp, trim craft he'd started out with. But then, if he could keep them alive long enough to get back to a proper berth, he'd spend two weeks in the engine room under Freddie's gruff instruction, gladly, fixing her up.

Right now, he just had to keep them all alive.

He tapped the decelerator as they approached, pulling them down to half-speed, and slipped the *Sweet Jenny* in alongside the *Chasseuse*, just close enough that she wouldn't cause the proximity alerts to go off. Then he throttled down. "Alright, Freddie. Let's show them what the *Sweet Jenny* can do," he said through the comm. "Fire at will."

The *Sweet Jenny* rocked as she discharged a broadside. Moments later, the precision weapons crackled out across his screen in bright arcs, slamming into the *Chasseuse* alongside the broadsides. The *Chasseuse's* full shields were up, but most of their power was focused forward, towards the *Verity*. And even on full power, they weren't enough to hold off the *Sweet Jenny's* guns.

The first gunner compartment on the *Chasseuse* exploded a

moment later, a flash of light that always made Silas's stomach lurch —he'd been in enough battles to know what that meant, how many sailors had died screaming.

But this was war, dammit, and he didn't have time to worry about any of that, any more than he had when he was serving in the navy.

Freddie focused her fire on the next gunner compartment, and he pulled the *Sweet Jenny* up and past the *Chasseuse* as her guns turned towards them.

The *Sweet Jenny* couldn't afford a direct hit, not unless they wanted to go up like the gunner's compartment on the *Chasseuse*. She was smaller and faster than the Rosette ships, but in a battle like this one, there was no maneuverability that would save them from the targeted guns. He'd either have to get them out and away, or get in so close the enemy ships couldn't afford to use their heavies for fear of hitting an ally.

And right now, he wasn't trying to get the *Sweet Jenny* away. He was trying to save the Level naval ship with Gracie aboard, if she was still alive.

He pulled back on the controls, swinging the ship around the *Chasseuse*, and plunged into the middle of the Rosette formation.

They hadn't been expecting visitors, and hadn't closed ranks to keep a smaller ship from being able to penetrate their formation, and he slipped the *Sweet Jenny* into a gap between three ships.

"Fire, dammit," he snapped through the comm, and the *Sweet Jenny* rocked as she released broadside after broadside, virtually unopposed.

Silas scowled down at the screen, his heart pounding.

The Rosette ships had recovered quickly, swinging around to face the new threat, but Freddie was firing heavily enough that they had to hang back or risk being taken apart.

But it wasn't enough. The ships hemming in the *Verity* had shifted at his attack on the *Chasseuse*, but not far enough to give her a clear jump-path.

"I'm going to swing back around and bring us past the *Chasseuse* again," he said through the comm. "Focus on damaging her as much as possible—I don't care if it's showy, I want to take down shields, gunner compartments, airlocks, whatever we can. We won't take her down, but I want them to believe we could."

Jumper tapped a quick acknowledgement through the line, and Silas brought the *Sweet Jenny* back around. The *Chasseuse* had seen them now, and she'd be waiting, but so far he'd been running the *Sweet Jenny* on half-throttle.

"We'll be moving quickly. Best sight in now, you won't have time once we start running," he muttered through the comm. "Price, get the jump coordinates through to Hollis. Tell her to jump the moment she has space, don't wait on us."

From the corner of his eye he saw Price's nod of acknowledgement.

He hit the throttle to full, and they swept past the *Chasseuse*.

The burst of focused fire from the *Sweet Jenny's* guns arced out in a blaze of brilliance, raking the *Chasseuse's* flank. The *Chasseuse's* guns were firing as well, but the gunners clearly hadn't expected the speed the *Sweet Jenny* was capable of—the shots trailed them, and even as the gunners adjusted their aim, they were past, and swinging around for another sweep.

Silas gritted his teeth.

Of course, they couldn't afford another sweep. Now that the *Chasseuse's* gunners knew how quickly they'd be moving, they wouldn't get past again without a hit they couldn't afford with their damaged shields.

Then he saw it, and breathed out a quick sigh of relief—the two ships hemming the *Verity* in had come around, pulling up to keep the *Sweet Jenny* from making another run past the *Chasseuse*.

For just a moment, the *Verity* was free.

He stared at his screen, his breath coming far too quickly.

Then the *Verity* flickered and disappeared, and his entire body sagged in relief.

They'd done it. They'd got the *Verity* out.

He glanced back down at his screen, and bit back a curse.

They'd gotten the *Verity* out, and in exchange, the *Sweet Jenny* was entirely hemmed in.

"Orders?" Ari snapped.

Silas glared at the screen a moment. Then he grinned a tight grin and hit the comm. "Jumper, Freddie, get ready. I'll take us straight at the Chasseuse's bow. Aim the precision weapons in on her bridge. If we can blow the bridge, with as short-crewed as she is, they won't be able to stop the chain reaction. It'll take her down, and we'll jump out through the hole she makes."

There was a moment's silence. "Well, lad, subtlety ain't your forte, is it?" Freddie grumbled back. "Jumper'n I'll do what we can, but I'm warning you—Jumper's been doing everything he can to get the shields back, and it ain't going to happen. We can take a hit from a precision weapon, maybe two. But they hit us with a broadside, it's over."

"I know." His tone was short. "But we don't make it out in the next few minutes, we're not going to. I don't think they'll bother trying to take us prisoner again." He turned to Ari. "I need you ready to go into jump the moment we're clear."

"Aye," she said. Her face was set, but he could see in her posture the same relief he'd felt, knowing Gracie, at least, was out, and

Temple and Toothpick and Vee.

It was the same as having a ghost compartment in the crew quarters—some of the crew would survive, even if the rest died horribly. At least they'd saved some.

He pulled in a deep breath, and turned the *Sweet Jenny* back to face the *Chasseuse* head-on.

With luck, they wouldn't realize what he was about to do. With luck, they'd assume he'd try to bring them alongside again, hit them with another broadside.

With luck, they wouldn't realize the *Sweet Jenny's* shields were down and he had no one in the mechanic's room to keep her running if they took a hit.

He shoved the throttle forward, and snapped, "Fire at will!"

The screen in front of him lit up with the shots from the *Sweet Jenny's* precision weapons, laser-focused on the *Chasseuse's* bridge.

The *Sweet Jenny* shook with the glancing blow from one of the *Chasseuse's* precision weapons, but again, they seemed to have caught the ship off-guard.

The *Sweet Jenny* was coming in fast. He held the throttle forward, despite everything in his brain screaming to pull back, to get out of the way before they were in too close to turn aside.

Freddie and Jumper were still firing, and from the corners of his eyes he saw the screen tracking their shots, saw them impacting against the *Chasseuse's* shielding.

Another shot from the *Chasseuse's* precision weapons hit, full-on this time, and the *Sweet Jenny* shuddered. He could feel her straining under his fingers—if Freddie had been in the mechanic's room, she could have adjusted whatever needed to be adjusted to give him back power, but she wasn't, she was at the guns giving them their only damn chance to survive this.

He gritted his teeth and pushed the throttle harder.

The *Chasseuse's* shields were glowing now with the volume of shots impacting off them. The other Rosette ships had come around, but he was in too close—they couldn't possibly get off any shots without risk of hitting the *Chasseuse*, and the *Sweet Jenny* was in too close and moving too fast for them to intercept.

They were less than a minute out from impacting against the *Chasseuse's* bridge, close enough that he could see the shots sparking against the shields through the clear plex of the cockpit viewport, without the benefit of the screens.

He tightened his hand on the throttle.

A few more seconds and he'd have to pull up, and they'd be open to shots from all sides. The *Sweet Jenny* wouldn't last a minute.

Freddie and Jumper were still firing, Ari bent over the jump controls.

The *Chasseuse's* shields glowed a dull red now, and he was close enough that he could make out the small movements as it tried desperately to get itself out of the way of the *Sweet Jenny's* approach.

In a moment he'd be too late to pull up …

Freddie shouted something through the comm, and for half a second he simply stared at the screen, trying desperately to understand what had gone wrong—she was shouting, and Ari was shouting too, and Jumper was tapping something through his comm line—then he saw what they'd all already seen: the thin cracks in the shield around the *Chasseuse's* bridge.

He jerked back on the throttle automatically, pulling the *Sweet Jenny* up. She was slow and sluggish under his fingers, and he wasn't sure, for a moment, that they'd make it in time. She pointed her nose up past the bridge of the *Chasseuse*, to the dark of space beyond, just as the widening cracks in the shield split.

There was a blinding flash of white, then the ship's bridge was simply … gone, a wide, gaping hole in the place where it had been.

Silas shoved the throttle forward, begging the *Sweet Jenny* for every bit of speed. They had to get past, they had to get out before the *Chasseuse* went down, because an explosion of that magnitude would take the *Sweet Jenny* out with it.

Smaller explosions echoed down the length of the ship as the *Sweet Jenny* finally, reluctantly obeyed his commands.

"Got clearance, going into jump!" Ari shouted. He heard it dimly, but his attention was focused on the massive Rosette flagship alongside them, the little bursts of flame running along her length, growing larger with each burst.

They were in too close. He'd miscalculated, he'd brought them in too close, they weren't going to get out, not without Freddie in the mechanic's room to give him running power …

"Jumping!" Ari shouted, and his stomach lurched.

For a moment he couldn't quite realize what had happened, staring at the fuzzed-out screens blankly, waiting for it to make sense. And then Ari had grabbed his arm and pulled him to his feet and was shaking him, slapping his shoulder and shouting, and Freddie was shouting through the comms.

"We did it, you idiot! We did it!" His brain finally made sense of Ari's words.

For a moment, he thought his legs would give out in relief. Then he was whooping and shouting along with the rest of them.

19

Hollis

Hollis found she was holding her breath as Officer Davis counted down to coming out of jump, staring at the screen in front of her as if she could force it to clear faster by her very gaze.

It fuzzed a moment, recalibrating as they exited the FTL jump, and then cleared.

Hollis sucked in a breath. The sight of the Level naval ships on the screen, within easy running distance, was a bone-melting relief.

She focused on the relief, rather than the memory of the *Sweet Jenny*, hemmed in by Rosette ships on all sides, firing desperately with no clear jump-path.

Mad Dog trusted Silas to keep her ship and her crew alive. Hollis could hardly do less.

"Captain. Orders?" Emmett's voice through her comm line held the same desperate relief that she felt.

She managed a small smile.

Her entire body ached, and she felt half-delirious with tension, the tightness in her muscles pulling at her injury. Thank God, at least, that she'd listened to Archibald—Emmett would be bodily holding her up if she was on the bridge right now, and no one on her crew needed to see that.

"Run in slowly," she said, tapping her comm. "Broadcast our ship vis tags, and send out a distress call and a request to talk to whoever the hell is in charge. I'd prefer it not be Commodore Webb, but I'll speak to whoever will listen." She grimaced at the thought. "If you can't get through to the commodore, or whoever's in charge now, at least try to get me through to the *Consolation*. Mate Ainsley might listen to me now."

"Aye, Captain." There was a note in Emmett's voice that told her he didn't find the idea of speaking with Commodore Webb any more appealing than she did.

He turned away to the ship's comm, and Hollis stared numbly at the screen.

She'd known, intellectually, that the Admiral had sent three fleets to Blackrock. But it wasn't until she saw the mass of ships spread out in front of her that she understood what that meant.

She could hardly blame the Admiral—what Mad Dog had almost done to Commodore Webb's fleet was horrifying. But leaving the Level almost completely unprotected …

From the looks of it, the ships had just begun their attack, but the impact of the weapons against the pirate stronghold was blistering.

Even as she watched, an explosion rocked out from the surface of the moon, a widening bubble on her screen that tightened her muscles unconsciously, the remembered panic of shouting at her bridge crew to get back, get them back, her navigator dead on the floor, her ghost ripping the young bridge officer's throat out …

She shoved the memories aside with an effort. Her eyes were glued to the screen, her hands tight around the arms of her chair.

The naval ships had clearly been expecting the blast, but they'd underestimated how powerful it would be. And it was powerful, absurdly powerful, she could see it in the way the ships, even pulled back farther than Webb's fleet had been, foundered as it hit them.

Again, there was that knot of unease in the back of her brain. Those were military-grade weapons, stronger, even. Those were weapons the Level itself didn't have …

Almost unwillingly, she found her gaze pulled to Mad Dog.

The woman's eyes were only half-open, pain-lines drawn into her face, but her expression still bore that mocking amusement.

"You got the weapons out," Hollis said, almost under her breath. "You got the weapons off the *Agate*, damn your eyes. How in the hell did you do that?"

Mad Dog's expression didn't change, but Hollis could feel the woman laughing at her.

She gritted her teeth, her entire body tight with dread.

That had been on her. Somehow, Mad Dog had slipped past her in the rush and panic of the *Agate's* last few minutes, and she'd taken the weapons off, and the ships lost to the pirates at Blackrock, and the deaths, and her own navigator's death …

"You did what you could, Captain Ives."

The pirate captain's words were so unexpected that it took Hollis a moment to understand them.

She turned to the woman, braced for an insult, but there was a surprisingly sympathetic look on Mad Dog's face. "I was always going to take those weapons, lass," she said, her words laboured. "From the moment I intercepted that broadcast, I'd have taken them. Didn't figure you'd be able to get the crew off, but you did, and you can take credit for that. Ain't many who would have. But you were never going to stop me taking the weapons, not a naval captain in the service who could have."

Her words were forced and slow, as if she had to work each syllable out past the pain.

Hollis frowned. She should be revelling in Hollis's defeat, not … whatever this was. "We are not allies, Mad Dog," she snapped. "Not now, not ever."

Mad Dog managed a small smile. "You may be right, at that," she whispered. "Just wanted you to know. May not see eye to eye, you and me, but you're a sight better'n most naval captains I've gone up against. Takes nerve to do what you did, lass, and brains. Ain't many as could have done it."

She lapsed into silence, her eyes falling closed, as if exhausted by the effort of speaking.

Hollis watched her for a few moments, her heart beating quick and unsteady, and she wasn't sure if it was fear, or anger, or the sheer disorientation of it.

Shaking her head, she turned back to the screen.

The ships in the rear of the formation had turned at the *Verity's* approach, and she breathed out a sigh of relief. "Mate Greene," she said, tapping the comm. "I assume you got word through—"

"Captain." Emmett's voice was tight with worry. "I broadcast our vis-tags and sent out a distress call. They're refusing any calls from us, and blocking communication."

Hollis swore, and leaned over the screen.

The ships were approaching, but now that she was looking closer, she could see what she hadn't noticed before—the way they were coming in formation, as if they were coming up on an enemy ship.

She closed her eyes, cold dread starting in the pit of her stomach.

"Greene," she said quietly through the comm. "Keep broadcasting our vis-tags, and keep trying to get a distress call through. Try the *Consolation,* if no one else will listen. But … I think we'd best check how the mechanics are coming on the shields and the guns."

"Aye, Captain." Emmett's voice was tense.

She turned back to the screen. "And put me through the line, if you would," she snapped. "It's possible they'll accept a transmission if it comes from me."

Aye, Captain," said Emmett again, his voice sharp with worry.

Hollis drew in a deep breath and tapped through the broadcast line. "This is Captain Hollis Ives of the *Verity*," she said, trying to keep her voice calm. "Request to speak with the flagship of the fleet."

The only response was a static fuzz.

She cursed.

Emmett was right—it wasn't only that they were ignoring the *Verity's* broadcasts. They were actively blocking them. Even if Ainsley or the captain of the *Consolation* would have listened to her a second time, she wouldn't be able to get through to them.

The ships by now were close enough that she could see their vis-tags clear on her screen. The *Valiant* and the *Ransom*, two-hundred-crewed each, and fitted out with in impressive array of heavy guns, if she remembered correctly.

She hesitated for just a moment longer. Then she drew in a long breath.

"Mate Greene," she said through the comm. "Prepare the gunner crews on our functional guns, and get crews on the shields."

There was a moment's pause. "Captain. We're going to fire on naval ships?" Emmett's voice through her private line was thick with horror, and she heard in it the same realization that had hit her like a blow to the stomach.

"We are going to damn well defend ourselves, Mate Greene," she snapped. "You may inform the crew of the circumstances—we are unable, at present, to establish communication with the fleet, and they appear to have decided we are a threat. Please instruct the bridge crew to prepare for an engagement."

"Aye, Captain." His words were hollow with a mixture of horror and shock.

Hollis could feel it herself, crawling through her veins.

"Firing on a Level naval fleet, Captain Ives." Mad Dog's voice was still a weak rasp, but a little stronger than it had been. "Didn't think you had it in you."

She spun on the pirate. "I am not going to let them shoot down my ship, the devil take you!"

Mad Dog smiled, a small, brief smile. "You were willing enough to let me shoot you yourself down, if it came to it."

Hollis closed her eyes a moment.

Her heart was pounding too fast, sickness curdling in her stomach.

Mad Dog was right. Once she fired on a naval ship, there was no coming back from it.

"I won't sacrifice my crew," she said at last, in a low voice. "They've been nothing but honourable throughout. They've followed my orders, even when perhaps they shouldn't have. They've risked their damned lives, over and over, gone far away and beyond the requirements of duty because I asked it of them. And I will be damned if I let them die for it while I have a chance of saving them." The words came out harsh in the quiet of the med bay.

Mad Dog studied her for a moment. "Even if it means firing on the navy," she said. "Even if it means being hanged for treason."

She drew in a deep breath. She could still hear Foster's words from the skiff: *Your crew deserves accolades for what they've done, I've never seen a crew volunteer for a mission like this one, knowing what it would entail.*

But you'd never think to demand it, not for yourself, and not for them."

"I'm a naval captain, Mad Dog. I'm loyal to the Level and to the Navy, and I won't question my duty. But—" She leaned forward. "I will not abandon my crew. They damn well deserve better than to be shot down by our own side. If that's treason, then yes, I'll happily hang for it. But I won't stand by while this happens without doing everything in my goddamned power to stop it." She turned her back on the pirate captain, tapping the comm line through to Emmett again. "Greene. Please put me on the ship's comm. I'd like to broadcast a warning before we start firing."

"Aye, Captain." Emmett's voice was still sharp with worry. There was a moment's pause. "The ship's comm is yours."

Hollis tapped through to the general broadcast line. "This is Captain Hollis Ives of the *Verity*, paging the fleet," she said, her words clipped. "Request that you stand down, or we shall be forced to defend ourselves. Repeat, please stand down, or I will instruct my crew to fire on you." She paused a moment. "I feel compelled to state that the order to fire will come from me, personally. My mates and crew are following my orders under protest. But I'll ensure they follow them, by God. This is your last warning."

She tapped off the comm.

It wouldn't do much—perhaps it wouldn't do anything, and most likely, if the naval ships attacked there would be no one on the *Verity* left alive. But it was the best she could do for them at present.

"Captain Ives! Every one of us here agreed to this course of action, I protest—"

She realized she'd half-way expected her second mate's outraged tones through the comm, and she almost smiled as she opened the line. "Greene, should this ship become a democracy I will damn well inform you. In the meantime, I'm your goddamn captain, and you'll not countermand my words."

From the corner of her eye, she could see Mad Dog still watching her, the faintest hint of humour tugging at the corners of the woman's mouth.

Hollis blew out a quick breath and turned her back on the woman, glaring down at the screen in front of her.

She swore under her breath.

The naval ships were coming in a tight formation. With the *Verity* as damaged as it was, they wouldn't stand much of a chance.

"Greene," she said through the comm line, "I believe our best chance is to hit them hard the moment they're in range. We don't have the gunpower they think we do, but best not let them find out. We want them to hang back, if at all possible." She scowled down at the screen, trying to identify the vis-tags. Her stomach was tight with dread.

"Aye, our shields will do best if we're at a distance." Emmett's voice was tight with strain. "Might survive for a bit."

"Thank you, Greene," said Hollis at last, biting her cheek. "Give the orders, if you would."

"Aye, Captain." Emmett's tone was grim.

"The *Sweet Jenny*?" asked Mad Dog softly.

Hollis closed her eyes, tried not to picture the ship as she'd last seen it.

It was a pirate ship, one the navy had been trying to take down for decades. She could hardly mourn its loss.

But Foster was on that ship.

And she couldn't help seeing Silas's face as he'd turned for the ship, the sharp worry in Ari's expression when she glanced back at Mad Dog. The way the *Sweet Jenny* had thrown herself into peril to save the *Verity*.

"She hasn't come through, Captain," she said at last, quietly. "I'm … sorry. And if she does—" She turned back to the screen, and tried to bite back the despair in her tone. "If she does, I'm not sure we'll survive long enough to see it."

20

The tension on the streets of the Level was palpable—Judith could feel it in the air as she made the short walk from her apartment to the Admiralty offices in the morning, and she could see it in the faces of the people on the streets when she stepped out in the afternoon for a bite of lunch.

It was even more prevalent in the Admiralty offices themselves—every person was on edge, and every loud noise sent half-a-dozen officers or aides or dignified senior bureaucrats jumping in a distinctly undignified way.

Judith couldn't blame them.

The news coming through was almost universally bad.

They'd pulled back every ship within a twenty-four-hour jump range of the Level. But it was far, far too few ships. Even with commandeering merchant ships and drafting the last-year Academy students into service, they had barely one fleet, most of it untrained and untested, and dismally short on weapons. They wouldn't stand a chance against a fleet of Rosette warships, trained and ready for battle.

The wealthier families, she knew, were already making arrangements to evacuate themselves and their families for the countryside, although what protection they thought that would afford them, Judith didn't know. More than one had tried to arrange transport off-planet, to one of the better-equipped resource planets —it spoke to the level of panic that Levellers who'd never traveled at FTL speeds would be willing to accept the cellular damage such travel caused, the potential to turn ghost, and the accompanying limitations to existing in civilized society, it brought with it.

She'd struck down all such requests, and made it clear that any captain with a space-worthy ship who should accept an offer despite this would be facing treason charges. The navy needed first priority on all the ships, and she refused to give up the Level just yet.

But she'd seen how the civil authorities were rounding up the army reserves, drilling the peacekeepers—brave enough when their only foes were unruly civilians and the Ghost Army, who they vastly outnumbered, but reduced to a shaking, terrified mass now that they might be sent up against trained and armed enemy soldiers—and preparing for war on the Level.

She couldn't blame the civilians for their panic.

But nor could she help a grim sense of justice when she thought of all the civilians who weren't wealthy enough to evacuate to the country or try to pay for passage off-planet.

Gracie may hate her for what she'd become, but she'd sworn her life to the navy because she truly believed it was the Level's best chance for protection—not just the wealthy families and the politicians, but the poor, the destitute, the sailors who'd seen trauma and were unemployable on merchant vessels, the mass of seething, miserable humanity that made up the Stacks. They were under her protection, as well as any of the well-to-do families, and she'd not abandon them to curry favour with the wealthy.

And she'd be damned if she'd give them to the flames without a fight.

"I'm doing it because it's important, Grace!" Judith snapped, doing up the buttons on her dress jacket.

"The Admiral insulted your family to your face." Grace's voice was low, with the kind of danger in it that had been enough to intimidate captains and Academy instructors both. "You don't owe her anything, and you certainly don't owe her your presence at her goddamn promotion."

Judith pulled in a long breath, and turned to face her lover. "I will always side with the navy, Grace," she said quietly, even though her heart was pounding. "I believe in it. Even if it's wrong sometimes, even if there's corruption and cronyism, I will side with the navy, because it's the best chance we have to protect the people who look to us for safety. You can disagree if you choose, but you know me, Grace. You know I'll always choose what I believe is right."

Grace closed her eyes a moment, the anger seeming to drain from her, replaced with weariness. "I know, Jenny," she said in a whisper. "But sometimes I wonder if we agree on what's right."

For a moment, Judith wanted to go to her. She wanted to tip Grace's chin up, kiss her until the strain left her face, kiss her until her hands strayed to Judith's hips, her breasts, her bare skin, kiss her until the hurt on her face and the weariness in her eyes was forgotten and their bodies were tangled together and there was no room for fear or anger or misunderstanding left between them.

But instead, she finished doing up her buttons and turned away to the door, leaving Grace standing silently in the barrack dormroom behind her.

The aide burst through into Judith's office with hardly a knock. "Admiral! Admiral, we have word from Rear-Admiral Hayes at Blackrock! I'm sorry, but you asked to be informed immediately if that should happen."

Judith looked up from the documents in front of her.

The circle of admirals and vice-admirals around the table turned as well to stare at the messenger, and the aide shrank back a little at the combined weight of the stares.

Judith sighed. "Bring the message in, if you please." She was certain she'd managed to keep her voice calm, but her heart rate had sped up, her pulse jumping at the words.

The aide stepped inside the office, his movements jerky with nerves, and came around behind her chair. "Here you are, Admiral," he said, pulling up an encrypted note and sending it to hover over her wrist comm.

"A moment, please," Judith said to the others around the table, and tapped the note open.

"Admiral Usher," it read. *"Received your message. Have just spotted the* Verity. *Assume your order to shoot the ship down still stands. Please confirm."*

Judith sucked in a quick breath at the painful jolt of hope, and pulled up another note on her wrist comm, tapping through the message.

"Do not fire on the Verity *at this time."* She wrote in quick taps. *"Repeat, do not fire on the ship at this time. Likely to be enemy ships in pursuit. Leave off attack of Blackrock, call all ships into formation, and prepare to engage Rosette warships."*

"Please send this on to the rear-admiral through the quantum-entangled message system," she snapped at the hapless aide, encoding the note with a quick motion, then sending it over to the aide's comm. "This is highest priority, and it must get through immediately. Please wait for confirmation, then inform me."

"Of course, Admiral," said the aide, with a nervous nod of respect. "At once." He scurried out of the room.

"What was that?" York asked, frowning at her.

"The fleets have emerged from jump at Blackrock. Rear-Admiral Hayes has sighted the *Verity*," she said, turning to him.

There was a moment of stillness, while her words sank in. And then she saw on the faces around the table the same sudden spark of hope she'd felt.

"We may be saved, then," said Savoy slowly, but there was a hint of desperate hope in his tone.

"If the aide gets word through in time," she said.

She drew in a deep breath and closed her eyes.

Her hands were trembling, and she wasn't certain whether it was relief, or worry—that something would go wrong, that her message wouldn't get through, that the Rosette ships would jump into the middle of a battle already being waged on two fronts—because she knew damn well the *Sweet Jenny*, at least, if she was with the *Verity*, wouldn't go down without a fight—or worse, that the Rosette ships hadn't follow the *Verity* through the jump, and they'd wake tomorrow morning to Rosette warships docked in the Level ports, despite everything she could do to prevent it.

At last she opened her eyes and straightened. "God willing, word will get through. But I'm not prepared to bank the survival of the Level on that happening," she said. "So, admirals, let's return to work."

They turned back to their documents.

But there was a lightness, a repressed, desperate hope in the air that was only overlaid by the tension, and she wasn't sure there was a one of them that wasn't surreptitiously watching the door for the aide's return, with good news or ill.

21

Silas

Price stood behind the copilot's seat, their hands clasped on the back of the chair. Their face was set into the bland expression that Silas had come to expect from them, but their knuckles were white, and there was a tension to their posture that he could almost feel.

"Coming out of jump in three. Two. One. Coming out." Ari's words were terse, her voice sharp with worry.

There was a brief jolt of disorientation, and then the *Sweet Jenny's* screens fuzzed back into focus.

Silas stared for a moment, then cursed. "What the hell are the naval ships doing?" he snapped, turning to Price.

"It looks like they're preparing to fire on the *Verity*." Their voice was clipped, their face a shade paler than usual, but their tone was still, somehow, perfectly proper. They glanced over at Silas. "Permission to page the *Verity?*"

"Granted," he said bitterly. "Ari, give Price the comm. If the navy's determined to fire on the *Verity*, I doubt very much it'll make a difference whether or not they're calling through to the *Sweet Jenny*."

Price hesitated the barest moment. Then they nodded, tapping

194

the comm line. "This is Mate Price, from the *Sweet Jenny*, paging the *Verity*."

There was a moment of silence, and then Hollis's voice through the line, tight with strain and ragged with relief. "Thank God!" She paused. "They won't accept our transmissions. We've tried. I believe our only option is to hit them hard enough that they'll back off, until …"

She didn't finish the sentence. All of them knew what it contained. Until the Rosette System navy came through, a small fleet of war ships in an ambush staged by himself and Hollis.

Or, until it was clear the ships weren't going to follow, and they were shot down, and the Level was left completely defenceless.

"Damn them," Silas hissed. "Damn those short-sighted, narrow-minded, self-important asses!"

Price glanced at him, and he could see from the wryness in their expression that he hadn't said anything they weren't thinking.

"Put me through to Silas, please, Price," Hollis said, her tone going businesslike once more.

Price tapped through the comm to the captain's chair, and Silas leaned forward. "Ives," he said. "I heard what you said to Price."

He paused.

If he'd been in the navy, he'd have known exactly what his duty was: sacrifice the *Sweet Jenny* if he could save the *Verity*, and if he couldn't …

Then let the *Verity* be shot down, and save the people on board his own ship.

If he were Gracie, he wasn't sure what he'd do, but he knew damn well saving Hollis and her crew wouldn't enter into it. Would she tell him to leave her behind, get the rest of the crew safe?

He didn't know.

But in the end, he was neither. He wasn't Gracie, and he wasn't the navy's, not anymore.

"Our shields are all but down, but our guns are still functional," he said at last. "We're going in. If we take down one of their damn ships, I'm guessing the others will hang back, no?"

There'd been a time, not even a month previous, where he'd have hesitated to fire on Level naval ships.

It was almost shocking how much had changed since then.

There was another short pause. "Very good, Silas," said Hollis at last, something distant and sick in her voice. "Please proceed."

The comm clicked off.

"That won't hold them," Price said quietly. "It will only make them more determined to kill us."

"I know," Silas snapped, not looking up at them. "But right now, it's the best damn thing we've got. Get up to the gun room, if you please, Freddie's up there and she'll tell you what to do."

"Aye." Price's voice was curt and businesslike, and they turned for the door.

When they were gone, he looked up and met Ari's eye.

He could see from the look on her face that she'd figured out the same thing he had.

"Hate to say it, Sil, but I agree with Price."

"I know!" he snapped, then he ran a hand over his face and sighed. "I know. There's no way we get out of this alive. We run that maneuver without shields, there's no way they don't take us down. But—" He shook his head.

"But Gracie's on the *Verity*," Ari finished softly. "And Vee and Temple and Toothpick. And if they take the *Sweet Jenny* down, maybe the navy'll see fit to keep the *Verity* aloft at present."

He nodded.

She was still watching him, and once more he was struck by how expressive her face was, how every thought was written across it for him to read—the strain, the worry, the fear, the exhaustion.

She gave him a small smile. "Well, Sil, guess Gracie picked right after all. Always figured I'd die under Gracie's command, but figure I can make do with you."

He stared at her for a moment, then smiled back reluctantly.

He cleared his throat and turned back to the comm. "Freddie, Jumper, Price, you ready? We're going in on my count. We want to cause as much damage as we can first run through, because I don't think we'll live through a second one."

"Aye, Sil," came Freddie's voice, and Jumper's staccato taps through the line agreed.

He glanced at Ari, raising his eyebrows, and she nodded.

"Alright," he said quietly. "Take us in."

Ari hit the throttle, and the *Sweet Jenny* jolted forward, her damaged running engines straining. Silas tapped a line through to the *Verity*. "Ives, we're going in."

"Acknowledged," she snapped back.

Then they were in range. He tapped the comm. "Fire at will."

The *Sweet Jenny* shuddered with her first broadside, and he had to grab for the desk to keep from getting thrown from his seat.

He gritted his teeth and stared down at the screens.

It was clear that the remainder of the naval ships had recognized the *Sweet Jenny*. The ships that had been approaching the *Verity* were turning off, coming towards them.

The *Sweet Jenny* shuddered with the release of another broadside, and Silas could see through the screens the soft explosions in the naval ship that showed where the *Sweet Jenny's* guns had cut through the shields.

He drew in a breath and tried not to imagine the terror in the gunner compartments, tried not to remember when that had been him, young and frightened.

He heard Gracie's voice in his head: *"You'll not lay the crimes of the Level on me, lad."*

Jumper's taps through the line alerted him, and he glanced over.

One of the ships, the *Destiny*, by the vis-tag, had come up around him. "Jumper," he said through the line. "All power to the shields, please. Freddie, you and Price give those bastards everything we have."

"Aye Captain," came Freddie's grim voice, and Jumper tapped his acquiescence.

They all knew, without Silas saying it, what it meant—after their two skirmishes with the Rosette System naval ships, they didn't have enough shield power left to hold up to a broadside, not from a two-hundred-crewed naval ship.

He glanced over at Ari. She met his eye and gave him a wan smile. "Don't worry, Sil," she said, an attempt at humour in her voice. "I've done worse if Gracie asked it."

"Worse than being shot down?" he asked, trying to grin.

She gave a short, humourless chuckle. "Maybe not, then."

She pushed the throttle forward, but the *Sweet Jenny* was already running as quick as she could. There was no way she'd get out of range of the guns before they were shot down.

There was the bright flare on his screen of a naval broadside being released, and he winced unconsciously, bracing himself.

His hands were trembling, he noticed idly. He hadn't expected them to, he'd faced death enough times. But, he supposed, it was different when you could watch it coming.

It was Ari's sharp gasp that made him glance down at the screen again.

He stared for a moment in sheer disbelief. And then he whooped, hitting the comm. "It's the *Verity*!" he called. "The *Destiny's* pulling back, the *Verity* hit her with a full broadside! They must have got their guns back online!"

There was a moment of silence, then Price cursed quietly through the line. "Bloody hell, I didn't think she'd actually do it."

Silas couldn't read from their tone whether they were impressed or horrified.

"Thank Our Lady she did," said Freddie, through the line. "We'd be space-dust by now if she hadn't."

"Get back on the guns, both of you," Silas snapped through the line, recovering himself. "If the *Verity's* going to war against the navy, she's damned well not doing it alone."

"Figure not," said Ari, grudging respect in her tone.

The *Sweet Jenny* shuddered as Price sent off another broadside with the heavy guns, and Ari maneuvered them skilfully around, coming up behind the naval ships which had turned at the new threat.

"Even fighting alongside the *Verity*, we ain't going to last long against the damn navy," said Ari under her breath.

"I know," said Silas shortly. "But I don't see that we have any better options right now, not unless you plan on abandoning Gracie and the others."

She gave a short nod, turning back to the screen. "Not saying I disagree."

"Where the hell are the Rosette ships?" he muttered, glaring at the screen. "Did they decide not to come after us after all?"

Ari shook her head, her eyes still focused on the controls. "Maybe we scared the bastards off."

Silas blew out a breath. "They had nine functional naval ships."

Ari glanced up at him, raising an eyebrow. "Well, Sil, why don't you explain that to—"

He hissed in a quick breath, holding up his hand for quiet, and stared down at the screen.

The Level naval ships had ceased firing, and were pulling back, turning towards the location of the *Sweet Jenny's* jump path.

"Silas?" Hollis's voice crackled through the line, sharp with strain. "What in God's name did you just do?"

"I didn't do anything," he managed, still staring at the screen. "Did they finally accept your broadcasts?"

"No." She paused. "I have no idea what the hell they're playing at."

Silas and Ari watched, Silas holding his breath, as the Level navy formation swung around.

And then he noticed the blurry smudges on the edges of the screen.

They clarified, forming into shapes.

For a moment, he wasn't completely sure he could trust his eyes.

Then he was grinning in utter relief.

"They followed us!" he said, tapping the line. "The Rosette fleet followed us through!"

22

Silas

For a few moments Silas simply watched, boneless with relief, as the Rosette ships and the Level ships exchanged volleys. Then he tapped through the comm. "Looks like we've bought ourselves some time," he said quietly. "Stand down, but stand by. I don't know what Hollis plans on doing next."

It felt strange watching the ships battle without engaging himself, like something crawling and itching under his skin. Price seemed to feel the same way. They stood rigid at their place behind the copilot's seat, hands clasped so tightly on the back of the chair that Silas found himself wondering if they were trying to hold themself still, or to hold themself from falling over.

He turned back to the screens, his breath catching in his chest at every broadside, hands tightening unconsciously on the arms of his chair.

But the Level navy was winning. It was inevitable—the Rosette ships had jumped after them with no reconnaissance, into the centre of a solid three fleets of Level naval ships.

He closed his eyes, forcing his attention away from the screen, and tapped through the ship's comm. "This is the *Sweet Jenny*, paging the *Verity*," he said quietly. "What's your damage?"

Hollis's voice through the line was dull with exhaustion. "This is the *Verity*. We've lost three gunner compartments, and our shields are offline."

He grimaced, sickness swirling in his stomach. Three gunner compartments. Unless they'd managed to find survivors, that was sixty sailors dead. "Running engines?" he asked.

There was a pause. "We have one functional running engine." Hollis's tone was clipped.

He cursed under his breath.

"They can't run," he said, turning to Ari. He tapped through the line. "Freddie, Jumper, what's our status?"

"We can run, but we'll be running slow," said Freddie. "That last maneuver didn't do us any favours."

Jumper's terse taps through the line didn't carry any better news— the shields inoperable, most of the heavies offline.

"We're not fighting our way out of this either," he said, dropping back in his seat.

The tension of the last ... however the hell many hours it had been, was finally starting to catch up with him, bleeding through his muscles and seeping through his brain.

The battle between the Level ships and the Rosette ships had been over, really, before it had begun—the Rosette ships were fighting gamely, but if he was any judge, they'd be offering up their surrender in a matter of minutes.

He didn't realize Price had come to peer over his shoulder until they spoke, startling him enough that he almost jumped.

"I'm not certain that the Level ships have given up on taking the *Sweet Jenny*. Or the *Verity*, for that matter," they said quietly.

Silas closed his eyes. "I know. But I'm not sure what our options are at the moment."

Once, he'd have said the navy would never fire on their own, not after something like this.

Once, he'd have told himself that only pirates would do something like that. Only people without honour, like the people down on Blackrock—

He sucked in a quick breath. "What if we ran through to Blackrock?"

Price turned to stare at him. He ignored them, and glanced over at Ari.

She shrugged. "Don't figure as anyone on Blackrock'll be feeling too charitable towards a naval ship. But if Gracie tells them, it's possible they won't shoot down every last damn one of the naval bastards on sight."

Silas turned back to the comm. "I may be able to get through a line, even through the naval blockade," he said slowly.

Ari nodded. "Figure you should be able to, at that. Gracie's got the ship kitted out."

He glanced back at Price. "Will Hollis agree?"

Price blew out a breath. "I don't know." They paused. "May I?"

Silas nodded and stood, gesturing them to sit.

They hesitated, then did so. He guessed, by the way their body slumped unconsciously into the seat, that they'd been avoiding sitting down because they weren't sure they could keep themselves awake if for one moment they relaxed.

They straightened again with an effort and leaned forward, tapping the comm. "Captain," they said in a low voice.

Silas moved back a little to give them space, and Ari rose, coming over to join him. "You figure we'll be able to get through to

Blackrock?"

Silas sighed. "I don't know. But it's the best chance we have. I doubt the Level navy will stay at Blackrock, now that they see the threat to the Level."

She nodded. The muscles in her jaw stood out from how hard she was clenching her teeth, and the sick, haunted look that hadn't left her face since they'd found Gracie sprawled bloody and unconscious on the floor of the Rosette ship made him want, irrationally, to take her into his arms, hold her until a little of the tension melted from her shoulders.

But instead, he turned back to the comm.

Price looked up at him, and he couldn't read their expression. "She agreed," they said quietly. "Your captain swore to speak for us, and Captain Ives agreed to go." They pushed themself to their feet with an effort, stepping out of the way to let Silas slip back into his place.

He tapped through the comm, and gestured Ari over. "This will be better coming from you," he said. "I don't think there are many on Blackrock who are overly fond of me."

Ari managed a smirk, despite everything, and came over beside him, leaning over the comm. Her body pressed up against his, and he was tired enough that he had to consciously remind himself not to let himself lean in, relaxing into the warmth of her.

"This is the second mate of the *Sweet Jenny*, paging Blackrock," she said into the comm.

For a few moments, there was no answer. Then, at last, a voice Silas recognized, hoarse and faint. "This is Abigail. That you, Ari?"

Ari closed her eyes and dropped her head for just a moment in exhausted relief. "Aye, Abigail, it's me. Captain's in a bad way, and I need a favour from you."

"What do you need, lass?" Abigail's voice was cracked and broken over the weak connection, but Silas could hear the sharp worry in it.

"Need you to let me bring a naval ship into port. Captain's on board, on account of they're the only ones with the medical equipment to keep her alive, and Temple is too. We'll bring the *Sweet Jenny* in after her."

There was another long moment of silence from the other end of the comm, then Abigail's voice again. "Didn't figure you were going to ask me for a goddamn miracle, lass."

"Well, you'd best figure out how to get me a goddamn miracle, or Mad Dog ain't going to live through this," Ari snapped.

Abigail heaved a sigh. "Lass, folks around here ain't feeling friendly towards the navy at the moment, and for good reason. But I'll see what I can do. Meantime, bring her in close, but keep the *Sweet Jenny* in front of her, or I don't know if you'll keep the other captains from shooting her down on sight."

The line clicked off, and Ari peered down at the screen.

"We can make it out here, I think" said Silas in a low voice, pointing. "They won't be able to shift to block us without breaking formation, and they won't dare do that as long as the Rosette ships are still fighting."

Ari gave a sharp nod, and Silas tapped through a line to the *Verity*. "Captain Ives. Instruct your navigator to follow my course," he said, and upon Hollis's brusque acknowledgement, he turned to Ari. "Chart us a course, Ari?"

She nodded and slid back into the navigator seat.

"We'll have to get out quick-time," he said. "If they figure out what we're planning, they have enough ships that they'll figure out a way to bring someone around to stop us."

"Don't figure the *Sweet Jenny* or the *Verity* have much quick-time left in them," she muttered, but she bent over the screen.

Silas turned back to his own screen, swearing under his breath. If they got out, it'd be a close thing.

"Got us a course," Ari said at last, looking up.

"Send it through to the *Verity*, then I'll take us out," he said tersely. "Freddie? I need everything we have on the running engines."

"Aye, Sil," came Freddie's grim voice.

"*Verity*. Stand by. Ari's sent you through a course, but we won't have much time to spare. Get everything you have through to your running engine, and stay on my tail," he said through the comm.

Then he pushed the throttle forward.

The *Sweet Jenny* shuddered and bucked under his hand, but she started forward. He gritted his teeth at her unresponsiveness, and sent up a silent prayer to Our Lady.

If the *Sweet Jenny* was moving this slowly, the *Verity* would be even worse off.

And they had to get out the narrow gap before the navy had time to send ships around to shore it up. Whatever the hell reason the navy had decided to fire on the *Verity*, he wasn't confident they'd given up on it.

He watched the screen, half his attention on the narrow gap ahead of them, half on the blip on his screen that was the *Verity*, biting the inside of his cheek hard enough that he tasted blood. He almost gasped with relief when he saw the *Verity* swing around, slow and clumsy, to come after them.

But sure enough, Level naval ships were already starting to shift in response.

Silas swore steadily under his breath as they approached the gap.

One of the ships fired off a warning shot.

"Jumper, fire one of the precision guns back at her," Silas snapped through the comm. "Don't hit her, but let her see that we could."

Jumper tapped an affirmation through the comm line.

Every muscle in Silas's body was shouting at him to push the throttle all the way forward, take the *Sweet Jenny* out as fast as she'd go. But the *Verity* couldn't move that quickly, and he couldn't risk getting too far ahead.

The *Sweet Jenny* was in the gap between the ships, the *Verity* close enough on her tail that there was barely space between them on his screen.

The nearest ship fired off another shot, this one close enough that the energy from it fuzzed across the cobwebby remnants of the *Sweet Jenny's* shields.

Then they were through, and there was clear, open space in front of them.

"Abigail? How's that miracle coming?" Ari said, tapping the comm.

There was a moment of silence. And then Abigail said, "I've got you safe passage, lass, with the promise that Mad Dog'll be answering for it when you get in."

Ari grinned, relief washing across her expression. "Knew you could do it, Abigail," she said. "Bringing her in now."

Silas dropped his head back against the seat for a moment in sheer relief.

In the background, over the general comm, he could hear the first of the Rosette ships broadcasting an offer of surrender, but it didn't matter.

They'd made it out.

23

Hollis

"Captain!" The navigator's face over the screen was bright with a desperate relief. "We made it through. Clear skies ahead."

"Thank you, Davis," Hollis mumbled. She was slumped back in her seat, too weary for even her pride to push her body upright. "You did well, Officer."

The woman's jubilant expression was echoed across the faces on the bridge, and Hollis could feel the same relief seeping into her muscles and weakening her joints.

At some point, she'd have to reckon with the fact that she was bringing a naval ship into a pirate base. She'd have to reckon with that, and figure out what the hell she was going to do next, what the hell her crew was going to do next. But for now—they'd survived.

Despite every last damn odd being stacked against her, she'd kept them alive, and for now, that was enough.

"Mate Greene." Her voice was slurring with weariness. "Please ensure that we maintain our pace behind the *Sweet Jenny.*"

"Aye, Captain."

For the first time since the beginning of this hellish ordeal, she

208

heard a note of hope in Emmett's voice.

She sighed, forcing her eyes open, and turned back to the screen.

They'd made it out just in time—the Level ships had surrounded the smaller Rosette fleet, and from the looks of it, were sending out skiffs to accept the surrender of their captains.

The *Sweet Jenny* was hanging back, matching the *Verity's* speed, guiding them in. Even damaged as both ships were, they'd reach Blackrock in under three hours' run-time.

Her whole body drooped with the release of tension, and she leaned back in her seat. The pain coursing through her was a throbbing undertone to her entire existence, and the thought of dropping down on a cot and letting her eyes fall closed was almost enough to make her cry.

She forced her brain back to the business at hand. "Greene. Get people working on the running engines and the shields, we want to run in as quickly as we can."

They wouldn't be able to outrun the naval ships, but with luck, they wouldn't have to. The Rosette fleet's surrender would take time, and by the time the Level navy had the attention to send ships after them, they'd be safe in Blackrock.

"Ives. We're going to bring you in to …" Silas's voice stopped abruptly. Then he hissed out a low, vicious curse.

Hollis forced her eyes open and turned to the screen.

It took a few moments before her exhausted brain processed what she was seeing.

And then she simply sat where she was, staring at the screen. Despair seeped through her body, leaving numbness in its wake.

The Level navy had split its damn fleet, and sent ships to cut them off.

It was impossible. It was absurd, they should never have pulled ships off the attacking Rosette naval fleet to come after the *Verity*, even if the surrender was all but complete. It was an utter breach of protocol.

But they'd done it.

"Lass? What's happened?" There was a sharp note of worry in Mad Dog's voice.

Hollis glanced over at her.

Mad Dog had offered her a way out. She didn't have to, she'd done it of her own accord. And maybe she'd done it because she had crew on this ship, but … Hollis recognized the expression on the pirate captain's face.

She recognized it, because she'd worn it herself often enough these past few days. A captain who wanted, desperately, to save her crew, to save the people who'd trusted themselves to her, and wasn't sure she could.

Slowly, Hollis pushed herself upright and drew in a breath. "Silas," she said through the comm. "There's no way the *Verity* makes it out of this. Take the *Sweet Jenny* and go, that is an order. You still have room to jump, get the hell out of here. All I ask is that you swear that no harm will come to Price."

There was a pause.

"Go to hell, Ives," Silas snapped through the comm. "I'm not leaving my damn captain to be shot down." He paused. "Price is in full agreement, in case you had your doubts. We still have our guns, maybe we can do something."

There was nothing he or the *Sweet Jenny* could do, both of them knew it. But she could hear in his voice that he wouldn't listen to argument. And she could picture Foster's face, their bland expression with that implacable stubbornness behind it.

For just a moment, she almost smiled at the thought.

Then she tapped through to Emmett. "Mate Greene. Stand by. I shall attempt once more to contact the naval ships." Her voice was dull.

"Aye, Captain." Emmett sounded as hopeless as she felt.

She tapped through to the broadcast line. "This is Captain Hollis Ives of the *Verity*," she said. "We are a Level naval ship of the line. Request you stand down. Repeat, please stand down. We mean you no harm."

She paused a moment, waiting for a response, although she knew there was no response forthcoming.

"This is Captain Hollis Ives of the *Verity*, paging the *Resolve*," she tried again. "Commodore Webb. If you wish to try me for treason, do so, but for God's sake, do not shoot down my ship. I will turn myself in for a court-marital, but please do not shoot down my ship."

Again, no response.

There was a cold, tight knot of dread in the pit of her stomach, growing by the moment.

"This is Captain Hollis Ives of the *Verity*. Request that you stand down. Repeat, please stand down."

She waited a moment longer, then cursed, slamming her fist down on the desk.

After all this, after everything they'd survived, she and her crew were going to be shot down by the damned Level navy.

"Captain Ives."

For a moment, she thought perhaps she'd imagined the voice. Then she spun towards the comm.

It was silent.

She turned.

Mad Dog was watching her, and she couldn't read the expression on the woman's face.

"Why'd you tell Sil to get out?" The pirate asked.

Hollis drew in a deep breath. "My first mate is on that ship," she said quietly. "They didn't have to die, at least."

"You'd let a pirate crew live to save one person?" Mad Dog's tone was still mild, but there was an intensity under it.

Hollis drew in another long breath.

"Your crew risked their lives and their ship to save the *Verity* on more than one occasion. It would be poor repayment to ask them to die with us." She tried to keep the bitterness from her voice. "But it hardly matters, as it appears Silas feels no compunction to follow my orders."

Mad Dog was still watching her. The woman gave Hollis a small smile. "Well, lass, he's my crew, not yours. Hardly see how he'd be obligated to listen to you." She paused. "But you didn't have to offer to let them go. Wouldn't have expected it of a naval captain."

Hollis closed her eyes. "I hardly see that it's relevant at this juncture, as we're all currently about to be shot down by my own damn fleet."

"We might not be, at that," said the pirate captain in a quiet voice. "Figure there may be a way to get them to rethink."

Hollis frowned. "What the devil are you saying?"

Mad Dog raised her eyebrows. "I'm saying, lass, that if you call in, tell them you've taken Mad Dog, and you're willing to turn me in— figure they might answer you then."

There was a moment of silence, as the words percolated through Hollis's exhausted brain.

Then she stared.

"Best do it quick-time, Captain Ives," the pirate said. "Don't figure they'll give you much time to talk."

"And the *Sweet Jenny*?" Hollis asked at last.

"Let me talk to the *Sweet Jenny*," said Mad Dog. "I know my crew. Figure they ain't going to jump, so best the navy think you've taken them, too."

Hollis nodded, still watching Gracie. Then, at last, she turned back to the comm and hit the broadcast line.

"This is Captain Hollis Ives of the *Verity*. Request you hold your fire. I have Captain Mad Dog of the *Sweet Jenny* aboard, and I'm willing to trade her for my ship."

"Hollis? What the hell?" Silas's voice through the broadcast channel was sharp with a mixture of betrayal and disbelief, but Mad Dog tapped her own comm.

"My orders, lad." Her voice was hard.

Then there was a sound that Hollis had all but given up on hearing—the crackle of an incoming broadcast.

"This is Rear-Admiral Hayes of the *Steadfast*, paging the *Verity*." The woman's voice was sharp and businesslike.

Hollis stared, then tapped through the broadcast line, her hands shaking. "This is Captain Hollis Ives of the *Verity*."

"Captain Ives. Please confirm you have Mad Dog on board as your prisoner."

Hollis glanced over at Mad Dog.

The woman nodded. There was an expression on her face, something wry and resigned, but she just said, "Best ask your Chief Medical Officer to restrain me, and put up a guard before you put through the visuals."

Hollis glanced over at Archibald. "Officer Smyth?"

He was already snapping whispered orders to the medics.

Hollis turned back to the comm. "Will visuals be sufficient?"

"Send through the visuals, Ives."

She glanced over her shoulder.

Mad Dog had been hastily restrained, and two of the *Verity's* officers were standing with their energy pistols pointed at the pirate's head.

Hollis tapped through the visuals. "I hope this is sufficient," she said, turning the screen so that Mad Dog was visible.

There was a pause. "And the *Sweet Jenny?*" the Level rear-admiral asked at last.

Hollis drew in a breath. "The *Sweet Jenny* has surrendered to my ship. My first mate is aboard, and has taken command of her."

There was another long pause, and Hollis prayed that Silas wouldn't say or do anything to refute her words.

At last, Hayes said, "Very good, Captain Ives. Instruct your first mate to bring the *Sweet Jenny* aboard the *Verity,* and we'll escort you back to the Level under guard."

Hollis wanted to curse at the woman, ask her what the hell they were being brought in for.

But she simply nodded. "Aye, Admiral. I will instruct my navigator to follow your coordinates. Please note, however, that we have only one functional running engine, and we are unable to jump without being given specific jump coordinates via comm that we can set in manually."

"Acknowledged. Instruct your officers to stand down. The *Verity* will not attempt to jump, or use her running engines, without my specific command, or we will shoot you down. Any unauthorized action on your part will result in the *Verity* being shot down. Do you understand?"

"Acknowledged." Hollis tried to keep the bitterness from her voice.

"Very good. Stand by for instructions."

The comm clicked off, and Hollis was left staring at the blank screen.

24

Silas's stomach was sick with dread as he put the *Sweet Jenny* down gently in the *Verity's* hangar bay.

Hollis had promised to turn Gracie in.

He knew damn well she wouldn't have done it unless it had been the only path open to her. Hell, with her stubborn sense of honour, she probably wouldn't have done it without Gracie's explicit permission. But he couldn't help the sting of betrayal, planted the moment he first heard her words through the broadcast line.

He didn't look at Ari or Price as he shut down the controls. He couldn't bring himself to.

They'd all agreed—they wouldn't leave the *Verity*. He and Ari wouldn't leave Gracie, and Price wouldn't leave Hollis.

But Gracie had put him in charge of her ship, dammit. Of her crew. And he still wasn't sure he'd done the right thing.

Still … He glanced over at where Ari sat, her face pale, a muscle in the corner of her jaw working. Price, standing beside her, looked almost as tense as Ari did.

He wasn't sure, honestly, if he'd had another option, even if he'd wanted to. He wasn't sure if they'd have obeyed, if he'd tried to put the ship into jump and leave Gracie and Temple and Toothpick and Vee to be shot down with the *Verity.*

And dammit—he didn't want to.

He remembered the moment, weeks ago, on the outside of the *Sweet Jenny,* the edges of a solar flair sweeping closer and his line cut almost through. He'd made a mistake, and by all rights Gracie should have left him to die. And back on the *Resolve,* when Temple had shoved Silas out of the way and taken the shot meant for him— none of what they'd done made sense. None of it was for the greater good. They simply hadn't been willing to let him die, not because he deserved it, but because he was their crew. That was all the reason they'd needed.

And he'd realized, suddenly and irrevocably, when Hollis had called through, told him to jump away—he no longer gave a damn about his duty, or about the greater good.

He wouldn't abandon his captain or his crew. He wasn't damn well going to leave Gracie and Temple and Toothpick and Vee at the mercy of the Level, even if all he could do was die along with them. And he wasn't going to try to force Ari or Price or Jumper or Freddie to, either.

For all his talk of duty, back in the navy, it had just been an excuse to avoid the responsibility that came with his actions. He'd told himself he was just following orders, but every decision he'd made from the time he was old enough to make them had been his own. It was just that now, he finally understood that.

He pushed himself to his feet, and finally, forced himself to turn to Ari and Price. "I suppose the *Sweet Jenny's* safe enough where she is," he said.

Ari nodded without looking at him, a short, jerky motion.

Price met his gaze, and he saw in their eyes the same tight worry he felt. "I suppose there's no point in delaying," they said. "Permission to disembark?"

Silas gave them a tight smile. "Permission granted. We'll join you, Mate Price."

They nodded, turning towards the door, and he glanced once more at Ari.

She looked sick, and so pale it was almost frightening. She didn't meet his gaze, but he put out a hand, catching her arm as she tried to step past him. She stiffened, but didn't pull away.

"Ari," he said in a low voice. "It'll be alright. We won't let them take Gracie without a fight, and I doubt Hollis is planning to just hand her over either. We'll figure something out."

She turned, studying him for a moment, and he could feel her whole body sag. "You don't know the captain like I do, Sil," she said, her voice quiet. "Much as I don't think much of your goddamned Hollis Ives, Gracie's the one who agreed to this."

He squeezed her arm. "I know. But this isn't the end. We'll figure something out, alright? I promise."

She closed her eyes wearily. "Figure we will," she said, but her voice was dull, and he could tell she didn't believe the words.

The others were gathered in the airlock when he and Price and Ari joined them. Jumper jerked his head in a nod, and Freddie gave him a grim smile. "Well, lad, I guess we see how this plays out, no? You ready for me to open the airlock?"

"Thank you, Freddie," he said, fighting to keep his voice steady.

She nodded and tapped the control, and the doors hissed open.

Naval sailors were waiting at the base of the gangplank. Silas recognized one of them as the *Verity's* second mate.

"Captain Ives has asked to see you," he said stiffly, once Silas was standing on the deck of the *Verity.* "Mate Price as well." He turned to Price, concern sharpening his tone. "God's sake, Price, you look like you're about to collapse. Shall I send someone with you?"

Silas glanced over quickly. Price stood stoically beside him, but he caught the way they swayed a little on their feet.

"I think I'll make the med bay." Their voice was thick with exhaustion. "I'm not sure I'd make it much farther than that, though."

"I'll walk with you. Lean on me, or I'll think you're as bad as Ives."

"God forbid," Price said in a wry tone. "Very well. Thank you, Greene."

Mate Greene stepped over to Price, glancing over his shoulder at the remainder of the *Sweet Jenny's* crew. "And the rest of you?"

There was still a note of distrust in his voice, but it was much more muted than it had been.

"Lead the way," said Silas. "We'll follow."

When they reached the med bay, his eyes found Gracie instantly. She was laying in the cot where he'd left her, still hooked up to far too many sensors and wires. Her eyes, though, were open, her gaze as piercing as ever.

He hesitated, glancing over at Hollis. She was already deep in conversation with her two mates, but she looked up and met his eye for just a moment. And he knew, suddenly, that he'd been correct— this had been Gracie's idea.

He gave Hollis a brief nod, then made his way across the room to Gracie, joining Ari and the others.

Gracie looked up at him, and there was something dangerous in her expression. "Told you to keep my crew safe, Sil," she said. "Thought we had an agreement."

He clenched his teeth. "We did, Captain. But if I remember correctly, Vee and Temple and Toothpick are your crew too." He paused. "And you're my crew. You knew damn well we wouldn't leave you."

She watched him a moment, then, at last, she nodded. "Figure I did, at that, lad. Can't say as I agree with you. But I ain't surprised." She raised her eyebrows at him. "That's saying something. Wasn't the navy taught you that, was it?"

He gave her a tight smile. "No. Learned it from my captain."

She watched him a moment longer, then smiled. "Good lad."

"I told you," he said in a low voice. "I'm yours, Gracie. Body and soul. Those weren't just words."

"I know they weren't, Sil," she said.

"The hell were you thinking, Captain?" Ari's voice was sharp. "The hell were you thinking, letting that bloody Ives trade you for safe passage?" There was pain under her words, sharp and raw.

"Ari." Gracie's voice was still mild, even weak and exhausted as it was. "Steady, lass." She put out a hand and caught Ari's arm, and Ari drooped a little, her stiff posture wilting at Gracie's touch.

Gracie paused a moment, studying Ari. "You've shipped with me how many years now? More'n a decade, at least. You've shipped with me since you were a skinny little thing with eyes too big for your head and feet too big for your body. Toothpick's been with me longer. You remember when we brought Temple on, don't you? Vee? Freddie? Jumper?" She smiled, just a little. "When you came onto my crew, I made a promise to you, lass. Maybe it wasn't in words, but I made you a promise, taking you on. And I ain't going to break it." She gave a small shrug. "I hate the Admiral and the Level and everything on it. Don't think that needs saying. I'd have taken down that naval fleet without a qualm, if our Captain Ives hadn't been a mite too clever." She glanced up a moment, and her eyes caught Silas's. There was something in her expression that told him the decision to turn herself in to the Level hadn't been quite as easy as her words would indicate—but he didn't see a trace of regret there, regardless. "But I ain't going to let that make me sacrifice my crew. Ain't going to sacrifice something I love for something I hate. That'd make me no better'n they are." Her voice faltered, and Vee swore.

"Get on with you, all of you. Captain needs to damn well rest, she ain't out of danger yet."

"Come on, Ari," said Silas quietly, taking her arm and pulling her away. "We'll talk when she's had some rest. It's a two-day trip back to the Level anyway, more if they want to hold guard on the ship the whole time. We have time to figure something out."

Ari let herself be pulled away. When Silas glanced over his shoulder, Gracie was watching him, and she gave him a small nod of approval before Vee was there, fussing over her, blocking his view.

He glanced around quickly, then drew Ari out of the crowded med bay and into a small side room off the corridor. He closed the door behind them, then turned to her. "Ari, listen," he began.

She turned, finally, and met his gaze.

There were tears in her eyes, and tear-tracks down her cheeks, and the sight sent a shock through him.

"I don't want to bloody listen, to you or anyone else," she hissed. "I just want—" She broke off, her voice choking.

Silas put his arm around her and pulled her in. She stiffened for a moment, then sagged against him. Her shoulders were shaking, her muscles tight with strain. He pulled her head down gently against his shoulder, and stroked her hair, and leaned back against the wall, holding her as she sobbed.

She smelled of blood and sweat and ship grease, her hair tangled and stiff with it, and he could feel the trembling exhaustion in the shape of her body pressed against him, her tears hot against the filthy collar of his borrowed shirt.

There wasn't anything at all he could say—he couldn't tell her it would be alright. He knew how much the Level hated Mad Dog, how long they'd wanted to kill her.

So he just held her, and stroked her hair, and let her cry.

25

Hollis

"Captain." There was a weight of relief in the word that Hollis recognized, even before she turned.

Foster stood there, leaning on Emmett's arm, face drawn and so exhausted that she was hit with a sudden jolt of panic. "Price? God's sake, are you hurt?"

They gave her a wan smile. "No, I was treated with nothing but respect. I'm just tired."

"Just tired." Archibald's voice was scathing. "I should think so, considering neither you nor the captain have slept in longer than I care to consider. Greene, you too. God save me from the hubris of the commanding officers on this damn ship."

"We need to discuss our next steps." Hollis was so far beyond exhaustion at this point that the world had become sharp and over-bright and brittle, like if she blinked, it would all shatter like glass around her, and she wasn't completely sure whether what she was looking at was real. Except for Foster and Emmett—she knew they were real, because their faces, the concern and weariness and exhaustion and the stupid, absurd loyalty, were something her brain couldn't have conjured up on its own.

Emmett raised his head. "With respect, Captain, Officer Smyth is right—we can discuss next steps when we've had a bit of rest. We're not in any immediate danger, and our hands are tied until Hayes gives us her orders. May as well take advantage of the lull. You look like death itself, and Price is about to fall over, if I'm any judge. I wouldn't say no to a bit of shut-eye myself, if it were on offer." His voice was gruff and tired, and for a moment she was so overwhelmed with fondness—for him, and for Foster, and Archibald, and every last person on her crew who had followed her through this nightmare—that she had to blink back tears.

"Captain? Are you alright?" Foster's voice was coming from far, far away.

"I'm alright," she murmured. "Greene, as always, your insight is appreciated. Go find somewhere to lie down. Smyth, see to Price—I expect they're hurt worse than they're letting on, besides being half-dead from exhaustion. And I'll put myself into your hands until I'm needed again." She could hear the words coming from her own mouth, strange and distorted and so very distant.

"Price, you heard the captain. For God's sake lie down, and I'll have someone over to see to you. No, don't say anything, you won't be any help dead on your feet, and I'm perfectly capable of handling Ives, now that she's damned well willing to listen to me."

Archibald's words were still coming from so far away.

Hands lifted Hollis upright, voices murmuring words her brain was too tired to translate, and then she was lying down, something soft under her head.

"Captain. I'm going to start you on painkillers, your body isn't going to hold up to much more of what you've put it through, and there's no emergency for you to deal with at present."

She tried to nod, although her muscles weren't obeying her as they should.

Something pricked the inside of her arm, followed by a wash of relief, flooding over her like a warm bath—the shocking lightheadness at the absence of the pain she'd grown so accustomed to that it felt like part of her very being leaving her feeling like she was floating over her own body.

She felt her eyes falling closed, and for once, she didn't try to stop them, and the warm darkness of sleep took her before she had time to think anything else.

She woke to pain, swirling around her hot and heavy. When she blinked her eyes open, she was still in the med bay, with no idea how much time had passed.

"Officer Smyth?" she croaked. Her tongue felt heavy in her mouth, the words coming out thick and unwieldy.

He was beside her a moment later. "Captain, thank God you're awake. I was getting worried."

"What happened?" she managed.

He gave a small, tight smile. "Just what I was worried about—you kept yourself upright through all of that, but now that you're not in the middle of an emergency, your body's decided to call in its debts. You'll recover, I think, but it'll get worse before it gets better. How are you feeling?"

She grimaced, and he raised an eyebrow in grim amusement. "I'll up the painkillers then, shall I? Don't worry, we'll pull you through, but you won't have a choice this time, I think. You'll be flat on your back until you recover, will you or no."

"Price? Greene?" She struggled to push herself up, then gave it up as a bad job. Archibald was right—her muscles were making it clear that they'd no longer obey her commands.

"Price is still sleeping. They haven't woken up since I made them lie down on a cot. I've treated their injuries, but they're not as bad as they might be—just sheer exhaustion, at this point. Greene is awake. I've told him he needs more rest, and thank God he's not anywhere near as stubborn as you two, but he's been keeping an eye on things, making sure the ship's running while you and Price recover." He reached over, adjusting something over her head. "There, that should help with the pain in a minute or so."

"What's happened while I've been out?" Hollis muttered. Her lips were cracked and dry, and there was a dull ache that permeated her entire being.

Archibald turned back to her. His expression was concerned, but she'd known him long enough to know it was more for her than for the situation. "Nothing much. Rear-Admiral Hayes sent through jump coordinates, and we're headed back for the Level. They sent most of the fleet on ahead, but there are six ships left here guarding us. It's been a day and a half, and it'll be two days more—they're taking no chances. Short jumps, and under guard the entire time." He glanced around the med bay and lowered his voice. "Mad Dog will recover, I think, but that pirate medic, Vee, is dealing with the same thing I am—apparently you and Mad Dog are more alike than you are different when it comes to injuries. Mad Dog's relapsed, and I'll be honest, I've not seen injuries that severe in a long time. But with the med tech we have aboard here, she should pull through. Temple is already better than he was, and that's gone a long way to keeping the pirate crew happy."

Hollis nodded. The pain was beginning to fade, but so were the clarity of her thoughts. "I'll need to talk with Mad Dog before we get in," she said, and she could hear how her mouth slurred the words. "Price, too. Wake me when they're able to talk."

"Aye, Captain, I'll do that." His voice was wavery and indistinct, and then it faded into blackness once more.

Archibald was right—when she woke again, everything hurt, her entire body a singular dull pain that clouded her thoughts and pulsed under her skin.

"Captain. You told me to wake you when Price was up."

She turned at Archibald's voice, the movement shooting another wave of pain through her body.

His forehead was creased in a frown of concern, and she could see the weariness in his face. Price stood beside him, paler than usual, the dark circles under their eyes aging them a decade, but the desperate exhaustion of before was gone from their face.

"Captain," they said with a small smile. "It's good to see you awake."

"And you." Her throat was dry, her voice hoarse from disuse. "How are you feeling?"

Again, they gave her a small, wry smile. "From the looks of it, Captain, I'm feeling better than you are. Although I suspect that's not saying much."

They dropped into a seat and turned to Archibald. "Thank you, Officer Smyth. I promise I'll keep the captain from overexerting herself."

"See that you do," muttered Archibald in a sour tone. "I had to cut back on the painkiller dosage to keep her coherent enough to talk with you, so I doubt she'll have the energy to try—but I've learned never to underestimate her." He turned on his heel and stalked off back to his duties.

Hollis found herself smiling after him, despite the pain.

For a few minutes, she and Foster sat in silence.

Archibald said he'd turned down the painkiller, and he must have, considering how she felt. But her mind was still hazy, like she was floating a little way outside of her body, the pain a distant thing that wasn't fully connected to her.

"There's hardly much use discussing next steps, is there?" she said at last, to break the silence. "I expect next steps will be whatever the Admiralty says they'll be."

A flash of anger flickered across Foster's features. "You saved the damn Level, Captain. You saved the fleet, and then you saved the Level from an attack it wouldn't have survived—with three full fleets at Blackrock, they wouldn't have been able to stand against a fleet of Rosette naval ships. And they're treating you like a goddamn criminal. They would have shot us down, for God's sake, without a word of explanation."

Hollis shook her head wearily. "I know," she said. "But it wasn't just me that did all that. You, Greene, Smyth, the crew—every person on this ship is a hero."

"And Mad Dog?" they asked quietly.

"Mad Dog had just as much a hand in saving the Level as we did." Hollis could hear the steel in her own voice. "She did it for selfish reasons, perhaps. But without her, the Level would have been overrun, and we'd not have been able to stop it."

Foster was watching her. "Selfish reasons?"

Hollis managed a wan smile. "Saving her crew. You were there. The navy will give us up to save themselves. Mad Dog will give up her revenge, her goals, her life to save her crew."

They were quiet for a little longer. "You told Silas to jump out with the *Sweet Jenny*, when you knew the *Verity* wouldn't get out," they said at last.

Hollis nodded. She couldn't quite bring herself to meet their eyes.

"I didn't think the Captain Ives I served under a few weeks back would have dreamed of letting a pirate ship go, never mind one as notorious as the *Sweet Jenny*. Not for anything. As you said, if I'd died, it would have been no more than my duty."

Hollis was quiet. When at last she looked up, they were still watching her, studying her in that way they had. She met their eyes. "The navy didn't deserve your life along with mine. They didn't deserve the lives of my crew. They didn't deserve any of it, but they were going to take it, regardless. I wasn't going to give them you, too."

Foster was still studying her, a small frown creasing between their eyebrows, as if they were trying to figure her out.

She reached out, even though her hand felt almost too heavy to lift, and grabbed their arm.

Foster's eyes widened a little in surprise, their gaze dropping to her hand.

"You deserved a better captain, Price." Her words were starting to slur again, her tongue too thick and heavy to form them properly. "You were right—you deserved more than this. I'm sorry."

"Captain—" there was a note of pain in their voice that she was too tired to parse.

She squeezed their arm. "Whatever happens, know this—I will do everything in my power to protect you. It may not be much—it appears the Admiralty has marked me as a traitor. But I'll do what I can, I swear it. I'll not leave you or Greene or Smyth or any of the others to suffer for my decisions."

"You were trying to save them." Foster's voice was tight. "Every damn thing you did was to protect the navy. And they're going to crucify you for it."

She smiled a little. "They'll try, perhaps."

"Captain Ives—"

She squeezed their arm again. "You're a good first mate, Price. A far better one than I ever deserved. Tell Greene I'm sorry I couldn't do more, but I'll do my best for you when we're back on the Level."

Her hand dropped to her side, her muscles unwilling to hold it up any longer, and she dropped her head back on her pillow, letting her eyes fall closed.

"The navy doesn't deserve you. It doesn't deserve any of us." Foster's voice was low and hard.

She smiled, without opening her eyes. "Perhaps not. But it has us, nonetheless."

By the time the *Verity*, under heavy guard, was within running distance of the Level, Hollis had managed to meet with Foster and Emmett again, and with the pirate crew. Mad Dog had been mostly silent, her face a mask of pain so thick that Hollis wasn't entirely sure the woman understood what she'd been saying. Ari stood next to her, face sharp with a mixture of anger and desperation. Silas had been mostly silent as well, the tension in his face and body reminding her that he, too, had served in the navy, been forced to hide every trace of feeling or emotion until it had become second nature.

She'd promised them the same thing she'd promised Foster— protection, to the best of her ability.

She wasn't sure what that ability was, wasn't sure she'd be able to keep any of her promises.

They'd had no contact with Rear-Admiral Hayes since Hollis had agreed to turn Mad Dog over to the navy, except for the brief, barked orders, and the woman had refused to accept any of her broadcasts. The most recent communication had been a terse order for Hollis to present herself, in person, on the docks once the *Verity* reached port. She was to bring Mad Dog with her, to turn over to the Admiral for trial.

One look at Mad Dog told Hollis this was impossible. The woman's relapse had been much more severe than Hollis's own, the wounds going septic despite the best care of Vee and Archibald. The *Sweet Jenny's* crew barely left her side, and Hollis wasn't sure Vee had slept at all, except in small cat-naps at the edge of her captain's bed, but Mad Dog had been drifting in and out of consciousness for the last twenty-four hours, moving restlessly in her sleep and muttering odd, disturbing phrases that made no sense.

Hollis herself dreaded the thought of forcing herself upright, and moving, even in a hover chair, sounded like a nightmare come true. But even Archibald agreed, reluctantly, that in this, at least, none of them had a choice.

"We're approaching the docks, Captain."

She looked up. Foster stood over her cot, their face cut with concern.

She forced a smile and, with an effort pushed herself into a sitting position. "Help me up, if you would, Mate Price? I think a hover chair will be my best option at this juncture."

"Aye, Captain." Foster's words were clipped and precise, like they had been when she'd first met them. She knew them better now, though, and she could hear through the stoicism in their voice.

She pushed herself upright slowly, supporting herself on the side of the cot. Her legs shook, and even with Foster holding her steady, it took her a moment to find her balance enough to settle herself in the chair.

Emmett appeared a moment later at her other side. From across the room, she could feel the eyes of the *Sweet Jenny's* crew.

She turned to them. "I'll do my best for your captain, Silas," she said. "I swear it."

He nodded tersely, and she turned back to the clumsy task of moving her hover chair forward.

Armed sailors waited outside the airlock door, and they fell into step with Hollis, Foster, and Emmett as they made their slow way down the gangplank.

Hollis hardly had the energy to care. She was shaking with pain by the time her chair was on the solid ground of the Level, and every bit of her attention was focused on staying upright.

"Captain? Are you alright?" Foster's voice in her ear was low and worried.

"I don't believe not being alright is an option, currently," she whispered back.

There was a small contingent of uniformed figures at the end of the dock. Hollis recognized the man in front as Vice-Admiral Williams. She was in too much pain to try to recognize the figures standing behind him, besides their Admiralty uniforms. A contingent of armed sailors and peacekeepers stood behind them, as if they thought Hollis was a starving, rabid dog who couldn't be trusted not to attack if allowed off leash.

The docks seemed to stretch on interminably, and she wasn't entirely sure she'd make it to the end of them. She focused on staying upright, letting Foster and Emmett direct the chair.

Once, the thought of appearing like this in front of the Admiralty would have made her hot with shame. Now, she hardly cared, as long as she could stay conscious.

When she came to a stop at last in front of the three vice-admirals, her armed escort gestured Foster and Emmett back. She felt them stiffen, Foster opening their mouth as if to protest, but she shook her head. "Please," she said in an undertone.

Her two mates hesitated, then did as directed, both stepping a couple paces back and leaving her to stand alone.

Vice-Admiral Williams looked her up and down, his gaze dispassionate and evaluating—a butcher examining livestock.

"Captain Hollis Ives." His tone bore no warmth. "It appears you are determined to be notorious."

She didn't bother answering. Nothing she said would convince them, she knew that much.

"I've had a report from Commodore Webb," he continued at last. "He informed me that you had been relieved of command by direct order, and your first mate appointed as acting captain. And he informed me that despite that, you and your ship's officers disobeyed direct orders."

Hollis lifted her chin. "We saved the fleet, Admiral. I hardly think that merits an apology."

He raised his eyebrows. "Captain Edwards saved the fleet, from what I hear. You were attempting to sow panic in the midst of an already fraught situation."

Hollis drew in a steadying breath.

She'd been right. They'd made up their minds already, and nothing she could say would dissuade them.

"If I'm to be court-martialled for it, I request that I stand for trial alone," she said, meeting his eye. "You can hardly fault my officers for following my orders."

"If I may?" The sharp voice made her look up, and for the first time, she focused on the figures standing behind Williams.

Admiral Judith Usher stepped forward. Williams stepped back quickly, allowing her to pass.

The Admiral was an imposing woman. Hollis had always admired her, looked up to her with the sort of hero worship that she'd learned, so recently, to despise.

She narrowed her eyes.

She was no longer a sailor before the mast. She was a goddamned captain, and she'd go to the devil before she let herself be intimidated. Not after everything she'd just come through.

"Captain Ives." The Admiral's voice was crisp. "I've heard the report by Commodore Webb that Vice-Admiral Williams has referred to." She paused. "However, I have also heard the report from First Mate Ainsley, of the *Consolation*, a report corroborated by Captain Edwards. It appears that the captain was alerted to the possibility of sabotage by her first mate, who in turn informs me that he was alerted to the possibility by yourself. That you had attempted to warn the Commodore, and your warnings had been ignored. That, in fact, your attempt to warn the Commodore was the very thing that led to your field-demotion."

Hollis stared at Admiral Usher, her mind trying to shape itself around this new information.

"It's true." Another man stepped forward, and it took Hollis a moment to recognize him as Lucian Ainsley, simply because of the sheer unbelievability of it. "I won't say Ives and I have ever been friends, but I won't take credit for someone else's actions."

Admiral Usher smiled, just a little. "Mate Ainsley has been arguing stridently for your reinstatement," she said. "I've heard the same from other captains. Your quick wit in finding the trap Mad Dog set, and your bravery in going after the *Sweet Jenny* in a damaged ship in order to lead her away from the stranded fleet, did not go unnoticed. Add to that the fact that you took back your captured ship, taking several Rosette officers prisoner in the process, and led the Rosette naval ships into a trap, after by all accounts taking Mad

Dog and the *Sweet Jenny*, and there are voices calling for not only your reinstatement, but for you to be awarded highest honours. So." She levelled her gaze at Hollis, a hint of amusement playing at the corners of her mouth. "Turn over the captured Rosette officers, along with Mad Dog and the *Sweet Jenny's* crew, and we shall ensure you and your crew are taken care of while we discuss the matter."

Hollis closed her eyes for a moment.

She felt dizzy, disoriented, and she wasn't entirely certain whether it was the Admiral's words, or the ache of her injuries.

This had been everything she'd dreamed of. Honoured by the Admiralty, lauded, recognized by the other captains as an equal— this was what her younger self had bled and sweat and worked herself to the bone for.

But she wasn't her younger self any longer.

She didn't regret wanting it—that had been all she'd known. But she wasn't that person anymore, desperate to prove herself, desperate for someone to recognize her humanity.

Foster had been right. She didn't need their recognition. And she refused to give up her humanity to earn it.

"No."

Admiral Usher frowned. "I'm sorry?"

"No." The word came out flat. "I will not be turning Captain Madox or her crew over to you, without your word that no harm will come to them."

The Admiral's frown deepened. "Captain Ives." There was something dangerous under her tone. "I hope you remember who you're addressing."

Hollis managed a small smile. "I have nothing but respect for you, Admiral Usher. I appreciate your promise to honour my officers and crew for their outstanding actions that went above and beyond the call of duty. But Captain Madox and her crew assisted my escape from the Rosette flagship, and saved my life and the lives of my crew on more than one occasion. And then, when my own navy threatened to shoot me down, after I had led the Rosette naval ships away from their planned attack on the Level and into a trap where they could be dealt with without endangering our own population, Captain Madox voluntarily surrendered herself and her ship to my control to save the lives of myself and my crew. In return, I promised her that neither she nor her crew would come to harm if I could prevent it." She met the Admiral's eye. "I understand that there may be nothing I can do to prevent it. But if you take Captain Madox and the crew of the *Sweet Jenny*, you'll step over my dead body to do it. Because I'll not see them harmed, not while I have breath to stop it."

Vice-Admiral Williams stepped forward, grabbing Hollis's arm roughly and dragging her up out of the hover chair. Pain burst through her body at the unexpected movement, and she gasped, black spots dancing before her eyes. "You forget who you're talking to," he snapped.

Hollis didn't have the breath to answer. From the corner of her fuzzy vision she saw both Foster and Emmett start forward, almost reflexively, before they were grabbed and restrained by their guards.

"Judging from the looks of you, while you have breath left in your body may not be long at all, Ives." William's tone was cold.

"Perhaps not."

Hollis's mind was spinning with pain, but she recognized Foster's voice, low and perfectly clear. "Perhaps you're willing to shoot down in cold blood the captain that saved your entire fleet, and then saved the Level. But I swear to you, if you do that, there is not a soul aboard the *Verity* who won't rebel. If you shoot Captain Ives, or drag her away and charge her with treason, you'll be dealing with a mutiny of every damn sailor and officer on the *Verity*. How will that look, Admirals? Shooting down the ship that saved the Level? Shooting down in cold blood, not only the hero of a captain, but every sailor and officer who sailed under her, right here on the Level's own docks?"

"That is enough! I'll have every one of you dragged in front of a court-martial," Williams snapped.

Something had pulled open inside of Hollis, she could feel the hot rush of it under the pain, and her muscles were going slack despite her best efforts, her vision blurring.

But she could see the defiant look on Foster's face, the grim determination in Emmett's posture.

"Ives," said Vice-Admiral Wright, stepping forward. "Consider what you're doing. You'd risk your life and your reputation for a pirate captain, who's dedicated her life to taking down naval ships and naval captains?"

"She gave herself up to save her crew," Hollis muttered. "I hardly think, as a naval officer, that I can condemn her for that. She, at least, has never broken her word to me."

The man holding her arm shook her, and she stumbled.

"Unhand my damned captain," Foster hissed.

Lucian stepped forward. "Vice-Admiral, I protest." His voice was tight. "She's clearly injured. Surely we can deal with this like civilized people."

"Enough!" Admiral Usher raised her hand. She turned to Hollis. "This insubordination will go on your record, Ives. I've done my best to protect you, but that can only go so far. This discussion is far from at an end." She paused. "But in the meantime, I will give you my word that neither Captain Madox nor her crew will be harmed. Will that satisfy you?"

"She's badly injured. She'll need care." Hollis forced her lips to form the words.

"As will you, it appears," said Admiral Usher wryly. "Very well. Will you allow me to send medics aboard the ship to transport Captain Madox to a hospital, on my word that neither she nor her crew will be harmed?"

"Yes." She was barely able to form the word. The pain danced through her body like a wildfire, too bright and brilliant and white-hot to allow her to focus on anything else.

"In the meantime, we will take the captured Rosette officers into custody, but you and your crew will be confined to your ship, as will the crew of the *Sweet Jenny*. You will receive what medical aid and provisions you require, but you will not leave the ship. Am I clear?"

"Acknowledged." The word slurred in her mouth.

Admiral Usher snorted and turned to Williams. "For God's sake, unhand her! She's hardly about to attack anyone."

"Aye, Admiral," the man said, reluctance clear in his tone. He let go his grip on Hollis's arm, and she staggered, swaying for a moment before catching her balance.

"Thank you, Admiral," she managed.

"For the love of God—" Foster's voice was strangled, but she only heard it from the corner of her mind. The blackness that had been creeping up the corners of her vision rushed over her in a wave, strong enough to block out even the pain.

She felt, distantly, her legs giving out, and then she felt nothing at all.

26

"Jenny!" Gracie twisted the handle to the barrack dorm room and pushed the door open with her hip.

Jenny was sitting bent over her desk, her long hair falling over the charts spread out in front of her, a frown of concentration creasing between her eyebrows.

For just a moment, Gracie almost couldn't breathe, looking at her.

Jenny Usher. The star she charted her course by. Her life and her soul together.

"Grace?" Jenny looked up, her face relaxing in that small, fond smile that she never gave to anyone but Gracie. "What's the occasion?" She gestured to the bottle and the two champagne glasses in Gracie's hands.

Gracie laughed and deposited them deftly on the table, then pulled Jenny up and into a lingering kiss. "I'm drunk on you Jenny, and I can't think of anything else," she said. She spun Jenny around, laughing, and after a moment Jenny was laughing too.

"You're absurd, Grace." Her voice was clearly trying to be stern, and failing badly.

Gracie hopped up onto the desk and pulled Jenny close, her hips fitting between Gracie's thighs, her body pressed against Gracie's. Gracie bent to kiss her again. "We graduate in a month, Jenny. A month from today, and we'll be given our assignments. We'll be back into space."

Jenny hummed in amusement. "You've never been one for sitting still, have you? I thought they'd throw you out more than once."

Gracie tipped back her head and laughed. "They'd not dare. Even if they wanted to, they'd not risk your wrath. You'd walk into hell and browbeat the devil if he tried to take me." She tilted Jenny's chin up, looking into her lover's eyes.

She could see herself reflected there, in the deep blue of them. And for just a moment, she was watching herself drown in the depths of Jenny's eyes.

Something odd twisted inside her, sharp and unexpected.

"Grace? What's wrong?" A flicker of concern crossed Jenny's expression, and Gracie pushed back the odd mood.

"It's nothing." She paused. "They're sending out the fleet tonight, with the new Starfire nav systems, my mam sent me a message. She's heard great things about the new technology. It'll bring the navy a decade forward at least." She grinned and slid off the desk, twisting the cork off the bottle deftly and pouring a thin stream of the pale, effervescent liquid into each of their cups. She handed one to Jenny and took one for herself. "This is the future, Jenny. In a month you and I both will be promoted. We'll be captains, I'm sure of it."

Jenny looked up at her, face still serious. "How are you so sure?"

Gracie winked at her. "A feeling. Good things are coming, my sweet Jenny. They'll be in need of captains soon enough, no doubt, and who better than the two of us? If there's anyone here with higher marks than yours, I haven't seen them, and I know it hurts the instructors' souls to give me good marks, as much as they're sick of me, but they can't in good faith help it. I study more for that than any other reason."

Jenny shook her head, laughing despite herself. "You're incorrigible."

Gracie leaned forward and planted a kiss on Jenny's cheek. "That's why you love me." She touched the edge of her goblet to Jenny's. "To the future, my love."

"To the future," said Jenny, and she tipped her head back and drank.

Gracie watched her.

It was true. She was drunk on Jenny Usher, in a heady, breathtaking way that no rum or champaign could match. She had been since she'd met Jenny, five and a half years ago—stumbling drunk, her head turned around and her life awash with colour.

She drained her glass in one swallow and set it down on the table, and Jenny rolled her eyes, laughing.

"God's sake, it's champaign, Grace, not rum! It's wasted on you."

Grace grinned and pulled her lover into her arms, taking the half-full glass from her hand and placing it on the table beside Gracie's empty one, and danced her across the floor of the small, cramped room until they were both laughing and breathless. "Soon, my love," she whispered, leaning in. "Soon it'll be you and me among the stars again. Captains the both of us, then admirals. I can feel it."

Jenny leaned closer, her body pressing against Gracie's, the shape of her, the way their bodies fit together, mingling with the brightness of the champaign to light a heady desire in Gracie's veins.

She adored this woman, loved her like she'd never loved anyone before. She would have laughed at the sentiment once, perhaps, but she knew without a doubt —Jenny was the only woman she'd ever love.

Jenny was her life, her soul, her compass, and in a few months they'd be back among the stars, captains of their own ships, and the world had never been more beautiful.

"Grace."

"Jenny?" she mumbled.

Her head throbbed, and for a brief, incongruous moment she wondered if she'd drunk too much in the taverns outside the Academy the night before.

But it wasn't that. It wasn't just her head that ached—her whole body hurt, a patchwork of sharp pain connected by a dull, nauseating ache that seeped through her muscles and settled in her bones.

Memories filtered back, the decades draping over her like a heavy blanket.

The Academy was years ago, so, so far away that it was hardly a memory, and she closed her eyes against the weight of the years, the decisions she'd made, the path her life had taken.

So much had changed since she'd been a bright young Academy student, preparing for her first command. So much hurt, and pain, and suffering. So much that could never be undone.

The burn on her arm, the impossible, mind-numbing pain of the brand searing its way through nerves and flesh. How she'd curled in around the pain, trying to hold on to consciousness, trying to force her body to move, to react, because if she was found she'd be hanged.

Stumbling through the streets of the Stacks, exhausted and bone-weary, pain flooding her body and dulling her mind—the raw stripes of the lash across her back, bruises from the prison guards' fists, the flesh of her palms torn raw from her escape, the burning torture of the brand on her forearm—and still, all of it a bare shadow to the pain branded across her soul.

"Grace. Can you hear me?"

She blinked her eyes open, the familiarity of the voice compelling the action without her conscious thought.

She was lying in a cot in a hospital—at least, it wasn't a ship's med bay. But it wasn't the hospital in the Stacks, she would have recognized that.

And beside her bed sat Jenny Usher.

For a moment, her pain-fogged mind tried to make sense of the scene, merging the picture of Judith as she was now, with her tired eyes and greying hair, with the Jenny she'd loved in the Academy, and who'd betrayed her to her death.

And then the world steadied, and it was Admiral Judith Usher seated at Gracie's bedside.

Gracie managed a small, ironic smile. "Jenny," she rasped. Her voice was hoarse, and the effort of speaking ached in her throat. "Didn't think to see you here. You plan on having me doctored up so you can parade me in front of the Level before you hang me?"

"You're not slated to be hanged." There was a note of something Gracie couldn't identify in Judith's voice. "Captain Ives and the entire crew of the *Verity* have threatened mutiny should I hang you, it appears. And with matters as they stand, Ives is something of a folk-hero. I can hardly afford to hang all of them."

It took a moment for the words to penetrate the haze of pain. When they did, Gracie raised her eyebrows. "Hollis Ives threatened mutiny?"

"If I didn't give my word that you and your crew would be unharmed." There was a wry note to Judith's words.

Gracie huffed a quiet laugh, which turned into a cough that left her doubled over in pain.

Judith turned, ringing a bell by the door. When a doctor appeared a few moments later, she snapped, "What kind of hospital is this? This woman is clearly in pain."

"I'm sorry, Admiral," the man said, not meeting Judith's eyes. He stepped over to the bed. "Patient. What's your pain level at the moment?" His voice had gone cold and hard.

"God's sake, she can't answer you. That should tell you everything you need to know." Judith's voice was sharp and imperious. "We are a civilized society, doctor. Whether or not you admire your patients, you have a duty to keep them from pain as much as you're able, do you not?"

"I'm sorry, Admiral," he muttered again. His tone was resentful, but he turned back to Gracie. "I'm going to increase the painkiller, that should help." Gracie closed her eyes as he fiddled with something above her head, then stepped away. "There you are, Admiral," he said. "She should be more comfortable in a moment."

"For your sake, I hope so." Judith's voice was frigid, and Gracie had to hold herself back from laughing at the sheer incongruity of it.

The painkiller did its work quickly. She could almost feel it flowing through her veins through the needle in her arm. Her body still ached, but the pain was more distant than it had been, and its absence left her more clear-headed than she'd felt in a while.

"Well," she said at last, turning her head on her pillow to look at Judith.

The sight of the woman still sent a jolt of something through her body—she'd thought, once, that it was anger. But perhaps she'd been wrong. Perhaps, this whole time, it had been hurt, pain masquerading as fury to make itself more bearable.

"Hollis Ives hasn't stopped surprising me, it seems." She paused, watching Judith. "Ain't going to say I agree with the lass, but your navy don't deserve her. You don't deserve her, Judith." Her voice was quiet, but hard as steel.

"I'm not sure what you mean." Judith said stiffly.

Gracie smiled, her expression dangerous. Her heart was pounding, her chest tight with a mix of pain and fury. "You ordered the ships to fire on her, didn't you? You ordered them not to accept the *Verity's* broadcasts."

She could tell by the way Judith's posture stiffened that her words had hit home.

"She took the *Verity* after you, damaged and with no backup," Judith said at last, her words distant. "I couldn't risk the possibility that you'd taken the ship."

Gracie smiled a little broader. "Couldn't risk that I'd taken the ship, could you? Figure you could have found that out easily enough if you'd instructed them to accept the broadcasts. I have some skills, I suppose, but imitating your Captain Ives ain't one of them." She shifted a little, turning her body towards Judith. "That wasn't the reason, was it, Jenny? You were afraid I'd turned her, same way as I turned Silas Hunt. You were afraid that she'd listen to what I had to say, against you and against the navy. You were afraid of what she'd tell them, weren't you? And you were willing to shoot her down, along with her three-hundred-and-fifty-crewed ship, to prevent that."

Judith closed her eyes. She was quiet for a long time. "Did you tell her?" she asked at last.

Gracie watched her for a moment, then lay back on the pillow, suddenly weary. "No. I should have. But she's a smart lass. She'll figure it out herself soon enough."

"I suppose she will," said Judith softly.

"She's as bull-headed as you and I ever were, and clever as hell, and she don't know the meaning of the word fear," said Gracie. "But you were wrong about her, Jenny. Never once considered turning on the navy, not even when your ships were preparing to fire on her, on your orders. She shot back in self-defense only. But you'd have killed her for it anyway."

"I'm running a war, Grace." Judith's voice was sharp with sudden anger. "For all your talk of justice for the Stacks and the pirates— how much justice will they have, do you think, if the Rosette navy firebombs our ships? If the Level burns, the Stacks burns with it, and from the looks of it, you've seen what the Rosette System thinks of pirates. You may not agree with me, but I'm the only one right now with the power to drag Parliament along with me, equip our ships and our crews so they're not shot down with every soul aboard, over and over and over again. What did you want me to do?"

Gracie watched her.

She could still see hints of the old Jenny there, even after the years and the heartbreak.

"Couldn't help yourself, could you?" she asked quietly. "Even after all this time. You'd betray them as trust you for the Level, sacrifice them without a second thought."

Judith narrowed her eyes. "That, at least, isn't true." Her voice was hard, sharp with pain. "Everything I've done for the Level I did because I felt it the only option. But don't insult me by saying I never gave it a thought. I put my career on the line for Hollis Ives, more than once. I'd have protected her if I thought I could without sacrificing the Level. I had to weigh her life and the lives of one ship's crew against the possibility of hamstringing our navy at a critical moment. But never once did I make a decision without feeling every bit of the weight of it."

"Perhaps," said Gracie. "Perhaps you did feel the weight of it. But you did it anyway."

They were silent again, for a long while.

At last, Judith said, "The doctors have told me you'll recover. It was touch and go for a bit, but they say you'll recover, without permanent damage."

Gracie nodded, still watching Judith. "And after that?" she asked softly.

Judith leaned forward. "That's why I came." She paused. "Gracie. Join us. This is war, and we need people with strategy and tactics, and I'm only one woman. They want to hang you, every last one in the Admiralty and the Naval High Command, but if I can tell them that you and I put aside our differences for the war, they'll accept it.

They'll have no choice—every one of them knows how brilliant you are. And we need you." She shook her head. "You don't have to forgive me, Grace. You can hate me until the day I die. But we need you. The Level and the Stacks and your precious pirate crews, all of them will be sacrificed if we lose this war."

Gracie closed her eyes, the burning, white-hot anger enough that for a moment, she thought it might consume her.

"Hang me, then, Jenny," she said at last, when she'd regained control enough to speak. "Hang me in front of the damned Level, and hang your Captain Ives and her crew with me. Or if you don't have the stomach for that, let me go. But work with the navy that betrayed me? Work with the Level? That, I won't do."

"Not even to save your own damn stubborn life?" Judith snapped. "There's not another way out for you. I've gone through every last option, there's no other way I keep you alive."

"Then kill me," Gracie spat. She drew in a long breath through her nose, fighting for calm. "Kill me, Jenny, and let my ghost haunt you. Because I'll die before I do this."

Judith closed her eyes, and even through the hot, burning anger, Gracie could read her the way she'd always been able to, see her bracing herself for whatever she'd say next.

Jenny had always lived and breathed for the Level. She'd always had that iron core to her, bright and hard and ruthless, that part of her that would never bend, never break, never compromise.

And Gracie's mistake had been that she'd lived and breathed for Jenny.

"You're willing to die for this, Grace." Judith's voice was soft, but Gracie could hear the pain in it. And under the pain, that same bright, uncompromising ruthlessness. "You're willing to let me hang you. But your crew?"

Gracie sucked in a quick breath.

"Don't worry, I won't hang them myself. I can't, without risking a mutiny of the *Verity's* officers and crew. But Silas Hunt will be tried for treason. There's nothing I can do to prevent that. His family, too, an aunt and uncle, some cousins—the youngest of them eleven or twelve, I believe. Just old enough to think about starting in the navy, but they'll likely hang along with him. It won't be in my hands, but you know how these things go—how could they not have known? How could they not have seen what was happening? Temple, too, he has family on the Level. Not an important enough man for the authorities to track them down before, but now? A treason charge for him, and they'll be swept up in it. And Ari. She won't hang, her family's far too important. No, I think the authorities will send her back to them, keep it hush-hush. She'll be kept under lock and key, of course, but she'll be back with her family. A touching reunion, no doubt."

Gracie closed her eyes, too weary, suddenly, to keep them open. "Please, Jenny."

The rough hospital blankets brushed against the old brand-scar as Gracie eased herself back on the cot, the damaged nerves sending a jolt of pain up her arm, sickening and soul-deep. "If you ever loved me, don't ask this of me. Please."

Her whole body hurt, the pain of the torture and the pain of the memories and the pain of seeing Jenny again, after all these years, coiling together as if it would choke her.

She was so tired. She was so damn tired, and she wasn't sure if the nausea rising in her stomach was from the pain or the exhaustion or from the crushing weight of despair.

"What's your choice?" Judith's voice was implacable.

She'd known. Deep down, through the torture and the flight and the desperate fight for survival, she'd known that the Jenny she'd loved was lost to her forever.

Or perhaps this was always who Jenny had been. Perhaps Gracie'd known that the whole time. Perhaps she'd loved her anyway, and dammed herself for it, walked into hell with her eyes wide open.

She'd refused to give Jenny up to the Rosette commodore, and she'd not regretted that, even during the torture. But it hadn't been only herself she'd sacrificed, in the end, although she'd always meant it to be. She'd dragged her crew along with her. They were here because of her. Because she still loved Jenny Usher, after everything they'd both done.

And in payment, Jenny had offered to destroy them.

As long as Jenny lived, her crew was in danger. And so Gracie would see her die for it.

She couldn't, anymore, pretend she'd ever stop loving Jenny. And she couldn't allow herself, ever again, another spark of mercy, or sympathy, or forgiveness.

"Damn your eyes." Her voice came out flat and emotionless.

"What's your choice, Grace?" Judith's words were hard and merciless and sharp as steel.

Gracie opened her eyes again, watching Judith. "I'd have walked through hell for you, Jenny," she said quietly. "I thought, once, you'd do the same for me. No, I won't sacrifice my crew. You know me well enough to know that. I'll not let you have them. I'll not let you send my Ari back to a family as never deserved her, I'll not let you put the death of their families on Sil's or Temple's conscience. That, I'll not do. They're mine, Judith. Your Level took everything else from me, but that, you can't have. I'll work with you, then, help you win your war, and you'll see to it that my crew is protected."

She pushed herself up on one elbow, ignoring the rush of pain, strong enough to make her vision waver. "And may God have mercy on your soul, Jenny Usher."

27

Hollis

"I'm sorry, Admiral, but I'm afraid I can't allow you to enter."

Archibald's words filtered through Hollis's consciousness, and she blinked her eyes open.

It had been three days. Three days that she'd been confined to her cot on the med bay, unable to lift so much as a finger. Archibald would have forbidden her from blinking her eyes, if he could have managed it.

Whatever had broken open inside her at Vice-Admiral William's rough treatment had frightened him, more than he wanted to let on. But he'd told her the day before, grudgingly, that there was a strong chance she'd live through it, now that she was actually getting some rest.

She'd spent most of the time since she'd been brought back to the *Verity* sleeping. She hadn't realized how exhausted her body had been until she'd collapsed. Now, with the sluggish lethargy induced by the pain and the lingering fever and the fact that, even if she had been on her feet, there would have been nothing she could do, she wasn't sure she'd ever leave her cot again. She seemed to exist in a dreamlike state, where nothing mattered and she could do nothing to change things, and, with the delirium from her injuries and the hazy, distant indifference that the painkillers induced, she found it hard to care.

A voice answered Archibald, sharp and crisp, and for a moment, Hollis's mind fumbled over the familiarity of it.

Then her eyes snapped open, and she sucked in a sharp breath.

Admiral Usher.

"I do apologize, Admiral. But the last time I allowed my patient to speak with you, you returned her to me half-dead, with internal bleeding I wasn't sure we'd be in time to staunch even with an emergency operation. So I'm certain you understand my hesitation." Archibald's voice was hard as steel, and Hollis almost winced at the irony dripping from it.

"Your devotion to your duty, and to your captain, does you credit, Officer Smyth." There was a wry tone to the Admiral's words. "However, I must insist."

She could imagine Archibald narrowing his eyes. "Captain Ives is —"

He'd find himself with a charge of insubordination at this rate.

"Officer Smyth," Hollis called, bracing herself against the pain. "A moment, if you would?"

Archibald made his terse excuse to the Admiral, and crossed over to stand by her cot. "Captain," he said in a low voice. "I don't want that woman or her ilk anywhere near you until we know what she wants with you. You saw what happened last time."

Hollis managed a tired smile. "I hardly think she's here to drag me from my bed, Smyth. And I won't have you face a court-martial on my account. Let her in, if you please."

It was entirely possible that they'd all face a court-martial. Their status at the moment was far from certain, and she knew well enough that the Admiral had the ammunition to charge all of them with attempted mutiny, if she had the wish to.

Archibald narrowed his eyes at her, but at last, grudgingly, he nodded. "Aye, Captain. If you're certain."

A few moments later, Admiral Judith Usher stepped into the med bay, making her way through the cots towards Hollis.

Hollis made no attempt to sit up.

She couldn't have done it even if she'd wanted to. And after everything that had happened over the past weeks—she was no longer sure she wanted to.

The Admiral didn't seem to expect it, at any rate. She pulled up a chair and took a seat beside Hollis's cot, and for a moment, the two of them sat in silence. The Admiral's face was drawn, and more weary than Hollis remembered seeing it.

"Captain Ives," said the woman at last. "I apologize for your treatment when you came to make your report. Williams has been disciplined for his actions."

Hollis raised her eyebrows.

She wasn't sure if it was the painkillers, or simply the fact that she couldn't stand the sickening, stifling make-believe of it all, but she found, suddenly, that she had no desire to pretend any longer.

Commodore Webb had stripped her of her command, naval ships had fired on her, ignored her broadcasts and tried to bring down her ship, she and her officers and crew had been treated like criminals, and she was laying on this cot because one of the vice-admirals had broken her injury open when she'd obeyed orders to present herself before them, taking out his anger on her like a petulant child.

"I suppose I'm meant to thank you," she said at last. "Forgive me if I ask to wait until I hear the fate of myself and my crew first."

The hint of a smile flickered across the Admiral's face. "I don't expect thanks. His behaviour was unacceptable by any measure." She paused. "As far as the fate of yourself and your crew—" She shook her head, casting a meaningful glance in Archibald's direction. "It appears, Captain, that your crew has bound their fate to yours."

The Admiral's words shot a sharp jolt of panic through Hollis's stomach. "Admiral," she said quickly. "I must insist that any punishment—"

Admiral Usher held up a hand. "Punishment? I was unaware that was what we were discussing."

Hollis fell silent.

"I can hardly punish the captain who saved the fleet, and then saved the Level. No, Ives, I had come, in fact, to inform you that the Naval High Command has agreed to bestow a medal of service on you for exceptional valour in an enemy engagement."

Hollis stared, unable, for a moment, to process the Admiral's words.

"Admiral," she began, then stopped.

"Yes, Captain Ives?" There was still that wryness in the Admiral's tone.

Hollis closed her eyes a moment.

The sheer unexpectedness of it curdled in her stomach, the disorientation almost nauseating.

"My crew, as well," she said at last, opening her eyes. Her voice was hard. "Every one of my officers and crew risked their lives. They deserve honours more than I do."

Again, the Admiral smiled. "I thought you might say that. While we can't bestow medals of service on every sailor before the mast, I believe mates Price and Greene, at least, should be similarly recognized. The remainder of your officers and crew will receive honours as well, and a bounty payment for each of the Rosette ships that were taken down in the course of the action. The High Command has agreed that a similar bounty will be paid to the families of those on the *Verity* who died during the engagement."

Again, Hollis stared.

The Admiral was joking, surely. In a moment her expression would go cold, and she'd explain what the Naval High Command intended …

But she didn't, just watched Hollis with that small smile playing on her lips.

"Mad Dog—" Hollis began at last.

"Is alive and well, and predicted to make a full recovery," said the Admiral brusquely. "I just came from speaking with her. She has agreed to work with us for the duration of the war, and in exchange, she and her crew will receive a full pardon."

Hollis was still staring.

But … She remembered the expression on Gracie's face as she'd watched her crew.

She'd told Hollis to trade her to the Level, to save her crew. What was it Silas and Ari were always saying? That Gracie'd not cut a crewmate's line to save herself?

Hollis had seen proof enough of that.

For them, Hollis had no doubt she'd do it. To save her crew, she'd work with the Level.

She wasn't sure why the thought made her sick.

At last, the Admiral stood. "Thank you, Captain Ives," she said. "I didn't want you to worry any longer than you had to. You are, of course, granted shore leave until your chief medical officer pronounces you fully recovered—I shall discuss the details with him, whether it would be prudent to leave you where you are or transfer you to a hospital—"

"I'd prefer to stay on my ship, if it's all the same to you," Hollis broke in.

Admiral Usher smiled again, that small, wry smile. "Of course. I'll see what I can do. While we are working out details, I think it best that you and your crew remain on your ship in any case." She turned, and her face went serious. "I thank you, Ives. For myself, and for the Level. You've done us a great service."

She turned and strode off, leaving Hollis staring after her.

Foster came to find her shortly after. "Captain?" Their voice was still cut with that same strain she'd heard in it on the docks. It hadn't really gone away since then, she'd seen it in their face and posture every time they looked at her.

She sighed. "Sit down, Price. The Admiral didn't try to kill me in my sleep."

Foster, at least, looked much better—the forced confinement wouldn't necessarily have meant they'd catch up on their rest, but Archibald had been in such a foul mood after her injury that not a one of them had dared cross him, and as a result, Foster and Emmett had been sleeping almost as much as she had.

Foster hesitated, then pulled out a seat, the gesture more forceful than necessary. "So," they said at last. "What's the verdict? Are they going to hang the lot of us?"

Hollis shook her head slowly. "No. We're to receive honours, it appears—you and I and Greene are to be awarded medals of service, and the officers and crew will receive honours and a bounty for each Rosette ship taken in the battle."

Foster stared at her for a moment. Then they cursed. "What the hell is the Admiral playing at?"

Hollis managed a small smile. "Mad Dog has agreed to work with the navy, it appears. For the duration of the war, and in exchange, she and her crew will receive a full pardon."

Foster was still watching her, their forehead creased in a frown.

They were slowly gaining back their usual equanimity, but she'd seen more emotion from them in the past few days than she had since she'd met them. Or maybe she was just getting used to reading their expressions.

"I don't know," she said at last, quietly. "I don't know what they're playing at. And I don't know what they did to convince Mad Dog to work with them." She shrugged a little. "But … it appears that, whatever their game, they still need us."

Foster closed their eyes a moment, and there was still that deep weariness in their expression. "We're going to war," they said quietly. "Of course they need us." They glanced up. "They need you, Captain Ives. They need the loyalty of captains like you, because that's how they convince sailors to die for them. Find a captain whose crew will follow them anywhere, and then send them into battle."

Hollis smiled, just a little, and reached out, taking their arm. "I'm a captain in the navy, Price. I made my choice when I signed up. And we can hardly let the Rosette System take down our ships without losing more good sailors than I can countenance." She caught Foster's eye. "Mad Dog agreed to work with the Level to save her crew. I'll do the same. Whatever this game the Naval High Command is playing, you and I are part of it now. As is the *Verity*, as is our crew. By the grace of God they decided to grant us honours rather than hang us, and I'll take every last one of those honours, if it means my sailors get some recompense for what they did. I'll fight this war. But I'll not lead my sailors blindly into danger again, not on the Admiralty's word."

The two of them were quiet for a few moments.

"A medal of service," said Foster at last, the ghost of a smile on their lips. "Who would have thought it?"

Hollis smiled back. "A captain from the Stacks, and a mate from the resource planets." She shook her head.

"The navy doesn't deserve you, Captain." Foster's voice was wry.

"No more than it deserves you." Hollis paused. "Price. I'm not, perhaps the captain you deserve, either. I only wish to say—"

"God's sake, Captain," Foster snapped. "I don't know another captain in the navy who could have done what you've done. Who would have had the courage and the audacity and the sheer, bullheaded stubbornness to try." They broke off, pulling in a long breath. "You're not perfect, Captain Ives," they finished at last. "Perhaps you've made mistakes. But I can't think of anyone I'd rather serve under." They gave her a small smile. "I told you, your crew would die for you. I include myself in that number."

She looked back at them for a moment, her throat suddenly too thick for her to speak.

"Well, Price," she said at last. "In that case, I shall do my best to ensure you do not have occasion to."

Price gave her one of their rare, quick, genuine smiles. "Aye, Captain." They glanced around. "So. War it is, then."

"War it is."

War. The best—sometimes the only—way for a sailor before the mast to gain a promotion. Opportunities for advancement, glory, bounty money.

And as the price of it, ships lost, sailors shot down, killed by cutlasses or pressure loss or ripped apart by ghosts. She'd seen enough of the ugliness of it to take no pleasure in the thought.

"We're naval officers, Price," she said, half to herself. "We'll serve where we're told."

Foster nodded, their expression serious.

She turned her head on her pillow. "We'll serve where we're told, Price, follow orders. We're at war, and we can hardly do less. But I'm serving the navy to protect my crew. Not the other way around."

Foster watched her for a moment, then gave her another of their quick smiles, like the sun appearing through clouds for just a moment—there, then gone. "Aye, Captain," they said.

28

Silas paced back and forth across the deck of the *Sweet Jenny.*

Ari looked up from where she was sitting leaned back against the wall of the ship, her energy pistol disassembled in front of her, and cocked an eyebrow at him, but she didn't say anything.

That was the worst of it—how none of them said anything. He could pace, because the restless energy prickling under his skin made sitting still unbearable, and instead of snapping at him or ordering him to for God's sake sit still, they just moved out of the way to make room for him and went back to whatever they were doing.

The freedom of it was disorienting, and almost uncomfortable.

They'd heard no word from Gracie. That was probably good news, honestly—they'd likely have been told if she'd died. But the uncertainty of it set his teeth on edge.

It was affecting all of them. Ari was much more quiet than was her wont, her face wan and pale, and Vee's mood had been so foul they'd all done their best to stay out of her way.

Temple, at least, was doing better. He was sitting up in his cot now, and he could speak without coughing, although he still tired far too easily. But his face was lined with worry, and there was a tension to his posture that hadn't gone away since the Level medics had carried Gracie away in a stretcher.

Silas sighed, and paced back across the deck, the sound of his boots against the hard metal loud in the quiet.

"You need something to do, lad?" Freddie called through his comm line. "Figure I could find some repairs here that'd keep your hands busy for a bit."

He sighed and tapped his comm line. "Aye, Freddie. I'll be down in a minute."

The last few days had been an exhausting buzz of activity. They didn't have all the spare parts Freddie needed, although the *Verity's* crew had been good enough to allow them free range of their supplies. But they'd worked through the basic repairs, everything they could do without a dry-dock and a supply of specialty parts.

He glanced over the deck one last time, and turned to head down to the engine room.

There was a sharp tap on the gangplank, the sound loud enough to startle him.

He glanced over at Ari, but she only shrugged. There was a tension in her posture, though, that told him her mind had jumped to the same possibility his had: Someone from the Level.

Someone with news, good or bad.

At this point he wasn't certain he cared which, as long as there was actual news.

He crossed cautiously over to the gangplank and tapped the comm line through to outside. "Hello?"

"This is Officer Morton, paging the crew of the *Sweet Jenny*," a voice from outside snapped, tone imperious.

"This is Silas, from the *Sweet Jenny*," he responded. "What do you want?"

"Please lower the gangplank. We'd like to speak to the *Sweet Jenny's* first mate."

He glanced back at the others. They'd frozen where they were on the deck, but Ari's hand was at the pistol at her belt, and Toothpick's fingers were wrapped around his cutlass.

"Let them in, lad," Toothpick said quietly. "May as well see what they want."

Silas nodded, drawing in a quick, steadying breath, and tapped the controls to lower the gangplank.

He stepped back, hand going to his own weapon as the gangplank creaked and groaned, settling on the deck below. But when he looked down it, the naval officers standing below were unarmed.

He let his hand relax.

"Permission to board?" the woman who appeared to be in charge snapped.

He glanced at Toothpick, who stepped forward. "Permission granted," the man said. He hadn't let go his grip on his cutlass, and he was taking no pains to hide the fact from the naval officers below.

Morton hesitated the barest second, but then stepped up the gangplank and made her way on board, the other officers trailing her.

"What did you have to say to us that couldn't have been said through a ship's comm?" Toothpick's voice was mild, but Silas could hear the danger under it.

The woman met his gaze without flinching. "I thought you'd appreciate hearing the news in person."

Silas's stomach dropped, sharp panic flickering through his brain.

"What news?" Ari had stepped forward as well, her voice hard.

The naval officer smiled. "Your captain is predicted to make a full recovery.”

Silas closed his eyes against the sudden wash of desperate relief.

The naval officer was still speaking. “She’s been granted a full pardon, as have each one of you, in consideration of her agreement to assist the navy in the war effort.”

Silas frowned, glancing quickly over at Ari.

She looked as puzzled as he felt.

“Assist the navy?” Toothpick’s voice had gone even softer, the danger in it more pronounced. “And why, pray tell, would we do something like that?”

The officer pulled up a note to hover over her comm, and flicked it towards him with a quick motion of her fingers. “Your captain’s orders, I’m afraid.”

Toothpick studied the note that had come to hover over his wrist comm for a few minutes, his forehead creased. “That’s Gracie’s note, true enough,” he said at last, looking up. “But I’d like to know what you threatened her with to get her to agree to it.”

The naval woman scoffed. “I hardly think it matters, does it? She’ll not hang, which is more than she deserves, and nor will the rest of you. You have your orders. I’d advise you take them and be grateful.” She glanced down at her own wrist comm. “The Naval High Command is working out the details. We can hardly let the *Sweet Jenny* and her crew out on the docks of the Level without causing a mass panic. But you’ll be released soon enough on recognizance, and on your captain’s sworn word.” She turned, and a few moments later, she and the other naval officers were gone back down the gangplank.

Silas stared after her.

His hands were clenched into fists, his palms damp with sweat. He could hear, vaguely, behind him, the others talking in low voices, but he couldn't focus on their words.

Back to the navy.

Back to the place he'd only just escaped from, back to the place he'd finally, finally realized had lied to him his whole life, and he was still reeling at how deep the lies had gone.

And Gracie was sending him back.

There was a hand on his shoulder, and he spun to find Ari standing beside him. Her face was still pale, cut with a grim determination, but there was sympathy there, too.

She gestured with her head, and he followed her back to the crew quarters.

They were empty, thank God, and he sank down into his hammock, dropping his head into his hands and closing his eyes.

He felt the hammock shift as Ari sat beside him, then the warmth of her body next to his.

"What the hell is Gracie doing?" he asked quietly, without opening his eyes.

Ari snorted. "Saving our lives, most likely. You know damn well that the navy'd never have let us go, Hollis Ives and her heroism be damned."

Mate Greene, his face pale with fury, had explained in curt tones what had happened on the docks three days previous. It had been the first time Silas had seen even the barest hint of respect in Ari's face when she spoke Hollis's name.

He drew in a long breath, not opening his eyes. "I can't do this, Ari." His voice was dull and toneless. "I swore to Gracie I'd follow her to hell and back, but I can't do this."

Ari was silent a moment. When she spoke again, her words were quiet. "Sil. Don't figure I can tell you what you can and can't do. Never served in the navy, but hell, I've seen the way they messed with your head." She snorted. "Only have to look at Ives to know the navy messes with peoples' heads, if you had questions." She sobered, putting a hand on his arm and turning him to face her.

Reluctantly, he opened his eyes. She was watching him, her face serious, her gaze searching.

"But you ain't the person you were back in the navy, are you, Sil? You saved Gracie's life, and mine, when everything you'd been taught said you shouldn't. You ain't one to take orders without question, not anymore. You don't believe their damn lies anymore."

He searched her face for a long moment. At last, he nodded. "You're right, Ari," he said quietly. "You're right. I don't." He stood abruptly, running his hand through his hair, then blew out a long breath, turning to her. "I'll go along with this, if that's what Gracie orders. But I'll not go against my own conscience. If the navy wants to take me, it'll have that, too—I won't lie for them any longer."

Ari studied him, then nodded, standing. "Figure you won't, Sil. And figure I won't either." She gave him a small smile. "Naval sailors before the mast, then, are we?"

He smiled back, despite himself. "Officers, at the least. If they have the *Sweet Jenny's* crew, they won't hide us below decks."

She grinned. "Figure that might not be all bad. I could get used to giving orders to naval sailors as want me dead." She winked at him.

Her face was still pale and drawn with strain, and he could see, under her grin, the tight ache of exhaustion and worry that she'd been carrying since they'd found Gracie lying in the brig of the *Chasseuse* in a pool of her own blood.

But she was Ari. She didn't need his sympathy, and she didn't need his pity. She'd spit the navy's condescension back in its face and laugh.

For just a moment, looking into her blue eyes, he had the sudden, unbearable urge to lean in closer …

He crushed the impulse ruthlessly, and managed a smile.

Ari would survive this, like Gracie had survived this. Like he'd survive it.

He was going back to the navy. But this time, it would be as his own man, not theirs.

He turned to Ari. "Well. Shall we go back on deck? I expect they'll let us see Gracie soon, and we don't want to miss that."

She gave him a small smile of her own, and the two of them headed back on deck.

29

Judith

"Officer Candidate Usher. A moment, if you please."

Judith glanced up sharply. The man who stood in front of her was a stranger, but she recognized him instantly. "Admiral Vernon?"

He nodded. "I apologize for startling you." He paused, and took her arm, drawing her around the corner of the Academy classroom she'd stepped out of.

She followed without protest. Her heart was pounding far too quickly, as if somehow she'd known, even then, that whatever this was, it would change the trajectory of her entire life.

"Usher," he said, once they were alone. "I … am sorry to be the one to bring the news. But I thought you'd best hear it from me, before you found it out on your own."

"What news?" The words seemed to stick to her tongue, her mouth dry with dread.

"The Starfire fleet," he began, and then fell silent.

She stared at him. "What about the Starfire fleet?" she asked at last, impatience forcing the words out.

He told her.

When he'd finished, she leaned back against the wall of the building, trying to make the words he'd said make sense.

The horror of it was so thick she wasn't sure her legs would support her.

"All of them?" Her voice came out in a strange whisper. "The sailors? Officers? Captains? All of them dead?"

He nodded. There was something like sympathy in his gaze.

"And why are you telling me this?" she asked, when he didn't speak.

She knew already. There was something sharp and frightened inside her that told her—there was only one reason he'd have come to seek her out specifically. Only one person whose family name was tied to Starfire, one person who the Admiral would have come to see over. But she had to hear it from him, she wouldn't believe it otherwise.

"Your ... lover. Grace Madox."

Even though she'd halfway guessed it was coming, his words felt like a punch to her gut.

"We have intelligence that this was intentional, that her parents were the ones who caused the disaster," he said in a low voice, as if he, too, didn't want to believe the words he was saying. "We need to know whether Officer Candidate Madox knew about their treason, and did nothing to stop it."

Judith closed her eyes. Her whole body felt weak, her head spinning with the sheer horror of everything she'd heard.

This couldn't be real. It had to be a dream, a nightmare. She'd open her eyes, and she'd be in her bed in the dorm room, Grace lying beside her, stroking her hair, whispering something soothing in her ear.

Grace. What she must be feeling right now, if she'd heard ...

She should be with Grace. She shouldn't be here, listening to some admiral, she should be with Grace.

But she couldn't move her feet, couldn't make herself straighten. That's how she knew it was a dream, she couldn't go to Grace, even though she was desperate to.

But no matter how long she kept her eyes closed, she could still feel the cold bite of the Level's early spring air on her face, smell the mist from the ports, brushing harsh and astringent against her senses, too real and clear for a dream.

"Her parents are guilty? Are you sure of it?" she asked at last, without opening her eyes. "Could there have been a mistake?"

"We've found conclusive evidence, I'm afraid. Believe me, Officer Candidate Usher, I was as upset by the news as you are. The Vice-Admirals Madox are personal friends of mine. But ..." He paused. "But for the safety of the Level, the integrity of the navy itself, we cannot afford to let personal considerations shape our response. So again, I ask you—do you have any information that Officer Candidate Madox may have been involved?"

Judith didn't open her eyes. She wasn't certain she could, without the hot tears gathering behind them spilling out across her cheeks.

It wasn't possible. Grace would never do something like that. Grace would never betray the navy.

Would she?

"I'd die for you, Jenny. I'd burn the world for you, and walk through the flames if you asked it." *Grace's voice in her memory sent a cold shiver through her that she couldn't entirely repress.*

Grace, the night before, her eyes sparkling with excitement. "Good things are coming, my sweet Jenny. They'll be in need of captains soon enough, no doubt, and who better than the two of us?"

The look on Grace's face that day in her first mate's cabin on shipboard, her hand cupping Judith's face. "If the navy asks me to give up those who trust me ... the navy can go to damnation."

Grace wouldn't have planned a horror like that, certainly. But if her parents had? If they'd told her, and she'd known, if they'd given her a reason that had made sense to her—would she have stopped it? Would she have spoken against it, even if she'd known?

"I ... don't know," she said at last, dully, opening her eyes. "She never spoke of it."

The admiral was watching her, his eyes sharp. "I don't expect you to know for certain," he said at last. "But you're the closest person to her. She'd not have been able to hide something like this completely." He paused. "She's been arrested," he continued. "We had enough evidence to arrest her, and to try her. But we need witnesses, for and against. And Officer Candidate Usher? I believe you could give the tribunal an insight into what your lover may have known."

Judith stared past him, her gaze blank, eyes unseeing.

"Thousands of sailors dead, Usher. Officers, captains, sailors before the mast, and ships blown to shreds. This could destroy the navy. If it's not rooted out, more people will die. I understand your hesitation. But you must decide where your loyalties lie—to a fellow officer candidate, or to the navy itself?"

For a long moment, Judith didn't answer.

"I'd die for you, Jenny. I'd burn the world for you."

Thousands of bodies, shattered and crumpled in death, strewn across space.

Grace.

Grace, the way her gaze softened when Judith stepped into the room, the way she threw her head back to laugh, the callouses on her fingers. The warmth of her, the naked vulnerability of her when they were alone, the adoration in her eyes. She'd never hurt Judith, she'd die before she did that.

The dead sailors, their broken ships spread around them in a starburst of destruction.

"I'd burn the world for you."

Grace.

Grace, Grace, Grace, the woman who had become her whole life, her whole heart, her whole soul.

"If the navy asks me to give up those who trust me ... the navy can go to damnation."

Her own voice, weeks earlier, across the barrack dorm. "I will always side with the navy, Grace. I believe in it. Even if it's wrong sometimes, even if there's corruption and cronyism, I will side with the navy, because it's the best chance we have to protect the people who look to us for safety. You can disagree if you choose, but you know me, Grace. You know I'll always choose what I believe is right."

Judith looked up at last, her gaze still distant. She wasn't sure, exactly, if she was seeing what was in front of her, or if she was seeing some vision of what would come after this. If anything came after this. If the world could continue, if her heart could continue to beat after this.

"I'll testify of what I know," she said quietly. "I won't lie. But I'll tell what I know, for whatever it's worth."

She hadn't known that words could cut you open on their way out of your mouth, like a fishhook being dragged from inside you, slicing you to ribbons as it came free.

She hadn't been sure she could continue to breathe, after she'd said it.

But she wouldn't take it back. Even then, she'd known in her soul that the one thing deeper than Grace, the one thing that was so much part of her that she couldn't give it up, was this: her duty to the navy.

Admiral Vernon was still studying her. "Very good, Usher," he said at last. "I and the navy thank you for your loyalty."

She hardly heard him.

She felt like she was bleeding out.

Maybe she was. Maybe the words she'd spoken had killed some vital part of her, broken it off and cut it open and left it bleeding and dying.

She straightened. "I'll do my duty, Admiral," she said quietly. "Thank you for informing me."

She turned and made her way back to her empty dorm, too numb to feel anything at all.

Judith looked up at the tap on her office door, startled out of her memories.

The distraction was a relief, even though she guessed well enough what it would prove to be.

"Come in," she called, and Vice-Admiral Edwin Wright stepped inside.

His face was cut with concern, his expression grave. "Admiral Usher. I just received the news." He paused. "You'd pardon Mad Dog?"

Judith took a deep breath. "Captain Madox is willing to work with the Naval High Command on our war plans, in exchange for a pardon for herself and her crew." She steeled herself against the memory. Against the sharpness of the betrayal in Gracie's eyes.

Edwin stared at her a moment, then sank into a seat.

Judith sighed. "Whatever else can be said of her, she's a brilliant strategist. We need every good person we can find—the war's begun, and it's caught us flat-footed, despite all my efforts. We avoided disaster this time by sheer luck, but the Rosette System won't have based all their strategy on that one attempt. I'll not waste a mind like Mad Dog's to the executioner's noose, not if I can help it."

Edwin shook his head. "Brilliant strategist she may be, but if you speak for her, Parliament will tear you apart. You're risking your career over this, Admiral. She's been the death of more good sailors and captains than I can count, and the Level is hungry for her blood."

"The risk is worth it." Judith kept her voice measured. "We need her if we want to win this. I'll find a way to convey that to them. I believe the fact that a fleet of warships appeared at Blackrock with no prior warning may help. We have informants in our ranks, and we need someone clever enough to take them down. Captain Madox fits the bill better than anyone I know. And as long as we have a hold on her crew and their families on the Level, she'll not dare speak against the navy."

He studied her for a long time, his gaze too perceptive for comfort. "Admiral," he said at last. "If that's your considered opinion, I'll respect it. God knows you're the one who's been holding the navy together singlehandedly these last few years. If you believe it's worth risking your career to bring Mad Dog on board, I'll defer to your judgement." He shook his head. "But Mad Dog is dangerous. She may not speak against the navy, she may help us win the war, but if she gets the chance—she'll destroy you."

She fixed him with a sharp glare. "It's a risk I'm willing to take."

He watched her for a long moment. "Aye, Admiral," he said at last, standing. "I'll follow your lead on this, you know that. But you know as well as I do—Mad Dog will stop at nothing."

He stepped out the door, closing it behind him.

When he'd gone, Judith slumped back in her chair.

Edwin was right. After what Judith had done, threatening Gracie's crew—Grace would stop at nothing to destroy her.

Oh, she'd serve the war effort, certainly. She was canny and whip-smart and far, far bolder than most, and she'd come, eventually, to the same conclusion that Judith had—that the safety of the miserable mass of humanity in the Stacks, and the pirates who looked to her for leadership, would be better served by the Level winning this war than losing it.

But she knew Grace, she knew her like she knew the heart in her chest. Grace wasn't one to forgive, and she wasn't one to forget, not something like this. She'd find a way to destroy Judith, take her down as thoroughly and viciously as Judith had destroyed her so many years before. And with this, Judith had just handed her the opportunity on a platter.

"Grace Madox is found guilty of treason, and is sentenced to death by hanging."

The judge's words sent a jolt through Judith's entire body, sharp enough to cut through the fog of numbness, and she couldn't bite back a gasp.

Hanging. They'd not told her that was to be the punishment. She hadn't been allowed to witness any of the trial, anything but her own part in it. She'd thought at worst the punishment would be dismissal from the navy, a dishonourable discharge.

Not hanging.

But there was a small, uncompromising voice inside her that told her that deep down, she'd known. She'd known that if Grace was found guilty, she'd hang.

That if Grace was guilty, she deserved to hang.

For the first time since she'd stepped into the courtroom, Judith's eyes flicked to the stand where Grace sat in chains.

Grace's face was pale, dark circles under her eyes, the strain of the past days written across her skin. She'd lost weight, and there was a bruise on her cheekbone, bright and angry.

But she looked up, and for just a moment, her eyes caught Judith's.

There had been times, after that, that Judith had been devastated, where she'd felt as if the breath had been struck from her lungs.

There had been the moment when she'd learned, beyond question, that she'd been wrong. That Grace had been innocent, that the Starfire disaster had been the fault, not of treasonous vice-admirals, but of incompetence and greed in the navy she'd given her life to serve—the utter, breathtaking horror of the realization that it was too late to change course. It was too late to save Grace, too late to take back what she'd done, because even if she shouted the truth from the rooftops, Grace would hang as a pirate, if she didn't hang as a traitor. Judith had chosen her path, and now she'd be forced to work with the very people who'd lied to her and used her, be forced to continue the betrayal that had destroyed her or let everything she'd done be for nothing, because bringing the truth out now would weaken the navy enough that it might collapse.

There had been the weeks and months and years after that where she'd walked through the world like an automaton, numb and dull and not really alive, where every hour stretched to eternity and every day bled into the next, endless and empty.

There had been defeats, failures, disasters, mornings she wasn't sure she could force herself out of bed.

But somehow, they'd all paled next to that one moment in the courtroom—the moment when Judith had looked into her lover's eyes, and known that she'd hang on the strength of Judith's word.

She closed her eyes.

Gracie would be just as useful to the war effort as she'd told Edwin. As she'd have to argue in front of Parliament. It would hurt her political capital, but she was comfortable that she'd be able to bring them around, because they all knew how brilliant Mad Dog Gracie Madox was, and how badly they needed such brilliance in this new war.

But that hadn't been why Judith had done it.

She could still see Grace's expression as she'd stepped down from the witness stand in that courtroom, the pale, shocked betrayal of the look that still haunted her nightmares.

She'd seen the woman she loved condemned to the gallows on the strength of her testimony once.

She couldn't bear to do it a second time.

In the end, after all her reasoning and logic and rationalization, it had been something so simple: she'd not watch Grace hang, not while she could prevent it. No matter what it took from her, no matter what it cost, she wouldn't watch the woman she'd once loved die.

The woman she still loved, no matter how much she'd tried to deny it.

She drew in a long breath, trying to calm the swirling nausea in her stomach.

"Kill me then, Jenny, and let my ghost haunt you." The pain in Gracie's voice. Grace had never been able to hide her emotions from Judith, much as she could from others.

Grace Madox had always been like that, proud and stubborn and headstrong. She'd have walked to her death without flinching if it was only her own life on the line.

And so Judith had saved her in the only way she knew how.

And she'd known, even as she was doing it, that she'd not survive it. Soon or late, Mad Dog Gracie Madox would find a way to destroy her, and she'd do it, without hesitation and without mercy. Judith had set that future, uncompromising and inevitable, in motion with her words, the same way she had in a courthouse so many, many years ago. She'd once again changed the course of her and Grace's lives in a way that couldn't be undone, and she'd doomed herself by doing it.

She smiled, just a little, the bare ghost of a smile.

She should be feeling regret, probably, or fear.

But she didn't. She didn't regret it.

The evening after their first kiss, standing in Grace's cabin, so close that she could feel the heat of Grace's body against her own. Grace's hand against her cheek, her eyes caught by Grace's like they always were, her heart pounding so that she was dizzy with it.

"You don't want this, Jenny, just tell me," Grace whispered against Judith's lips. "And I'll not do it again."

And Judith had leaned forward, closing the space between them, desperate and hungry.

She'd known, even then, what she was doing. She'd known this was a step she'd never come back from, that wherever this path led, it wasn't one she could

turn aside from.
    And she'd done it regardless.

She opened her eyes, still smiling that small smile.

Even after all these years—all the time, and the hurt, and the pain and the guilt and the betrayal—it seemed she'd still damn herself for Grace.

Thank you for reading!

I hope you enjoyed the book! Book four will be coming soon.

You might also enjoy the following, also by R.M. Olson:

The Ungovernable series (beginning with Zero Day Threat):

A mouthy ex-smuggler pilot, a grumpy demolitions expert, a tech genius and a hacker. They're pulling a job on the most dangerous weapons dealer in the System. They're stealing tech that could change the course of history. And every one of them has something to hide.
What could possibly go wrong?
"Spectacular and thrilling! Olson's debut novel is filled with compelling characters and endless excitement." -SD Simper, author of the Fallen Gods series

The Singularity Series (beginning with Redshift):

A scientist searching for the cure to an incurable disease, a canny elder stateswoman in game of politics that could spell the beginning of a new era or an end to humanity as we know it, and a cheerful assassin on the run.
Add in an emotional support murder-octopus and first contact with an unknown alien entity and, and it's an open question if the Joias System will survive this.

You can find the paperbacks on all major retailers.